Keren David is a journalist and YA star who has been shortlisted for *The Bookseller*'s YA Book Prize, the UKLA Book Award and the Branford Boase Award, and nominated five times for the Carnegie Prize.

Keren David started out in journalism as a teenaged messenger; she then trained as a reporter, and later worked for many national papers before moving to Amsterdam with her family where she studied art history, learned to cycle and failed to learn Dutch. In 2007 she returned to London, and took a creative writing evening class at City University. Her first book, the award-winning *When I Was Joe*, started out as a plot-planning exercise on the course.

Also by Keren David

STRANGER

KEREN DAVID

ATOM

ATOM

First published in Great Britain in 2018 by Atom

1 3 5 7 9 10 8 6 4 2

A CIP catalogue record for this book
is available from the British Library.

ISBN 978-0-349-00305-4

Typeset in Palatino by M Rules
Printed and bound in Great Britain by
Clays Ltd, St Ives plc

Papers used by Atom are from well-managed forests
and other responsible sources.

MIX
Paper from
responsible sources
FSC® C104740

Atom
An imprint of
Little, Brown Book Group
Carmelite House
50 Victoria Embankment
London EC4Y 0DZ

An Hachette UK Company
www.hachette.co.uk

www.atombooks.co.uk

For my friends Valerie and Robert Peake, with love.

Always remembering James Valentine.

CHAPTER ONE

1904

EMMY

I thought it was kinder to keep the truth from you, but now I'm doubtful. I was only trying to protect you. I was only trying to do the best I could. Forgive me, my darling. Forgive me.

He was naked and bloody as a newborn baby, and just about as ugly too. He was so skinny that his head seemed oddly big for his body, his features too large for his face. His hair was shoulder length and tangled, matted with dust and twigs. His face and limbs were scratched and scarred and rotten with dirt. The mud and blood had dried and mottled like rust on an iron gate, all apart from a fresh wound to his side which bled rapid and red. He gripped it with one hand, trying to stem the flow, but the blood oozed through his fingers.

Sadie had seen him first. Or at least she saw something, some movement among the trees at the edge of the forest that near-surrounded our little town. We'd been walking back from school, chatting about this and that, when she stopped dead, mid-sentence and gripped my arm.

'Emmy! What's that?'

I looked carefully, but all was still and dark.

'Was it an animal, Sadie?' Surely, I thought, a bear or a wolf would not come so close to town. The winter had been unusually mild. There should be plenty of food in the forest for predators.

'I don't—' Sadie's voice faltered, and she stared and blinked as the shadows moved, became flesh, stumbled towards us.

'Sadie!' I breathed. Fear and disgust were sour in my mouth, but I have never been one to panic.

The creature took another step towards us and Sadie clasped my hand tight. Then he made a noise in his throat, a whimper like a dog's whine, and Sadie shrieked. She let go of my hand and ran, splashing through the mud in her best button boots.

'Come on, Emmy!' she shouted, but I could not move.

He needs help, I thought. *He is hurt.*

I stood listening to the squelch of Sadie's progress through the quagmire that was North Road until, eventually, all I could hear was the wind in the trees, a woodpecker's drumming, and the boy's ragged breath.

'Do you speak English?' I asked, in a shaking voice. 'Do you understand me?'

He nodded slowly, but said nothing, gaping like an idiot.

His free arm dangled loose at his side – injured, I assumed. But I was wrong. His hand gripped a pistol.

'Drop the gun!' I ordered, though he'd made no move to use it.

He looked down at his hand, as though I had surprised him. He made a strange sound, a strangled cry, and flung the weapon into the long grass as though he could not wait to rid himself of it.

I felt powerful then, and vastly superior to Sadie who had turned tail and run. 'Good,' I told him. 'Well done.' His face twisted and he fell to his knees. His hand clutched at my shoe and I stepped backwards.

I took off my coat to cover his body as he lay on the ground. 'Help is coming,' I told him.

I laid my hand gingerly on his forehead. Although the wind was bitterly cold, he was burning hot with a fever.

'What has happened to you? Where do you come from?'

His mouth moved and I bent down closer to hear his words.

'*What are you?*'

I was confused, but relieved that he spoke English.

'What do you mean?' I asked.

3

He didn't answer. He seemed to be listening very intently to something – exactly what, I could not say. Then he scrambled to his feet, looking from side to side. My coat lay crumpled on the ground.

I was horribly aware of his nakedness. I knew that most girls would have screamed and ran, but I prided myself on being no ordinary girl. And after all, my mother had told me enough times that bodies were bodies. Nothing to be scared of.

'What are you doing? Stay still, you are hurt!'

'They are coming ... they will kill me.' His voice was little more than a groan.

'They?' I said, and as I did, I heard a noise behind me. I turned around to see Adam's cart approaching through the mud, two men riding abreast. Sadie must have run all the way to her family's farm, and sent her father and brother to find us.

'Whoa, Ben, stay back!' Mr Harkness shouted to his dog, his voice booming through the trees. 'What in the name of God is this?' I saw that he was carrying his rifle.

The boy's whole body tensed. He reached out and grabbed me, holding me tight to his chest, as if to shield him from harm. His arms were thin and rough, his body burning with fever heat. I felt his trembling breath on the back of my neck – the smell was overpowering.

I stared at Mr Harkness, then at Adam. The set of their faces told me I should be terrified but somehow, I was not. Not for myself, anyway – rather, I was scared for the boy.

'Tell him you will not hurt him,' I shouted. 'Don't you see that he's afraid?'

Adam ignored me, jumping down from the cart, his face grim.

'Take your hands off her!' he growled.

His voice, usually so kind and comforting, shocked me. This was a person I no longer recognised. I was flung into fear again, a state that had less to do with the boy who was holding me than the change in someone I thought I knew.

'Emmy!' roared Mr Harkness. 'What is this?'

'He's injured and needs our help. He is bleeding; he needs to go to the hospital – quickly!'

'Let go of her!' Adam was nearly upon us. Suddenly, the boy's grip weakened. He staggered backwards and Adam pulled me away by the arm. 'Run to the cart, Emmy,' he ordered.

'No, Adam, I—' I gasped, but Adam wasn't listening. He let go of me, his hand made a fist and his strong arm went back – 'No! Adam, no!' I screamed – and he struck the boy hard in the face. Blood poured from the boy's nose and he crumpled to the ground.

Adam paused. 'Emmy! Are you all right?'

'Never mind me!' I shrieked. 'He is injured, he needs a doctor. Get him to the cart right away!'

'But you – there is blood on your skirt and blouse.'

'There is nothing wrong with me,' I said, so angry that I wanted to make a fist of my hand and hit Adam with it. 'Why did you hurt him?' I was furious, tears burning my eyes.

Adam was bemused. Maybe he was expecting me to fall into his arms and call him my hero. 'Sadie said he was dangerous.'

'Sadie was wrong,' I spat back. God would forgive me for my falsehood. The boy was in trouble enough, and the gun was lying safely in the long grass now.

A look passed between Adam and his father. Reluctantly, they hauled the boy up into the cart and wrapped him in a blanket. I mounted alongside them and we set off for town, the boy moaning softly as the wheels bumped along the track.

Mr Harkness shook his head at me. Just because I had no father of my own, he thought it was his responsibility to tell me how I should behave.

'Emmy, you shouldn't have stayed alone with a madman. It wasn't safe, and you know it.'

He treated Sadie and me as though we were twelve years old, not young women of sixteen, poised to leave school.

'What will your mother say?' He meant well, but sometimes his concern was oppressive.

'He is wounded and in need of help. She would've done the same,' I said firmly. We both knew I was right.

6

'You may be correct,' he conceded. 'But you are not your mother and don't have her expertise in these matters. Be careful, Emmy, or you'll end up in trouble.'

CHAPTER TWO

1904

EMMY

There was a small track leading off the main road, a short-cut to the hospital. It was impassable by cart but I made Mr Harkness let me off so I could run ahead and warn Mother that an emergency case was coming.

By the time I arrived I was breathless, my boots, skirt and petticoat splashed liberally with mud. I burst through the hospital's main door, past the dozen or so patients waiting to be seen, shouting for Mother – my voice rough in the hush of the corridor. Charlotte, one of the nurses, rushed from the treatment room.

'Emmy?'

'Where's Mother?' I gasped.

'Are you hurt? What's happened? You're a sight!'

My words came out in a rush of emotion and panic. 'There's a boy on the way, he's badly hurt. You need to prepare for him – he's bleeding.'

'Emmy!' My mother was there at last. 'You do not need to shout. Tell us what has happened, calmly and quietly please.'

She did not ask if I was hurt, despite my blood-stained clothing. My mother never panicked, in any circumstance, which led some to call her cold and unfeeling. Her clipped English accent didn't help, and she deliberately made herself look as unattractive as possible, tying her yellow hair back into a severe bun, hiding her fine green eyes behind spectacles and rarely smiling. Mother did not care if she was liked or admired. 'The most important thing is that I am taken seriously,' she would often tell me.

I tried my best to steady myself and focus. I gave her an account of the way the boy had appeared from nowhere and fallen at my feet, omitting the pistol and the way that he had grabbed me for protection. She did not scold me like Jonathan Harkness. Instead she asked only about the things that she could fix.

'Fever, you say, and a wound? How fresh is the wound? Were there signs of infection?'

'He is so dirty that it is hard to tell. His eyes are sore and bloodshot.'

9

Mother frowned, and pushed her spectacles higher on her nose. 'Is he an Indian?'

I thought back to those bloodshot eyes. 'He's no Indian. His eyes were as grey as the sky, and any skin I could see was pale.' Paler than mine in fact, because I loved to be outside and I never wore a hat. With my freckles, high forehead, long face and unruly red-brown hair, no one ever called me a beauty, but luckily I never cared for that kind of nonsense. No one ever called me ugly either. In fact, Adam Harkness had silently admired me for so long that I took it quite for granted that he would continue to do so with no particular encouragement. I assumed he'd always be happy to bring me the first apples when they were ready to pick, give me lifts on his cart, or walk by my side whenever possible. I felt that my future might involve leaving Astor and Adam behind, although I didn't know where I might go, or why. But if I stayed, then maybe, one day, I might decide to marry him.

I thought I had the power to decide my own fate. I was wrong.

'He is probably a runaway,' said Mother. 'A farm worker or a chore-boy from a lumber camp. Charlotte, prepare the isolation ward. And Emmy, you can help too, but not in those dirty clothes. Come along and I will find you something to wear.'

A nurse's uniform was found for me, and I hurried to pull the rough dress on, kicking off my boots and replacing them with soft felt moccasins. I scrubbed my hands too, and then followed Mother down the corridor to the main hall of the hospital where we found a commotion.

The boy had regained consciousness somewhere between the cart and the hospital, and was struggling to escape Adam's custody, wriggling and lashing out, growling like an animal. His nose was still bleeding, and blood splattered across the floor and walls.

Around us, women shrieked and shielded their children, and men made to help Adam restrain him; but the boy managed to break free and took off shakily, staggering towards the exit. Within minutes he was floored again, flattened by the bulky figure of Jack Greengrass, the butcher's son, who was nursing a cut on his hand.

Mother clapped her hands. 'Silence!' she commanded. 'Everyone sit down!' She knelt beside the boy where he lay half-squashed under Jack and choking on his own blood. Jack's bandage had fallen off, and it felt as though the entire waiting area was blood-drenched chaos. I froze for a moment, but my mother's voice soon snapped me back to my senses.

'Charlotte,' she ordered, 'help Jack.' Then she leaned down to address the boy. 'We are here to help you,' she told him. 'Will you come quietly?'

His raw, sore eyes met mine. I saw a question in them. 'Come quietly,' I echoed. 'We will help you.'

He nodded slowly. Jack climbed off him and roughly pulled him to his feet.

Mother turned to leave and Adam and Jack seized the boy, half-dragging, half-carrying him in her wake. I followed. Behind me I heard the waiting room start to animate with gossip and gasping and the sound of Minnie, the maid, arriving with her mop and pail to wash away the blood. I felt bad for the boy – injured, confused and scared, naked and dirty in front of all those people.

Adam was waiting for me at the door of the isolation room. 'Emmy, are you all right? He could have killed you!'

Poor Adam. So loving, so protective, so completely perfect as a future husband. Above all, so patient. At sixteen, I did not yet appreciate how rare it is to find a man so kind.

'You should not have hit him,' I said. 'He was injured already. I knew he wouldn't hurt me.'

'And how did you know that? He looks half starved, but he fights like a wildcat.'

'I just knew. You should trust me.'

'No one ever "just knows". I can take you home now. Or why not come to us?'

I put my hand on the door. 'I must go and help Mother.'

'I'm coming with you,' he said, gently placing his hand on mine. 'Emmy – don't be stupid. You know nothing about this person.'

I paused. The touch of his hand made me feel shaky, and I was perilously close to leaning on him, and letting him comfort me. But I pulled myself together.

'I trust my instincts,' I said. 'And I am not stupid.'

Inside the room, the boy lay still on a bed, no more struggle left in him. Albert, the hospital orderly, pinched his nose, and Mother's deft fingers examined the wound on his torso, staunched by cotton padding, but still bleeding. He stared at her as though he had met the man in the moon.

'We must get him cleaned up and sedated,' she said. 'He has lost a lot of blood, but the wound itself is superficial. Emmy, leave us now; Adam, Albert and I will handle this. Charlotte, can you take over in the dispensary please?'

'I can help,' I protested, but Mother shushed me and pointed to the door. Charlotte and I left the room together, she to her patients, me to sulk in the passageway. I knew, and so did Mother, that there was nothing wrong in a nurse and a doctor tending to a patient, however naked he was. But I was not a nurse, and half the town still did not accept that she – even with her degree from the London School of Medicine for Women – was a real doctor.

The boy was not happy to be cleaned up, that was for sure. Even through the heavy oak door I could hear his cries as they did their work. It was an eerie sound, half-animal half-human, and I shuddered to hear it. Maybe I was better off in the corridor.

Soon enough Adam came to the door and called me in. First, I saw the pile of dirty towels, the mud-brown water in the pail and then the boy himself. Despite their efforts, his pale skin was still stained grey with grime. He was quiet now, lying rigid in the bed, but his eyes darted towards me as I approached. Again, I felt the force of that intense gaze.

His matted hair had been hacked off, and lay in a sad heap on the floor.

I did not wait to be asked before setting to work.

I picked up the pail and refilled it with clean, boiled water. I brought in a stack of clean linen too. I took a brush and swept his discarded hair carefully into a bowl. And as I tipped it into the waste, I touched my fingers to it, feeling silky strands among the clumps of dirt.

I washed my hands and went back into the room.

Mother was attempting to persuade the boy to drink a syrup to make him sleep. The first taste sent him into a frenzy, crying out and shaking, as though she were feeding him poison. The medicine cup flew across the room – another cleaning job for me.

Mother nodded to Adam, who clasped his strong arms around the boy. He resisted still, but could do nothing to stop my mother tilting his chin up and forcing the sedative down him. He tried to stop his eyelids closing, whimpering with the effort to stay awake. But he could not manage it for long and soon lay insensible, his mouth slightly open.

Asleep, with his hair all different lengths and his wide mouth slack, he looked harmless enough. Perhaps he was a halfwit and his family had abandoned him – I had heard rumours of that happening in the past, in the pioneer days, if a family were short of food. But I did not believe the theory, as soon as I had thought it. I had not liked being used as a shield, but it showed the boy was intelligent enough to protect himself.

Jonathan Harkness sometimes told stories of his childhood, when his father had settled the land that became Astor, and we could hardly believe that once the whole area had been nothing but forest, with nowhere to cultivate crops. But those days were gone. We had plenty now. Even at the end of a long winter Hannah, our housekeeper, made sure that we had a storeroom full of grain and preserves, and the railway brought supplies all season long.

'Hold these, Emmy,' said Mother, handing me some cotton padding and surgical scissors. 'You may leave us now, Adam. Thank you for your help.'

Adam tried to catch my eye as he left, but I was still annoyed with him. I felt my mother watching us, as I turned my head to my work. It was a relief to hear the door close behind him.

You are a reckless fool, Emmy Murray, I told myself, as Mother exposed the boy's torso, white as curd, ridged by ribs that seemed about to burst through the skin.

'Poor boy,' murmured Mother, and I looked closer, and saw beyond the wound on his abdomen. His body was criss-crossed with marks – new scratches, old scars. I winced to imagine how they might have been inflicted.

Blood was seeping through the dressing. Mother

15

gestured for me to change it. I shuddered at the sight – it looked far worse against his bare tattered flesh than it had when plastered with mud. I tried not to let Mother see my revulsion.

'He's young,' she said, as we watched him sleep. 'Barely older than you, Emmy.'

We cleaned the wound again and then she stitched it, neat as any embroiderer. I applied a new dressing, and she approved. 'Well done,' she said, rare praise indeed.

Now that our work had been done I could look at him properly. His nose was straight, his mouth generous, his features sharply defined, as though he'd been carved from wood with a very sharp knife. There was something forlorn about his skinny limbs; cut and bruised all over, he reminded me of a fledgling that had fallen from its nest. Then I remembered the strength of those arms that had grasped me and squeezed me tight, and the way his breath on my neck had made me shiver inside.

I tried to imagine his life in the forest. The darkness, the stony ground, the oozing mud. Creeping insects, snakes, bears, wolves and other wild predators. Rustling leaves, and all the time listening for animals and hunters, savage tribesmen and even ghosts. Always alert for anything that might hurt him. Did he sleep high up in trees to keep safe? Or had he found a cave or a tunnel from the old mining works that had been abandoned fifty years ago and nearly forgotten?

Charlotte appeared at the door. The father of a sick child had arrived and wished to see my mother. 'Shall I take over here?' asked Charlotte, but Mother said, 'No, Emmy can manage.' I was silently triumphant. Luckily there was no more blood to be seen; all I had to do was watch over the patient, covered up again now, and dispose of the old dressings.

Several times his eyes flickered, his mouth moving as though he were about to speak.

His foot poked out from under the bedcover. The dirt of the forest was still embedded in his skin, among the mass of cuts and scars. I looked closer. Were these truly the feet of a wild boy? Weren't the cuts too new, the skin too soft? I considered living barefoot. I thought of how the skin would turn tough and black, calloused and scarred.

It was so unusual to be looking at someone else's feet like this. It felt almost more intimate, more private than when he was fully naked. I could easily imagine the pain of walking barefoot on stones and through brambles, as the boy must have done.

Mother came back into the room and stood over the boy, appraising his state. 'He's stable now, Emmy. You can go home; run along before it gets too late. Hannah will have your supper waiting. Thank you for your help.'

I wanted to stay, but thought better of asking. I had remembered there was urgent business to attend to else-where; and I had no desire to give Mother any impression that I wanted to train as a nurse or doctor – not this close to my leaving school.

I made a bundle of my muddy clothes and changed back into my boots to walk home. I put my coat back on, because of the cold, but it was bloody and muddy, stained and smelly, and I felt strange wearing it, as though it were a pelt torn from an animal's back. I half ran along North Road until I reached the spot where we'd seen him earlier – I knew it by the trampled grass where he'd flung himself down. I tried to remember where he had thrown the pistol. I thought it would be easy to spot, even though the light was fading.

But although I searched until my hands were covered with cuts from the blades of grass, it was nowhere to be found.

CHAPTER THREE

1994

MEGAN

'Home at last,' says Dad as we drive along the highway towards Astor. 'It's good to see you, pumpkin, I've been so worried.'

I know he wants reassurance, *to talk about it*, but I honestly can't be bothered. Talking about stuff doesn't help, I've decided; and anyway, I'm hyper-exhausted from the flight. While everyone around me put on eye masks and inserted ear plugs and covered themselves with flimsy blankets to catch a peaceful night's sleep, I resigned myself to the in-flight entertainment. I started *Four Weddings and a Funeral* – my friends had all raved about it – but ten minutes of British fluff and charm was enough. I couldn't hack it and ended up watching *Jurassic Park* instead, which was kind of dull but contained nothing likely to cause distress, such as people kissing or falling in love or making plans for their future.

I accept I can't hide from everything that causes me pain, not for ever anyway; but no one needs another tragic, melancholy girl who can't cope with the consequences of her own actions, so right now I intend to do what I can: close my eyes, turn my face away, say nothing, switch the channel. And, right now, stare out of the window at all the green nothingness. It's so unlike London. The sky is bigger, somehow.

Dad interprets my silence correctly, *well done, Dad*, and changes the subject. 'Everyone's so excited to see you,' he says. 'Your grandma especially. And Grammy.'

'Yeah, right,' I say, realising immediately that I sound like a sulky brat. 'I mean, yeah, I'm excited too.' And I am. Sort of.

I asked Mom and Dad not to tell anyone what happened. It's not that I feel ashamed, it's just that it's no one's business except mine, and maybe Ryo's. Secrets didn't matter so much in London – thousands of miles away, a big anonymous city. But now we're driving towards Astor – the closest thing to 'home' I've ever really known, to Grandma and Bee and Great-aunt Betsy and Grammy – and I sort of wish they knew the truth without my having to say the words.

'You *could* tell them,' says Dad, as if he's reading my mind. 'They all love you so much.'

'Maybe,' I say, meaning no. Nothing has changed, and I was very clear then that this was not something for the annual Christmas round robin. 'It's over, Dad. I want to move on.'

We drive in silence for a while. I guess there are things Dad would rather not talk about, too. Mom, for one. We pass another road sign for Astor.

'Wait till you see the house,' says Dad. 'You won't believe it.'

My parents met in Astor. In high school, of all the clichés. Mom was new to town but Dad was Astor born and bred – as were pretty much his entire family back through the generations. Dad's great-grandmother, Elizabeth, was the town's first doctor, one of the first women in the world to receive a proper medical training. I remember when I was a little kid, sitting on Grammy's knee, hearing about her mother's work in the hospital and thinking even then that if she could do it back in the nineteenth century, then I could do it now. I *would*, too.

For most of my life I've felt certain I was meant to be a doctor.

Now, just when I've finished school, I've started to doubt everything. I still want to be a doctor in theory. I'm just not sure about spending my life in a hospital, or even a GP's practice.

'I've pretty much finished the downstairs,' says Dad. 'The bathroom's still a bit basic, but I'm getting there.'

'Cool,' I say. 'But I'm staying at Grandma's, aren't I? Like usual?'

'Well, we thought you'd like the choice . . .' His voice trails off.

When my parents bought the house in Astor it was a shared project, a dream of a joint future. No more globe-trotting, no more short lets, no more international schools. Rob and I would go to high school, grow up with our cousins, have somewhere to call home.

But the move never happened. As soon as they tried to put down roots, the further away we travelled. New York, Hong Kong, London . . . And all the while Mom and Dad growing further and further apart.

Then a year ago, when Rob started at Harvard, Dad gave the tenants notice and came back to Astor to work on the house. Mom stayed in London; I had a year more in school and she had her job. And at Christmas – Christmas! – they broke the news that this was a permanent thing. That they were splitting up. Dad's been back and forth, staying at a hotel when he's in London, which is weird. And Mom moved on pretty quickly. Right now, she's at some conference in Switzerland with her new 'friend', Fernando. Our family has simply dissolved, as though it never existed.

So here I am: in a car with my dad, stuck between a past I want to forget and a future I'm not sure I believe in anymore, heading towards a place full of history to see a half-built house that should have been a home for a family that has fallen apart.

I wonder how long they stayed together just because of me. I wonder why they couldn't keep it together for one more year to see me through school. A lot of things might have been different if they had.

Not that I'm blaming anyone or anything. My stupid mistakes are all down to me.

'I've been over at Grandma's a lot,' says Dad. 'I've been sorting out my dad's things. I'm finding a ton of stuff for the anthology.'

My grandpa Jesse died last year, leaving about a million books behind him. He was a reporter, way back, a war-reporter working for one of Canada's biggest newspapers. Dad is supposedly trying to put together a collection of his work. It's a dusty, difficult job because Grandpa never let anyone touch a thing in his study, and he wasn't the tidiest of men. My grandma Vera kept the rest of their house sparkling clean, but not his room. 'It's my belief that he actually likes dust and cobwebs,' she told me once, 'because if I even sweep one away he sulks for a whole week.'

'There's a load of family papers, as well as Dad's own work,' he tells me. 'I'm trying to sort it out. The local history library is interested – I've been chatting to the archivist there. Eleanor. You'd like her.'

Dad went on about Astor's history – first came the

miners, with the Native Canadians over to the west; but it was the Harkness family who settled and founded the town. I'm not sure if all this roots stuff is nostalgia or a way of dealing with his sadness about Grandpa Jesse, or if he's got a thing for this Eleanor, or he's trying to blot out the whole of his and Mom's marriage.

I can understand that sentiment.

We reach the outskirts of town, the surrounding forest stretching away into the hills.

'It's so good that you're here for Grammy's birthday,' says Dad. 'Did you manage to buy her a present? Or do we need to go shopping tomorrow?'

My great-grandmother is turning 105 in one day's time. She's one of the oldest women in Ontario, and definitely the oldest in Astor, and we're throwing her a party. Harknesses from all over the world are coming together to celebrate.

I tell Dad not to worry. I bought her a gift in London. It's a silk scarf, grey and red. Grammy might be old but she still cares about style – or she did last year, anyway. You never know with really old people, when they're going to slip into a world of their own.

Grammy has countless grandchildren and even more great-grandchildren, yet she seems to take a special interest in me. She always said that I reminded her of when she was a girl, loved telling me stories about when she was younger and used to run around the town with her best friend, Sadie.

She would never have allowed herself to get into a mess like I have, when she was my age.

She would have known how to cope.

She was so proud of her strong, sensible, clever great-granddaughter, doctor in the making.

I've let her down.

I don't think I can ever tell her the truth.

CHAPTER FOUR

1994

MEGAN

'Happy birthday to you
   Happy birthday to you
   Happy birthday, dear Grammy
   Happy birthday to you!'

My great-aunt Betsy leads the chorus. She's a loud laugh of a woman who spent her whole life as a farmer's wife and treats everyone like a stray sheep that needs rounding up. No sooner have we hip-hip-hoorayed than she's trying to spoon cake into Grammy's mouth like she's five, not 105.

Grammy accepts one mouthful and then pushes the plate away. She catches my eye. 'No need to look at me like that,' she tells me. 'It's my hands that are crocked, not my intellect.'

She's right. Her hands are well and truly crocked. Little gnarled claws, with knuckles like a bag of sharp rocks. Her hair is wispy and barely covers her skull, but her eyes are bright and sparkly and she's wearing a bright blue dress, with a yellow scarf tied jauntily at her neck. Grammy is better dressed than all of us put together, I think, glancing over at my second cousin, Bee. I mean, I'm no fashion icon but she looks *particularly* underdressed for the occasion – in a pale pink polyester uniform which is too tight and clashes with her hennaed hair. Fair enough. She works here at the care home and happened to be on duty today.

'Where've you been, Megan?' says Grammy, as if I should've been popping in daily for tea and biscuits.

'I only got here *yesterday*, Grammy,' I point out.

Aunt Betsy roars with laughter. 'She's just teasing you, Megan. Grammy's wicked that way. She knows very well who lives in Astor and who's visiting special.'

'You should come home more often,' says Grammy. 'I'm starting to forget who you are.'

'I had exams,' I say.

She nods. 'That's very good. Education. Qualifications. Make something of yourself.'

'I'm trying.'

She looks around at the crowd of people. 'All I ever did was have children.'

27

Twenty-seven of Grammy's direct descendants are here, packed into the dining room at her nursing home. It's a nice, light space and they've made it pretty with flowers, but there's still an institutional smell of bleach.

The smell of hospitals in general.

One in particular. But I push that memory away.

'You did more than just *have children*. You worked for the local paper.'

She sniffs. '*My* mother wanted me to be a doctor.'

'Oh. Well. Never mind,' I say, limply. I'm grateful when Dad comes over.

'Grammy, can we go through some more family history this week?' he asks. 'I want to get it all recorded.'

'Oh, I've done all that,' Grammy says airily, waving her hand as if to dismiss Dad and his plans. 'Jesse's got all the tapes somewhere. But no one's going to listen to them. Not till I'm gone. Who wants to hear an old lady blabbing on, eh, Megan?'

'It's Wilf, Ma, not Jesse,' prompts Great-aunt Betsy. 'Jesse's passed away now. You remember.'

'Jesse will never leave me,' says Grammy fiercely. Her eyes sparkle with tears.

Aunt Betsy pats her hand. 'I know, Ma, I know,' she says.

Grandpa Jesse was clearly her favourite child – her oldest son. She outlived him – as she did her other children, apart from Betsy, and her husband – yet believes he's still alive. Despite her claims to the contrary, Grammy's memory fades in and out like a radio signal on a long drive. I guess once you're as old as Grammy you've got more friends in the cemetery than you have in the world. It's unbelievably sad. Now, after everything I've been through, I wonder if this is her mind's way of shielding her from the pain of it all. If she ever remembered, she'd be devastated.

I remember Grandpa Jesse as a quiet, gruff man, not keen on talking about himself. When he was a war correspondent, he travelled far and wide. Then he came back to Astor, married Grandma Vera, and disappeared into his study to write books on the state of a world he'd seen through the lens of violence and destruction. They only had one son, my dad, but there were so many Harkness cousins at hand that it was like he had a million siblings.

Children are running around the room, and there's a jazz tape playing in the background. It's noisy and stiflingly hot and that smell of disinfectant is getting to me. I feel too weary and sad for all of it. For a moment I even miss Mom, though if she were here she'd be polished and shiny in a designer suit, trying to hide her discomfort.

Dad's over the other side of the room with some cousins. My dad is tall and dark, with bright, blue eyes and he must have been kind of good-looking back in the day. Now he's stubbly and paunchy, there are white hairs mixed in the black and he looks like the world's punched him in the face.

I don't much take after my dad, or my mom, come to that. My hair is dark and my eyes are grey, and my mouth is a bit big, under a long, thin nose. I'm short and skinny with sharp elbows and knobbly knees. I never used to mind the way I looked. I wasn't one of those girls who obsess over their hair or skin or body. But now that's changed. Now I wonder if people just see 'rejection' when they look at me.

A photographer from the local paper arrives and starts getting everyone to line up around Grammy. My cousin Jenna steps forward with her tiny little baby daughter, Emily, asleep in a car seat dressed in pale pink. Her head is covered with blonde hair, wispy as dandelion fluff. Her impossibly delicate fingers curl into harmless fists. Jenna lifts her from her seat and settles her into Grammy's arms. Everyone starts cooing and whispering, praying the baby doesn't wake up and spoil the picture.

Suddenly my face feels too hot. My eyes well up. I quickly mutter something about the ladies' room, push past Bee's mum and Grandma Vera, run along the corridor and through a door into what turns out to be a little garden. There are benches and flowers and a shady tree. I slump down on to a bench and burst into good old-fashioned tears, which take quite a while to stop. Annoyingly, I don't have a tissue, so I have to do my best with the end of my sleeve. Not a good look, believe me.

'Are you all right?' I don't recognise the voice (male, gruff, local) but I do grab the tissue that's appeared under my nose, although not very gratefully. I blow my nose and wipe my eyes. He doesn't do the decent thing and leave, but sits down next to me. Huh.

'Thanks. I'm fine.' Who the hell is this guy, invading my privacy?

Eventually I recover enough to glance at him. I don't think he's a cousin. The general Harkness template for men is blue eyes and blond hair, big muscles and a general solid, reliable, salt-of-the-earth kind of air, but this guy has messy dark brown hair and he's only a few inches taller than me, although he's stocky. His eyes are dark too, and he looks as awkward and embarrassed as I feel. I feel like we might have met, but it's hard to keep track of all the kids I've met in Astor over the years.

'Thanks for the tissue,' I add, willing him to go away and leave me alone.

'That's okay,' he says. 'You probably don't remember—'

'Oi!' There's a shout from across the lawn. 'Sam! Get back in there.'

He sighs. 'Bummer. He noticed. See you around.' He picks up a camera bag and trudges back towards the party. He stops to chat to the guy who summoned him over, who then strides towards me. He is tall, well-dressed and I suppose I'd think he was attractive if my default setting wasn't currently fixed to Japanese indie boys. I can't imagine wanting to be with anyone but Ryo, ever again. So that's going to be fun.

'I'm sorry if Sam was intruding,' he says, a little

pompously. At close range, he looks more familiar. I wrack my brains.

'I know you,' I say, 'don't I?' He holds out his hand for me to shake. 'I'm Ed Thompson. I'm the reporter from the *Astor Press* and Sam is my photographer.' The 'my' makes it clear that he considers himself to be the boss. 'I wondered where he'd got to. And now I can see exactly what distracted him. Don't worry, I'll administer a suitable reprimand.'

Ed Thompson! A year older than us, the local rich kid, the one sent away to boarding school, the one Bee and I crushed on for an entire summer! I do remember him, although clearly he doesn't remember me, probably because last time I saw him I was fifteen, gangly and giggly. I shudder to think. Anyway, he seems to have turned into a pompous ass. Same blue eyes, though. Same long, dark eyelashes.

'We have met, haven't we?' he says, looking puzzled. 'I'd never forget a face like yours, but I'm afraid I need a hint about your name.'

An intense two-year relationship has left me unpractised at random acts of cheesy flirtation. To my surprise I find myself smiling. Ed Thompson! Wait till I tell Bee.

'You're kind of young to be a journalist,' I say.

He nods appreciatively. 'Nice. Subtle interview technique, Ms . . . ?'

'Harkness,' I supply. 'Megan.'

'Oh, yes, Megan. From Hong Kong!'

'London now,' I say. I can see he's impressed.

To my intense frustration, the fifteen-year-old inside me is far too delighted by his appreciation, even though he's a pompous show-off.

'Are you here just for the party? When do you go back to London? Perhaps we could have a coffee before you go?'

'I'm here until September,' I admit.

'Really? And what's the appeal of Astor? Besides the prospect of a coffee with me, I mean.'

'Are you serious? My dad lives here now.'

'Well, that's good news. It's not often we get new girls in town. It's almost worth a story in the paper.'

'Oh no!' I say, before I realise he's joking.

'Then again, why would I want to alert the other guys to your presence ... So let's say I'm working on the story, but it'll need some more investigation before I can file my report.'

'No investigation needed,' I say. 'Girl comes to town, suffers jet lag.'

Ed smiles then, and it is the nicest thing about him. Wide and warm and full of perfect, white shining teeth, like an orthodontist's advert. His pale blue eyes are difficult to read. 'So, we're on for that coffee?'

I hesitate. My instinct is to hide away, avoid social occasions. But I know that's not healthy. And Ed's too cheesy to fall for, so I'm perfectly safe. Maybe it's a good idea. Something to laugh about with Bee, anyway.

'Maybe,' I say.

He asks for my number and I give him Grandma Vera's address instead. He can look the number up if he's that interested.

After he's gone I consider going back to the party, but decide to wait a little while. Just till it's safe; just until I feel ready to see my beautiful baby cousin without getting upset all over again.

It's not that I think I did the wrong thing.

I have no doubts about it at all.

I was never going to be a teenage mum, a statistic, a write-off.

It was clinical and sensible and nothing to write home about. It was quick and relatively painless and everyone was nice about it.

I'm not ashamed, I hardly considered *not* doing it, I have no regrets. No regrets at all.

It's just that somewhere at the back of my mind there's an image of me and Ryo and a baby. And it's all dappled and sunny and the baby is blowing raspberries and we're laughing, and I know it's bullshit, I know it's not real but . . .

Am I always going to feel like this?

CHAPTER FIVE

1904

EMMY

I hope you're still listening. I hope you want to hear this story. I know your mind is fixed on other things, bigger stories, a world of troubles, but this is important too. Especially to you.

Oh, but it was hard to concentrate at school the next day. Everyone had questions and hovered around us incessantly, demanding answers, vultures picking over every last detail of our story.

Sadie was much more forthcoming than I was (even though she had fled at the first sight of him, like a tabby cat chased by a terrier), but I made sure I was first to answer when Jimmy O'Neill asked if it were true that the boy had been carrying a rifle and had exchanged gunfire with Adam Harkness before being captured.

'No,' I said firmly, 'he was not armed.' I shot a look at Sadie and she said nothing. I felt relieved. She had obviously not seen the gun.

'Was he truly naked?' asked Amelia Farmworth, with a snigger. I had no time for Amelia. She was easily distracted in lessons, but too clever at making snide remarks. Her chief talent was curling her hair into crisp ringlets. She and her sisters Florence and Maria reckoned themselves queens of the school, but their airs and graces were built on the shaky foundations of their father's role as chairman of the town board. She left Astor eventually – she married a travelling salesman and moved to California. No one ever talked much about her again. I got the impression that it wasn't a happy match.

Anyway, back to the schoolyard.

'I'm not saying,' I told them, with an urge to protect the boy's dignity. But the hollers and giggles only grew louder, so I added, 'He was so black with dirt that it didn't matter anyway.'

Then William Bell announced that his sister had been in the waiting room when the boy was brought in, and treated us to a full-blown re-enactment of the event, with William down on his hands and knees, howling and growling and sending Lucy Lovage quite hysterical when he lunged at her. I was never so relieved as when Annie Partridge rang the bell for lessons to start again.

There were few others of our age in the school. Most of our classmates had left at fourteen to start learning their trade or work on the family farm. Just a handful of us were taking our diploma, with the thought in mind that one day we would teach school. We were nearly finished, and much preoccupied with the future. My mother was determined that I would go to university, and sang the praises of Canada's open-minded attitude towards women scholars, but I looked forward to the day that I could be free of my studies. Sadie, on the other hand, loved book-learning and yearned to be allowed to take a degree, but it was out of the question; she was needed at home. A year at college was the best she could hope for.

After school, we set off down the road together.

'Emmy?' she said. 'I feel so bad. You were brave and stood your ground when he came at us. And I ... I just panicked and ran and left you all alone like that.'

'You have nothing to feel bad for,' I reassured her. 'And he was not so very frightening.'

'Emmy, are you mad? He tried to strangle you! Adam said—'

'Adam saw no such thing.'

'He rescued you!'

I sighed. 'The boy was just protecting himself. He thought he was going to be shot.'

'So now you can read minds, Emmy Murray?'

We'd reached the fork where the road turned off to the hospital. Sadie carried on straight home, but I paused.

'Emmy. Come on,' she said.

'Go ahead without me. I want to go and see him. Find out how he is today.'

'Emmy, please. He is not safe.' She lowered her voice. 'And I am sure that I saw a gun in his hand.'

'No, you did not,' I said, fingers crossed behind me.

'I know what I saw.' Sadie was stubborn.

'You were only there for a few seconds. Your mind is playing tricks on you.'

We stood there, glaring at each other. Sadie opened her mouth and closed it again.

'If he had a gun, where is it?' I said, as though I spent a sleepless night wondering that very same thing. 'If he had a gun, and wanted to kill us, would I be here now talking to you?'

Sadie shook her head. 'Whatever you say. Go and see your wild boy. But Emmy—'

'What?'

'Remember who your friends are.' With that she walked off, along North Road, never looking back once.

Arriving at the hospital, I found Charlotte in the entrance hall.

'What are you doing here?' she demanded.

'I thought I might be useful . . . with the boy.'

'Hm. Well. You *might* go and sit with him, I suppose. He's safe enough, but your mother wants someone to keep an eye on him. It's a strain on all of us when there are so many others to look after. People who actually deserve our care.'

I thought of the scars on the boy's body.

'He deserves our care too, Charlotte. Anyway, don't you want to know who he is, where he has come from?'

She shook her head at me. 'Not everything is explained by science and medicine, despite what your mother might have told you. Some things are best left alone.'

With that she was gone, clip-clopping down the corridor like a cantering carthorse.

Albert was standing guard outside the boy's door. He raised his eyebrows when he saw me coming.

'You didn't ought to go in there,' he drawled.

'Charlotte told me I could,' I said. 'And the boy might talk to me.'

'Rather you than me,' he said, unlocking the door. 'If you ask me they'll send him off to the asylum.'

'I wasn't asking you,' I muttered and closed the door as he whistled at me.

The boy was starting to wake up, his body stirring under the bedclothes, his eyes flickering open. I was shocked to see that he had been tied down, each limb attached with strips of bedding.

'How are you?' I asked, making sure my voice was soft and unthreatening.

He stared up at me. I wondered how much he

remembered from yesterday. I reassured him, 'You are in the hospital. We are looking after you.'

He opened his mouth and closed it again. Then he tried to sit up in the bed.

'Help me,' he croaked. His voice was scratchy.

'We are helping you,' I told him.

'I must ... they will hang me. Like a bear.'

'Everyone wants to help you,' I insisted, although I wasn't entirely sure that was true.

He seemed agitated, and again struggled to sit upright. 'Like a bear,' he said again. 'Heavy, like a bear.'

Where has he seen such a thing, I wondered. What does he mean?

'Truly, you are safe,' I told him. 'Please, trust me.'

His eyes locked mine. 'Trust no one,' he said, his voice now deep and harsh. 'Trust no one. Run.'

He scared me, to be honest, and I was about to call for Albert when the door opened. The boy fell back on to his pillow and turned his head to the wall as Mother and her deputy, Dr Dupont, entered the room. He had, I knew, returned that morning from visiting his cousin in Montreal. What happened on his visits, three or four times a year, we never asked and he never told us. His hands were even shakier than usual for weeks afterwards though.

When my mother had been invited by our town board to set up her hospital, there were some folk who did not like that she was a woman, alone and with a baby, although her story was sad; she was widowed by typhoid after just a year of marriage to a teacher she'd met on the boat from England, bringing them to a new life in Canada. After a year in Toronto she was keen to explore the wilderness of her new nation, and Astor, just starting to expand into the Ontario forest, seemed the perfect spot. She was championed by half the town board and the local newspaper, and together they suppressed the doubters' objections. After all, many rural hospitals had been started by women who were only trained as nurses. Canadians could not afford to be fussy.

I was born three months after my father died and, according to my mother, I inherited his freckles, his unruly hair and his large feet. As to his character, she told me that he was kind, gentle and patient – qualities that I strived to emulate with, I feared, only limited success. There were no photographs of him, or letters. Everything I knew came from her.

Arriving in Astor, facing prejudice and downright hostility, Mother had made sure that her deputy was a man. Dr Dupont liked brandy better than doctoring, he was not deft enough for surgery, but he was there for those who thought that you might as well be treated by a 'performing monkey' – as Mrs Josiah Farnworth put it – than by a female physician.

Dr Dupont didn't like to take orders from Mother, but he didn't stir himself to object either. The Necessary Evil, she called him. And because he lived on the hospital premises, my mother was free to return home at night, although often she did not arrive until quite late.

Now Dr Dupont shuffled into the room, reeking of smoke, brushing ash from the sleeves of his jacket. My mother's mouth twitched, but she said nothing. We needed him, and he knew it. The boy's nose twitched too; his eyes were wild and scared. He started to speak again, but this time his babble was wordless. It was like listening to a baby or animal in distress and very different from the way he had been speaking to me. I could not tell whether or not he was putting it on.

My mother explained to Dr Dupont how the boy had been discovered. The doctor regarded me as she described the boy's wounds, his nakedness and the dirt on his body, and I was annoyed to feel my face growing hot. I turned away from them to stare out of the window.

'Pah,' grunted Dr Dupont. 'He'll be from a farm out yonder, or a house. A chore-boy finding the work too hard. Run away to the forest. I have seen it all before. But usually all that is found is a pile of bones, licked clean by the wolves.'

The boy's babble subsided at the mention of wolves. He did not protest or try to escape as Albert untied his bonds, pulled away his blanket and unbuttoned his nightshirt to show Dr Dupont and Mother his wounds. I hoped that if he were a runaway, his employer would never find him.

Mother's hands made the boy wince.

'Did that hurt?' she asked.

He did not answer, staring into space as though he did not understand. I knew this was not the case but did not betray him. Instead I wondered why I was the only person he seemed to trust. I may have felt pleased with myself, I confess.

'He's been beaten plenty of times. No doubt he deserved his punishment,' said Dr Dupont, spitting on his hands and rubbing them together. Mother grimaced.

'He fought us before when we tried to sedate him,' she said, 'so I thought we should do the job together. You may find him hard work to quell.'

Dr Dupont stood at the side of the bed and I thought I saw the boy cringe away. 'Give me the medicine,' the doctor commanded Albert, and he approached with the little cup.

'Prop him up,' said Dr Dupont, and Albert hauled him up with his meaty arms. The boy offered no resistance, although his eyes were wild.

'Open your mouth,' ordered the doctor. The boy clamped his teeth together and drew a deep growl from the back of his throat. Dr Dupont leaned in, close. 'Do as I say!' he ordered.

'Really, Dr Dupont,' said Mother, but the boy opened his mouth and, without warning, sunk his teeth into Dupont's fleshy arm. The doctor yelled in pain and dropped the cup. The boy took advantage of the confusion to push Albert aside and tumble out of the bed.

'Albert!' called Mother as he stumbled and Dr Dupont cursed and Charlotte fussed and the boy pushed past us and made for the door, his nightshirt flapping and his feet bare. Albert caught him just outside the door, grabbing the boy's arm and twisting it behind his back with enthusiasm. The boy fought, briefly, then flagged. Albert pushed him to his knees, Charlotte brought some more sedative and between them they forced it down his throat.

Mother looked on, her face betraying no emotion, but her forehead was pinched and her shoulders tense.

'You'll sleep now,' she reassured the boy, as his head drooped and his eyes blinked, and Charlotte changed his bedsheets with much muttering. Sure enough, he was out before the job was done and Albert had to lift him into the bed.

'We'll tie him down again,' growled Dr Dupont, showing the teeth marks that indented his skin. 'He is like an animal.'

'Oh, no—' I protested, but Mother nodded in agreement.

'He cannot be trusted, Emmy. We can't let him bite people, and he can't wander off whenever he is awake. We have no idea where he has come from. And Albert is not free to guard him all day and all night. We will tie him to the bed and lock the door, and he will be quite safe.'

There was nothing I could say. So I stood aside to let them tie him down, and watched as the key turned in the door, making him our prisoner.

'Home now, Emmy,' said Mother. I knew that there was no point arguing.

I walked home to Hannah, our maidservant, who had raised me since I was a baby. I was often teased at school for living with two old women. Hannah was seventy and Mother was just forty-five, but in those days she seemed freakishly old to be the mother of just one daughter. Some girls did have mothers as old as mine, to be sure, but they were different. They belonged to large families, were one of many children, and their mothers were worn-out husks. My outspoken, energetic mother, with her spectacles, her crisp English accent and her framed diploma, who spoke to men as her equal and did no wifely tasks around the house – there was no one else that remotely resembled her for hundreds of miles around. Not as far as I knew, anyway.

As for Hannah, she came to Canada from Scotland with a husband and three sons, but a bout of fever carried them all off. We were her substitute family, and although her official title was housekeeper, I looked on her as more of a grandmother.

Hannah and I sat and ate rabbit stew, and I told her about the boy, how he'd fought to escape. She tutted and sighed as I told the story.

'They should've let him go,' she said. 'He'll bring no good. And we can do nothing for him.'

'Oh, Hannah, you can't know that.'

'From the sounds of it, he's like a wild beast. You can't tame someone like that.'

'But he needs our help!'

'This is a small place, Emmy. People don't react well to strangers.'

'But we were all strangers here once! This town was made by strangers.'

I tried to argue further, but she shook her head and said, 'I don't say I like it, but I've been around a lot longer than you have, Emmy Murray, and I know what people are like. Now, have you no school work to do?'

I did have a page of arithmetic to complete. But as I puzzled over the numbers I found myself wondering about the boy's life in the forest. It was a place that had long been a source of curiosity to me, probably because I was warned so often about the dangers of exploring in the wild. Men worked in the forest, animals roamed there. But a young girl had to keep well away.

Had he trapped rabbits and make a fire to roast them? Had he lived on nuts and berries, drinking from streams and forever hungry? Did he know the secrets of surviving in the wild? Or was he as clueless as me?

That night I dreamt of wolves tearing my flesh as I lay helpless, bound by forest vines.

CHAPTER SIX

1994

MEGAN

Of all my Astor cousins, Bee is the one that feels more like a sister.

Whenever I came to Canada, she'd be there. Our friendship never seemed to suffer for the length of time in between, we'd always pick up easily from where we left off. We kept in touch with postcards and letters of course – airmail envelopes stuffed with wads of paper. I wrote to Bee about school and family, she replied with pages and pages of cartoon strips. Some faces in Astor are more familiar to me from her caricatures than from sight.

She's great company and always makes me laugh, and

she's got the best name. Bee Patience. 'It's not a name, it's virtually an instruction,' she says.

I should be excited and happy to see her. Instead, I have a nagging headache and a sick, scared feeling in my gut. I need to tell her everything, get it all out, cry on her shoulder just like always.

Except I can't. Not now.

Sometimes the closest friendships are the ones that fall apart, because if you share everything, one secret feels like a betrayal. With people who aren't so close, it's fine to keep big things to yourself. That's called privacy.

In my world – the international roundabout, the world of global citizens – people are very good at superficial closeness, you get used to it. But Bee was different. Now I don't know what to do or say to close the gap between us.

Since our last visit, a year ago, she's got a nose piercing, discovered eye liner and dyed her hair scarlet. She's still in jeans and lumberjack shirts though, still the same old Bee, still chewing gum and making mix tapes and drawing comics. We're sitting in Shakesville, a new place in the North Road Mall. And all I need to do is open my mouth and spill my story. Oh, God.

'So, what do you think?' she asks, gesturing at the purple plastic banquettes in our booth. The decor is designed to appeal to the discerning six-year-old girl – all pinks and purples, with a silver-topped bar.

'I like it,' I say. 'It's so different from anywhere I'd go in London.'

Bee winces. I realise my mistake.

'Not different bad! I love it, I really do.' Duh, Megan, can you sound any less sincere?

Bee takes a sip of her shake and says, 'It's so good to see you. How long do you think you'll stay?'

'I don't know. I've got a whole year before I start at uni. It's been a bit difficult lately . . . ' My voice trails off.

'I heard your parents were separating.' Bee leaves a little pause for me to tell her how horrible it's been. I just stir my Americano. She tries again. 'Difficult, huh? Remember when my parents split up? I sent you all those tear-stained letters. Thought my life was over. But, you know, you get used to it.'

'Yeah,' I manage. 'I mean, you were just a kid. I'm about to leave home anyway. I probably won't even notice it that much.'

'I suppose.' Bee's voice is uncertain. I'm glad I'm wearing shades.

'I was just so busy with exams,' I say. 'That's why I didn't write much.'

'I suppose it helped that you had Ryo to support you,' she says.

'Yeah, sort of. We were working pretty hard.'

Ryo was my defence, my comfort, my first support when Mom and Dad made their announcement – all very good-natured and grown up and business-like, because that's how Mom does things. I was okay, just about, as long as I had Ryo to hold on to. Overnight, our relationship turned into something that I needed, rather than wanted. I couldn't do without him. Like an addict, I felt as if I couldn't get enough. Every moment I *wasn't* with him left me anxious, paranoid, scared, confused ... kind of out of control. And then I had to go cold turkey.

'And now your dad's moved here full time?'

'He's done a load of work on the house,' I say. 'I'll have a permanent place to stay in Astor.'

Dad took me round the house yesterday. I could see that one day it was going to be beautiful – light, with large rooms and high ceilings, and a big garden too. I made all the appropriate noises of praise, picked out a room for myself, and chose a shade for the walls that matched my feelings ... a washed-out grey-blue. But I couldn't tell him or Bee or anyone how sad the house made me feel. There was too much space for Dad. Even Rob and I wouldn't fill it up. It was a house bought for a family, and now it's too late to be a home.

'Great!' she says, and I hope for a few questions about the house. I can cope with that. But no, she's too astute for that.

'I thought you were going travelling with Ryo?'

'Yeah ... I was.' I wait for her to take the hint. No luck.

'But you felt you needed to support your dad? So nice of you.'

'Yeah, something like that.'

'So, might Ryo come and stay here for a bit? I'd love to meet him at last.'

I take a sip of coffee, hot and bitter. Now is the time.

'I have to meet this perfect guy of yours!' she says. 'I feel like I know him already. How are you going to cope when you're studying in England and he's in Japan?'

I have to tell her. I have to say something.

I take a deep breath. Exhale. 'We've split up. He's back in Tokyo. He got a place to study math. He had been planning a gap year but, well, he kind of changed his mind.'

Bee's eyes widen. 'Oh, Megan, I'm sorry! I thought you guys were keepers.'

She's staring at me all concerned and caring, and I have no idea what to say at all. I dump a spoonful of sugar in my coffee and stir. But I'd already put sugar in. So now my coffee is undrinkable and I feel like a dork.

'Oh, Megan, I shouldn't . . . I didn't think . . . ignore me. I'm just too nosy for my own good. Sorry.'

This is my chance to tell her the whole truth.

'No, don't worry. It's actually . . . it's just, well stuff happened, you know. I'd like to tell you, try to—'

'Ladies!' Ed's standing over us, all blue eyes and bright teeth.

'Hi, Ed,' I say.

'Oh!' says Bee. 'Wow. Ed. Hi.' Her milkshake goes down

the wrong way and she starts coughing, her pale skin flushing pink. Clearly, she never got over our girly crush.

Ed slides into the seat next to her.

'We're going to have a coffee soon, aren't we, Megan? You into music? There's a band playing at the Old Hospital. Come.'

The Old Hospital is one of the town's landmarks and it was made into a bar and arts venue a few years ago. I can never quite believe that it was where Grammy's mother was a doctor. I wish they'd made it into a museum or something, so I could get a feel for how it had been back then.

'You fancy coming along to that?' I ask Bee.

'I've got a ticket, I'm going with Annie,' she says, looking at her hands.

'We can all go together,' I say, staring at Ed as fiercely as I can.

'C'mon, Bee obviously I meant you too. And Annie. Don't think I know her . . .'

'She works for your dad,' says Bee. 'In the ad department.'

'Does she?' It's clear that Ed isn't that interested. 'I spend most of my time in Editorial, although obviously Dad wants me to get to know the whole business. I'll have to pick Annie's brains, eh?'

I catch Bee's eye. She winks at me.

Ed stays and chats breezily for a while longer, about himself mainly; the stories he's working on, the gigs that are coming up. And then leans over to give me a peck on the cheek before leaving. He smells of citrus, and his skin is ever so slightly stubbly. A lot of girls would think he was a real catch.

As he walks past the window outside, Bee lets out a sigh and says, 'Oh, Megan, he likes you!'

And that's enough. We're laughing and laughing and it's like we are fourteen again.

I just can't tell her about the baby.

I can't tell her about the hospital and feeling so lonely, and the way Mom was supportive in a chilly, efficient, let's-get-this-over-with sort of way. And how Ryo didn't even show up.

Another time. Another time.

CHAPTER SEVEN

1904

EMMY

Sunshine filtered through the pine trees that surrounded the grey, stone hospital buildings. I was glad of my coat – clean again now, thanks to Hannah, and buttoned right up to my chin against the biting wind. Sadie and I had set off to see the boy as soon as school finished. She had agreed to come with me, despite her reservations. I felt he needed friends and I wanted Sadie to show some gumption.

The minute we arrived, Charlotte came bustling along the corridor, full of indignation about the boy and his nasty, cunning ways. He'd *tricked* Albert into untying him by pretending to vomit. He'd *pushed* Albert's head into a bucket. He'd tried, yet again, to escape!

'We had to chase after him, of course,' said Charlotte. 'Lucky for us he tripped and Albert pinned him down. What that man's been through ...'

I smiled a little at this story, but it soon vanished when Charlotte said that absolutely no one was allowed into his room. Rather, we were to go to Mother's office. Sadie, sensing an opportunity, decided that she should go home and so I trailed down the corridor on my own.

There were two men waiting outside Mother's study. I knew them instantly. Mr Jonah Goodfellow and Mr Wyngate Mitchell, both important members of Astor's community. On instinct, I adjusted my posture – walked taller, drew in my breath and tried to appear as composed as possible. Jonah Goodfellow was the local police chief. Short and round, with a bushy red beard and a mouth full of broken teeth, he had never been a supporter of my mother's cause. He was not ashamed to let it be known that he thought women doctors an abomination, flying in the face of nature, God and all that was right.

His companion, Mr Mitchell – tall and dark and generally considered quite dashing – did not share the same view. He owned and edited the town's newspaper. His trenchant editorials, arguing that the townsfolk deserved the best of everything, including medical care, had won the day. Mother had no time for men in general, but even she would admit that Mr Mitchell was intelligent and could be good company. He was the closest thing to a confidante she had, and I had, on occasion, found them together in her office, drinking whisky and discussing the town's affairs.

He always showed me particular interest, which I found uncomfortable and annoying.

'Emmy!' he said, 'The very person! You *must* tell us your story.'

'So you can print it in the newspaper? I don't think so.' I didn't care if I sounded rude.

'We are entitled to take an interest,' he said, raising an eyebrow at my surliness. 'After all, he is being treated in our hospital, has already bitten a doctor, and by all accounts was raving like a lunatic for all to witness when they brought him here.'

'If he is a lunatic, he should be in the asylum,' said Mr Goodfellow.

'I think he is perfectly sane,' I told them.

'You're the expert now, are you Emmy?' Mr Mitchell looked amused. 'I must say, your attitude surprises me, after all you've been through. Well, let's see what your mother has to say.' He knocked at the door, and did not wait for an answer before pushing it open.

Mother was at her desk, working on patient records, and looked less than pleased to be interrupted. They spent a little time on pleasantries, and then inevitably the questioning began.

'The boy, your patient,' said Mr Goodfellow. 'Who is he, and where does he come from?'

'Is it true,' asked Mr Mitchell, 'that he has been brought up by wolves and no one has any idea who he is?'

'No one knows anything about the boy and he is not yet in a fit state to give us any answers,' said Mother. 'It's a romantic idea, a boy raised by wolves, but not likely, I think. He comprehends English well enough.'

'English-speaking wolves, eh?' said Mr Mitchell, with a smirk.

I thought of the boy's growls. 'He might have spent time with wolves,' I suggested, and then bit my tongue. Why was I helping him create a story?

'Well that's as may be. Still, someone who is not a wolf will have to pay for the cost of his treatment here,' said Mr Mitchell. 'We shall need to print all the information we can gather to find his family or employer.'

'He is very likely a chore-boy from a lumber camp,' said Mr Goodfellow. 'Ran away because he found the work too hard.'

'Well no wonder if he did, the state of him,' retorted Mother. 'They work those boys half to death. Awake all hours, building fires and carrying water in the bitter cold.'

'It ain't lumber camp season now. Where has he been all winter, if that's true?' said Mr Mitchell.

'What if no one comes forward?' I asked.

'The hardship fund board will have to consider his case,' said Mr Goodfellow. His puffy eyes and bald head reminded me of a toad. A bearded toad, with an orange frill at his throat. 'If we think him worthy of our help, we will sponsor him.'

'And if not,' said Mother, 'then he will have received our care free of charge.'

'What exactly *do* you know of him, Dr Murray?' said Mr Mitchell, pulling a notebook and pencil out of his coat pocket.

'As I said, I have no details from him, neither of a family nor an employer,' she said. 'He has been too sick. He is mostly sleeping, healing from a serious wound. I do not even know his name. When I ask he says he does not remember.'

'Cannot or will not?' asked Mr Mitchell. I wished he would just stop his questions. He had a nasty, cynical look as though we were all agreed that the boy was lying and cheating to try and hide something.

'If he is in breach of a contract of employment, there may be a bounty,' said Mr Goodfellow.

'What do you think, Emmy?' asked Mr Mitchell. 'Young Sadie Harkness ran for her life. Why didn't you?'

'Quite simple, Mr Mitchell,' I replied. 'I did not run because I was not scared. I was interested and I wanted to help.'

My mother thumped her desk with her fist and the room fell still. 'Enough! There is no complaint against the young man in our care, is there? No one has reported a runaway or a theft. Indeed, it may be that he had no clothes because he was anxious not to be accused of stealing. So you can have no business with him, Jonah Goodfellow. And as for putting him in the newspaper—'

'News is news,' said Mr Mitchell. 'The town wants to hear about one thing and one thing only: this boy.'

'And we must question him,' insisted the police chief. 'He could be a dangerous criminal.'

'*Be not forgetful to entertain strangers, for thereby some have entertained angels unawares,*' said my mother. 'Hebrews, Thirteen, Two.' She always took mischievous pleasure in quoting scripture to the most holy of the community, which Mr Goodfellow would claim to be, although not Mr Mitchell, who rarely came to church.

'What if he has family far away who are searching for him?' asked Mr Mitchell. 'What harm can it do to tell his story and see who comes forward?'

'If he has a kind and caring family, they must have lost him some time ago,' she said, after a short pause. 'The marks on his body suggest he has not met with much kindness in recent years.'

Charlotte knocked at the door and then entered without waiting for permission. My mother frowned, but Charlotte rattled on regardless.

'Just to tell you, ma'am, that the boy is restless. I would like to dose him, as he never stops trying to loosen his restraints, and he is making me nervous.'

My mother rose. 'Please excuse me, gentlemen,' she said.

They both stood up as well. 'Is that the lad?' asked Jonah Goodfellow. 'Well, we'll just come along and meet him too.'

My mother opened her mouth, then shut it again. 'Of course. But please remember that he is very weak, and cannot take too much questioning.'

As we filed into his room, the boy stopped his struggling. Was he scared to see the unfamiliar men? Or, as I hoped, did he recognise my face and in some way feel soothed by my presence?

Jonah Goodfellow stepped forward. 'Young man, my name is Mr Goodfellow. I'm a policeman and I have some questions for you.'

To this day I have never seen anyone become so utterly still and silent as the boy did in that instant. He knew what a policeman was, that was certain.

'What is your name?'

Nothing.

'Answer me. What is your name?'

A very small shake of the head. 'I do not know.'

'Come now. Everyone has a name.'

'Not me.'

'Where do you come from?'

'I don't remember.'

'Had you been living in the forest for a long time?'

'I don't know.'

'Come now. This is not good enough. What can you remember?'

He gulped and looked pleadingly at my mother. I thought she might order the men out of the room. But she shook her head and said, 'Try to answer the gentleman's questions. You are not in trouble.'

'I remember coming to this place,' he said. His voice was surprisingly assured; I thought perhaps he was making an effort to impress and comply, so as not to attract suspicion. 'I remember being in a field, by a path, and she was there.' He raised a hand and pointed at me and I felt myself blush.

'And before that?' Mr Jonah Goodfellow was impatient for answers.

'I remember running. That's all.' He closed his eyes, exhausted from the effort now. 'Running, and the trees scratching me, and I was bleeding. Everything hurt.'

'But why were you in the forest, and where were your clothes, and where do you come from?'

He opened his eyes again. 'I don't know.'

'How did you get wounded?' I asked. 'Was it an animal?'

His eyes seemed to change, shifting focus away from my face. He shook his head. 'I can't tell you for certain. Maybe an animal, yes. I don't know.'

'This is a very comprehensive and convenient loss of memory,' observed Mr Mitchell.

There was silence, and my mother nodded to Charlotte to start preparing the medicine. 'That's enough for today,' she said. 'Mr Goodfellow, Mr Mitchell, my patient is still very sick, as you see. Leave him be and let him sleep and perhaps his memory will return.'

Mr Goodfellow grunted, but seemed satisfied enough. As we left the room, I glanced back to see Charlotte administer the medicine. The boy took it like a lamb, lay back on his pillow and closed his eyes.

'He doesn't sound like a farm boy,' said Wyngate Mitchell, thoughtfully, and true, if I had judged on accent alone, I'd have figured he was the child of educated people. 'But I guess he must be.'

At the door, Mother shook hands with the gentlemen. 'I'll be back,' Jonah Goodfellow told her, and he left right away.

But Mr Mitchell lingered. 'Sounded like a Yankee to me,' he said. 'But that's a long way for him to run. I will come tomorrow with a photographer, if that's all right with you, Dr Murray?'

Mother frowned. 'He is very weak physically. And he is suffering memory loss.'

'We will tell his story far and wide,' declared Mr Mitchell. 'That young man's secrets *will* be uncovered.'

She smiled at him, and he smiled back and I was jealous because my mother's smiles were infrequent.

'I wonder whether that is the right outcome,' she said. 'Sometimes secrets are better left buried. You know that as well as I do.'

CHAPTER EIGHT

1904

EMMY

I prayed every Sunday that no one would come forward to claim the boy, and after three weeks it seemed apparent that all the newspaper reports in the world would never elicit any answers.

Was it wicked of me to feel happy that he was alone? I had become convinced that he had run away from people who were hurting him. And I had become certain that I should be the person who made him better. Mother was not the only one who could heal people, after all. In some way that I didn't fully understand, I had come to think of this boy as *mine*.

In a week, his fever had gone and his eyes were no

longer sore. His wound was healing, and he no longer needed the syrup to sleep. He was eating normally too, quickly and with enthusiasm; the awful gauntness was less marked; he was starting to fill out. But his story remained bare as a skeleton. No new details had returned to him, not even his name, or, if they had, he did not trust anyone with them.

'Emmy must go and sit with him,' declared Mother one day at breakfast.

'Are you mad?' Hannah was not usually so blunt with my mother. 'Everyone in town says that he is a complete savage. Why would you put Emmy in danger?'

'He is no longer dangerous,' said Mother. 'I have taken him off the sleeping drugs. Soon I will take the restraints off too. He is not our prisoner.'

Hannah was about to argue back, but Mother quelled her with a look.

'He responds to Emmy. He becomes calm with her. Maybe he will tell her something of his story. And when we know who he is and where he has come from, and people see that she is perfectly safe with him, then they will not tell wild stories about savages and monsters.'

Hannah sighed. 'I only want to keep you safe, Emmy dear.'

'I think I know how to keep my daughter safe,' said Mother. 'Come after school, Emmy.'

So I did, although I felt a little like a spy, sitting at his side. I did not want to betray him, if his memories were bad. And how could they not be, given the scars on his body?

He woke, soon after I arrived.

'Hello,' I said to him. He was gazing at me – that unnerving, unblinking stare.

'Emmy,' he said. 'Isn't that your name?'

'It is. What's your name?'

'I don't think I have a name.'

'Everyone has a name!'

'Not me.'

'Well then. You need a name, so I shall call you Tom. For now. Just until you remember your real name, as I am certain you shall.'

'Tom,' he said, uncertainly, trying it out.

I asked if he liked it.

'I think so,' he replied, before lapsing into silence again.

His hair was cropped close to his skull now and his face was bruised and scratched. He had indeed put on some weight, which made him look more normal in proportion, but those grey eyes still dominated his face. He stared at me in a manner I'd never known before, nor since. It was as if he was searching deep inside me, with those rock-pool eyes, and it left me with a sense of being utterly exposed. In the small room, with silence between us, the feeling intensified to such a degree that after a short while I could not tolerate it further.

'Why do you stare at me like that?' I demanded.

'You are different,' he said.

I had no idea what to say.

'I never saw anyone like you,' he added.

'How do you know that, if you can't even remember your own name?'

'My name is Tom,' he said. 'You just told me.'

I smiled, despite myself, and he responded in kind. He looked relaxed, happy, and it gave me hope that he could leave the past behind. If the people who called him 'monster' could see him, I felt sure they would change their minds.

'Your own family could come and see you,' I told him. 'If you could only remember their names or any clues by which we might trace them.'

He shook his head.

'You honestly remember nothing?'

'Nothing.'

His denial was so abrupt that I felt snubbed, and more upset than the single word warranted.

'I'm sorry if you think I'm intruding,' I said, my voice shaking a little. 'I only want to help.'

'I know.' His face was troubled. 'You have helped. The doctor and the nurse and everyone here.' He jerked his head at the bare hospital room. 'I will miss it when I am well.'

'Even though they have tied you to the bed?'

'I know why they do that. It is in case I do something bad.'

'But you wouldn't . . . would you?'

His gaze faltered for the first time. He quietly turned his head away from me and looked at the white-washed wall.

'I'm sorry,' I started, and then, 'I didn't mean . . . '

He turned back towards me. 'What will I do when I am well again, Emmy? Will they take me then?'

'Who?'

'The policeman. Charlotte said they would put me in the jailhouse. Or the asylum. I don't know what that is.'

'They won't put you there,' I said, trying to sound reassuring. 'The asylum is for crazy people. And you are far from being crazy.'

In fact, many residents of Astor thought that was exactly where Tom should be. There had been a lively correspondence in the pages of the *Astor Press*. Mother had told Mr Mitchell that she thought it wrong to discuss a patient's treatment in public, but he said it was better that people's fears were aired and answered.

'They think I am crazy. They think I am an animal.'

'How do you know?'

'Albert. He said it.'

'Mother does not like the asylum. She never wants to send people there.'

She had visited the asylum last year and returned with stories of violence, over-crowding and little hope of recovery.

'I need to get away,' he said.

'But where to? You don't have any money. You don't even have clothes.'

'I don't know.' He shrugged. 'But they will kill me if I stay.'

'You mean the people here in Astor?'

'Maybe. Or others.'

'Absolutely not. You must stay and prove that you are no harm to anyone. Then you will be safe here *and* have protection from anyone ... from elsewhere.'

'Safe,' he echoed. He sounded as though he had no idea what the word meant.

It was stuffy in his room, so I went to open the window.

'Maybe you could have a job. Can you read and write? I don't think you are strong enough for farm work, not for a long time yet.'

He made a small noise which I couldn't interpret with my back to him. Something short of a laugh. When I turned to look at him though, there was no smile on his face.

'Are you all right?' I asked. 'Not in pain?'

He shook his head.

'So, can you read and write?'

This time I saw the disbelief in his eyes.

'Of course not.'

'What do you mean, of course?'

'I ... you're tricking me?'

I sat down at his side, wishing I could take his hand. He was clutching on to the side of the bed, as though it were a boat and he was pitching around on a choppy sea.

'I wouldn't trick you,' I said, trying to make my voice reassuring. 'Why shouldn't you read and write? Did you never go to school?'

He looked confused. Beads of sweat flecked his brow. 'Perhaps. I do not know.'

'Do you know about school? Sadie and I go to school. We learn all sorts of things – reading and writing and arithmetic, nature and history.'

Questions tumbled out of him and I tried to explain everything that I took for granted: the small school room where we sat in rows by ages, the Readers that we worked through, the succession of teachers who had come to Astor to pass on their knowledge, the way the pot-bellied stove in the corner of the schoolroom rumbled and smoked some days.

Tom listened in evident amazement.

'I always thought reading was too difficult ... or not allowed ... '

'Who told you that?'

'I hear a voice in my head,' he said, quite matter of fact. 'It tells me things. Things like reading is not for you. You are not worthy.'

'Whose voice? A man's voice or a woman?'

'A man.' He looked away from me. 'Please don't tell about it.'

'But it could be important!'

'The voice says don't tell. Don't tell anything, don't trust anyone.'

'So why are you telling me?'

I held my breath. He was lying quite still, his skin pale against the rough linen. I yearned to reach over, hold his hand and assure him that he could trust me.

'Because you brought me here,' he told me. 'And here it is so soft and easy to sleep. Like lying on a pile of bear skins.'

'Is that how you slept before?'

'No,' he said, looking directly at me. 'I never slept on a bed like this before. Not until I met you.'

I felt quite flustered, so I bent down and fished out my book from my bag. I'd chosen one of my favourites, *The Prince and the Pauper*, a tale of rags to riches which I thought he might enjoy too. And as I read about the pauper, Tom, being mistaken for the prince, I realised why I had chosen Tom for the boy's name. Did he feel as though he had been transported to another world?

He was quiet, listening, and I was not sure if he was bored or if the book was too complicated for him.

'Shall I continue?' I said, when I'd reached the end of a long chapter stuffed with difficult words.

'I like to hear you,' he said then. 'I like to hear about the palace where the people dress as butterflies. But I do not know some of these words.'

'They are difficult words,' I said. Then I showed him the page.

He narrowed his eyes. 'I don't know any of the marks.'

'These are letters. Surely you know . . . ' I stopped myself. 'Did you never learn your alphabet?'

'I don't think so,' he said, and his voice sounded so sad that I regretted being astonished.

'It will all come back to you.'

'I don't want to remember,' he said, and turned his head away.

I thought of the scars on his body. It seemed that his family or employers had hardly given him a day without a beating, let alone much in the way of education.

'I am sorry,' I said. 'I talk too much. Do you want me to go?'

He shook his head.

'Do you want me to read some more?'

He shook his head again.

'Can I get you anything?'

'No thank you.'

I felt I had failed him, but I did not know how. However, I understood that he was worried about what would happen when he was well enough to leave the hospital and resolved to think about what I could do to help.

I waited until evening to broach the subject with Mother. She was so preoccupied with work and worries that I had to judge my moment. I sometimes suspected that all my patience got used up waiting for her.

As we ate our soup she asked me about my day and I made her smile by telling her how I tried to entertain her patient.

'Mother, did you know he cannot read at all? He does not even know his letters. I am going to teach him.'

'It may be a question of memory. Perhaps your lessons will help him recover some of his past. He is very confused at the moment. I do not think he has much idea about anything.'

'What can have happened to him?'

'Not much that's good,' she replied. 'He has three rotten teeth which must be removed tomorrow. We will have to sedate him again.'

'He is worried about what will happen to him when he is well enough to leave. He wants to work. He is scared of the asylum and he is scared of this town and of most of the people here – Albert has been filling his head with all kinds of horrors, Mother. But we had a proper conversation today. He is quite sensible and I am convinced he is harmless.'

'Mr Mitchell thinks I should not have allowed you to have that conversation, Emmy. Mr Harkness too.'

'It's none of their business!'

'They care about you. They care about my reputation as well.' It was a rare thing for my mother to hint at self-doubt. 'But my responsibility is to my patient. And once he is cured, he may well prove not so mysterious after all.'

'We must show them that Tom is not anything to be scared of.'

'Tom?'

'He needed a name. I found one.'

'Emmy, you should not be too trusting. Perhaps he is manipulating our good will. He could have a criminal history. We do not even know how old he is. I think he is at least seventeen.'

Tom was as tall as me, and I was not small, although my head only reached to Adam's shoulders. Although Tom was lean, his arms and shoulders were strong and muscled. His jawline had a dark shadow and Mother had ordered Albert to teach him how to shave, although Albert protested that the savage would cut his throat if he were given a razor.

'Have you noticed, Mother, how he is scared of men? Dr Dupont, Albert, he shrinks from them all. That is why he fights and runs. He is different with women.'

'I have noticed,' said Mother. She sighed. 'Perhaps the Mitchells would have him. They have no child of their own.'

'Mother, no!'

Of all the gossip that I'd heard at Sadie Harkness's house, the Mitchell marriage was one of the most chewed-over morsels. Why a man generally reckoned handsome, witty and (when it suited him) kind-hearted was shackled to a misery like Isabella Mitchell, who looked and sounded twenty years older than him, was an enduring mystery to us all. According to Mrs Harkness, Isabella's father had helped Wyngate Mitchell set up the *Astor Press*, in exchange for him taking his daughter off his hands. But the marriage had never been happy, and at one point Mr Mitchell even left Astor for a year or so to take up a job at a city newspaper. Eventually, though, he had returned to his wife, his home and his small-town press.

'Perhaps Isabella would be happier, more friendly, if she had someone to care for,' said Mother, absently. 'It might be an act of kindness for all three of them.'

'No, please don't suggest it! She will be cruel to him.'

'Anyway, I doubt Isabella would take him,' said Mother. 'Certainly not if I suggest it.'

It was typical that while her husband stoutly upheld the value of a woman doctor in the columns of his publications, Mrs Mitchell quietly spread poison against the idea in the parlours of the town's smartest houses.

'I suppose you might ask Mrs Harkness?' I suggested. Sadie's mother was everything a woman should be. Good cook, devoted mother, the perfect housewife. She would give Tom a real home ... still, I knew I would begrudge seeing him grow closer to Sadie than to me. Even the thought of it made me jealous.

Mother continued to eat her soup, as though she had not heard me.

Eventually she said, 'No. Emmy, there is nothing else for it.'

I held my breath.

'We will take the risk and bring the boy here to live with us. There would be talk of course, but I am used to that. We will show the doubters that care and friendship can rebuild a person.'

I could hardly believe my ears.

I resisted the urge to throw my arms around her.

'He can sleep in the room off the scullery. Once he is feeling better he can help Hannah with the heavy work. And you can teach him his letters, and eventually he can find himself a job. He seems intelligent. No one has made a claim on him.'

'Oh, Mother, thank you!' I ran to hug and kiss her. She smiled, although, as always, she was uncomfortable with the show of emotion.

Later that night, I woke and became aware of a conversation downstairs, between Mother and someone else. I assumed it was Hannah. Though her voice was unclear and her words muffled, her tone was unmistakable: she was unhappy about the whole idea. Mother remained undeterred. She knew her own mind, and spoke it at such confident volume that I had no trouble hearing her every word.

'Emmy will be safe. I guarantee it. Would I put my own daughter in jeopardy?'

CHAPTER NINE

1994

MEGAN

Smooth, flirty, remarkably persistent Ed rang yesterday evening to say he'd pick me up for the gig at 8 p.m. I'm kind of surprised when he turns up at the front door at 11 a.m.

Grandma Vera greets him and calls me downstairs. She is *very* keen on Ed. She thinks he's the perfect distraction from Ryo, while my broken heart mends. Naturally, she doesn't know the whole story.

'You're about nine hours early,' I tell him, as Grandma retreats to the kitchen.

'I thought we could go for a coffee. We won't get a chance to talk tonight if there's going to be a whole crowd of your cousins there.'

'Just Bee,' I say, but he shakes his head.

'Bee and Sean and Kevin and . . . '

'Oh, all right.' I cut him off, grab my jacket and shout goodbye.

'Bye Mrs Harkness!' Ed shouts after me. 'I'll bring her back safe and sound!'

I restrain myself from clouting him on the head.

Ed's car, parked up outside, is sleek and new and it reminds me that he is more like the wealthy international school crowd I've been used to mixing with than most of my friends here in Astor. (As well as the *Astor Press*, his dad owns about twenty other newspapers around the province.) Ed's arrogant, sure, but I know lots of guys like that and he's easy to talk to. As we banter gently about music and film, TV and books and mutual acquaintances, I can't help comparing him to Ryo.

Ryo was a challenge. He kept me on my toes with obscure indie bands and arthouse movies. Ed's more mainstream – more radio playlist and Hollywood box office. I was never as cool as Ryo, never as cutting edge, and I had to work hard to keep up. Sometimes I worried I'd become *the girl who liked what her boyfriend liked*. At least with Ed I actually know what he's on about and get his references. And when I tease him about the blandness of his tastes, I enjoy being the cool one. Ryo never gave me that chance.

At the café, we order coffee, and chat about holidays in the Caribbean versus the Far East. But then Ed's phone rings. His cell phone. One or two of my friends have them – Ryo does, but his dad was an executive at NTT, which launched the world's first ever mobile phone service way back in 1979. Ryo used to tease me about being technology-averse, and he'd tell me that in a few years everyone will have a phone small enough to put in their pocket, but I've resisted so far. I don't want my parents being able to contact me day and night.

'Ooh, check you out, Mr Flash,' I say, teasing Ed, and he wrinkles his nose.

'I have it for work,' he replies, and answers it. 'Hey, Ryan. What's up?'

The voice at the other end is clearly agitated. Ed pulls out his notebook and scribbles furiously. I wonder idly what can be going on in Astor to cause such a frenzy. A fire? Some local political scandal? *A lost dog?*

As soon as the call's ended, Ed's on his feet, his face lit up with excitement, grinning that goofy smile again. He grabs his jacket.

'Oh! You're going?' I say. 'Don't worry about me. I'm sure I'll figure out how to get home.'

'Come with me, Megan – it's a real story for once. They've found a body uptown. You know, where they're building the new mall?'

Ed's glee is clear, and unsettling in the context. I can see that he's all about the big story, but it's not the most attractive quality.

'Not a very fresh corpse, apparently. Coming?'

I'm interested, I have to admit. Forensic medicine, even pathology, is something I've thought of specialising in somewhere down the line. I'm drawn to fields of medicine that stand at a remove from real, live patients. Dead bodies seem much easier.

He holds out his hand. 'C'mon. You can help me. Sometimes the cops talk more freely to a pretty girl.'

Honestly, the boy's a bit old-fashioned in his sexism, but I suppose he means it as a compliment.

'Well, as long as I won't be in the way.'

We pay up and go, leaving our coffees unfinished.

In two years Ryo never called me pretty. 'Your face is strong and wild,' he'd told me once. And he'd written some lyrics I was almost sure were about me, which included the lines, *'She's reflected in my brain/Like an angel burnt in pain.'* When I asked him what it meant, he'd said he couldn't explain it any further, and it was all in the ear of the listener anyway. Ryo wasn't into analysis or interpretation.

When I'd told Ryo the news about the baby, I presented it to him as a problem for which I'd already found a solution. He just nodded and said, 'That sounds like the best thing to do,' and then changed the subject to which film to see that night. A day later he rang and asked if I wanted him to come to the hospital. No, I said. He asked if there was a bill that he needed to pay. No, I said again. I'll never forget what he said next.

'Look, Megan, I don't know how to handle this. Shall we just pretend it never happened?'

That hurt a bit, but at the same time it was a relief. I guess we thought, or hoped, that by not confronting things we would move past them and carry on, with nothing changed between us. So I agreed, and we stumbled on for a month, hardly daring to touch each other in case our teenage bodies played another trick. And then I got a letter.

He'd changed his plans, he said.

He wasn't going to have a gap year after all.

He'd left the band.

And by the time I read this letter he'd be on a plane to Tokyo. Sorry and goodbye.

How could I blame him? I couldn't handle it either.

Ed interrupts my thoughts. 'You're very quiet.'

I yawn and tell him I'm still jet-lagged. I wonder how long I can stretch out that explanation.

We drive through street after street of houses, little rows of shops, schools. Everything is modern. There's not one old building. I never appreciated what I had in London when I was living there, but I suddenly find myself missing it. In London, you can walk along almost any street and see something from an earlier time – something Tudor or Victorian, that inspires your imagination.

'Amazing to think this was all forest until about thirty years ago,' says Ed. 'The environmentalists are always protesting – they're generally good for a story in a slow week.'

'They've got a point, haven't they?' I say. We've passed three mini-malls already.

'Yes, but so do the people who say we need to develop to create jobs and a growing economy for the town. Sad for the wildlife though. Mind you, who wants to be attacked by a wolf or a bear? That used to happen quite a lot. Okay, here we are.'

He slows down and pulls up behind two police cars and a van. It's a strange scene. On our left is a vast building site. Lots of workmen in hard hats, marking out the land. On our right is a timber house, with a bright red door. It looks about two hundred years older than anything around it, although it can't be – Astor is only just a hundred and fifty years old.

Police tape marks and cordons off a patch of green on the edge of the building site. Ed strides over towards a nearby policeman. I follow.

'Hey Andy, what's going on? What can you tell me?'

'Might've known you'd turn up. Back please. I'm making the area secure.'

'What's happened, what have you found?'

Andy frowns, but he clearly knows Ed quite well.

'Who's your friend?'

Ed turns to me. 'This is Megan Harkness. She's from London.'

'Hi, Megan,' says Andy. 'Pleased to meet you. I'm seeing your cousin Sarah.'

'Oh, right,' I say. I have at least three cousins called Sarah. 'Sarah the dental nurse?'

Andy beams. 'That's the one.'

'So, what've we got here?' says Ed. 'A corpse? Fresh?'

'Nah. Not so fresh,' says Andy. 'Off the record, I'd say she's been here quite a while. We've got forensics on the way.'

'How did they find her?'

'They were a day or two into this sector. They've found bones mostly. Some clothes. That's why we think she's female. Hair as well. Well preserved.'

'Anything else?'

Andy shook his head. 'Not until we get the full forensics report. She's been dead for longer than I've been alive, I'd guess. There's not so much you can tell from a skeleton, Ed. You could talk to your archaeologist friends. Weren't they making a fuss about building on this site?'

'That was last year, remember? When the town tried to build a car park on Native Canadian burial ground. The campaigners blocked it in the end.'

I nod towards the little cottage. It's kind of cosy-looking with its red door and rose bushes, and I can't imagine it with a shopping mall right next door.

'Who lives there?' I ask.

'Some retirees. Come here from the city, I think. One of our boys had a chat, but as I say, it's a body that's been there some time. Not much they can add. Not a pretty sight.

I wouldn't want something like that turning up right next to my backyard.'

'We'll go and get some reaction quotes,' says Ed. 'Thanks, Andy. I owe you a drink. Let me know any developments, eh?'

'Yeah, I'll be right in touch if I want to lose my job. The boss'll put out an official statement later on.'

Ed knocks at the cottage door. A lady opens it, suspicious and tight-lipped at first but soon thawing under the warmth of Ed's charm. He establishes that they've lived there for five years, they're horrified to learn of the grisly find and are even more appalled by the prospect of a mall next door.

'Thank you,' he says, eventually, but I have another question. 'Do you by any chance know how old this house is?'

'Oh, at least one hundred years, possibly older,' she says. 'That's why we loved it. We like to imagine all the people who've lived here before us, all their stories. I bet these old walls have seen a few things.'

'I bet,' says Ed.

'Real pioneers,' she beams.

We're in the car heading back into town when Ed has his idea. 'That house,' he says, 'must've been there when your great-grandmother was a girl. I wonder if she remembers it, a little cottage right in the forest?'

CHAPTER TEN

1994

MEGAN

Grammy is asleep when we get to the nursing home. She looks tiny and frail in a huge armchair that would comfortably hold someone three times her size. She's wearing a granite-grey skirt and a cerise turtle neck, a cool colour combination for an old lady.

I reach forward and take her hand, stroking it gently. 'Hi, Grammy,' I say.

She wakes up slowly, blinking her hazel eyes. She squints at me. 'Betsy, is that you?'

'No, it's me, Megan.' I laugh because I can hardly imagine anyone more different from me. 'Betsy,' she says again. 'Always laughing. One day you're going to learn that life's not all fun and games.'

'Aw, some of it is,' says Ed.

She stares at him. 'Well,' she says, eventually. 'Billy Thompson. I haven't seen you for so many years.'

Ed is shaken, I can see, but also pretty pleased. 'I'm *Ed* Thompson,' he tells her. 'Billy was my grandpa. And this here is Megan. She's your great-granddaughter.'

'Well, I know that,' she snaps. 'Do you think I don't know my own family?'

'Wilf's girl,' I add, to prompt her memory better. And then, 'Jesse's granddaughter.'

Her face is all smiles. 'Ah, Jesse, my beautiful boy. What would I do without him? My comfort and joy.'

Ed said, 'Mrs Harkness, I work for the *Astor Press*. I'm a reporter. I know you used to work there too.'

'Good for you, young man,' Grammy says briskly. 'Yes, I was at the *Press*, many years ago – but what do you want from me now?'

'Your memory, actually. Do you know a little timber cottage uptown, built in what used to be the forest?'

In an instant, Grammy is alert. 'No forest left now. It's all houses and shops.'

'But you remember the cottage? Back when you were working for the *Astor Press*? It's still there. Still standing.'

'They should've torn it down,' she says.

'Why is that?' Ed asks.

'Too much trouble,' she says. 'Terrible things.' Then she closes her eyes. 'I need to sleep.'

'Mrs Harkness . . . ' Ed hesitates. 'They've found a body right near to the cottage. It sounds like it's been there for a long time and I was just wondering if you could share any memories – of the people who lived there, when it was built?'

Grammy leans forward in her chair. Her wrinkled skin drains of colour, like a crumpled old tissue.

'They've found a body?'

'It's a female,' I say.

She shakes her head. 'I never meant it.'

I lean forward. 'What, Grammy?'

'I didn't mean . . . it wasn't my fault.'

'Of course it wasn't,' I say, trying to reassure her without understanding what for.

'I need to rest,' she says and closes her eyes.

CHAPTER ELEVEN

1904

EMMY

Mother broke the news to Tom the following week. I was at his side that day, reading to him as had become our habit. She offered him a room and a job helping Hannah with the heavier work around the house.

'The room is simple, but clean and private,' explained Mother. 'I could not pay you a great deal, but you will have somewhere to stay while your health recovers and perhaps your memory as well.'

Tom said nothing. The prospect of freedom seemed to have silenced him.

'Do you understand?' she asked. 'Is that something you would like?'

He watched us, warily, and I could see he was trying to make sense of Mother's statement. Then he smiled, a nervous smile, but better than his usual serious expression. 'Thank you,' he said. 'But I have no clothes.'

'We will organise everything you need,' she told him, and this time he shook his head in utter disbelief. He was happy, I thought. And I knew that once he had moved in, he would be happier still.

It was another two weeks before he was well enough to leave hospital. In the meantime, Hannah made new clothes for him and Mother purchased boots from the general store. Mother also spoke to those people she counted as allies – the Harknesses, Mr Mitchell – and asked for their support. Most of them grudgingly agreed to give Tom a chance. 'I know they think I am foolish,' she told me, 'but when they see Tom thrive, the whole town will have more confidence in me than ever before.'

Eventually the day came. He was still weak and pale, but shiny clean, his dark hair beginning to grow again. He looked almost nothing like the wild creature that Sadie and I had met just a month before. The only trace of wildness about him was his hands, balled into fists, betraying the tension he must be feeling.

At the last minute, Mother was called out to homestead just out of town, to attend to a woman who was expecting twins. It was left to me to accompany Tom on the journey home, along with Adam, who had volunteered to drive.

Tom emerged from the hospital, blinking in the spring sunlight. Adam glared at him, defensive from the outset. It felt unnecessarily intimidating and I found myself babbling to fill up the silence and sooth the hostile air. 'It's so kind of you to come and help us, Adam, and I do appreciate it very much, especially as it looks like it might rain.' Adam softened a little, and said to Tom, 'Can you climb up by yourself? Or shall I help you?'

'I can do it.' And so he did, clambering into the back, while I sat next to Adam.

'Giddy up,' said Adam, and along the road we went. Now and again, I twisted around to Tom, pointing out such landmarks as there were – the church, the school, the general store. Tom said nothing, but his eyes darted everywhere.

'What do you think of Astor?' I asked him.

He shrugged and smiled again. 'It is not like London,' he said.

I was amazed. 'You've been to London?'

'You read to me about London. All the people in the street.'

Adam snorted at this, and I laughed, and it soon seemed a more friendly atmosphere had settled between us all. I was proud that Tom had absorbed so much of *The Prince and the Pauper*.

'Mother was born in London. She can tell you about it.'

'Did you come from London too?'

'No,' I said. 'I was born in Canada, in the city. Toronto. Adam was born here though.'

'My grandfather was one of the first settlers who founded Astor,' said Adam with pride.

'We moved to Astor when I was a little girl. So I'm a newcomer, like you,' I told Tom, and he seemed to like that.

When we reached our house, Adam helped us both down from the cart, and I made sure to thank him warmly. I was indeed truly grateful – after their initial awkward encounter, he seemed to have accepted that Tom was no threat. But then he leaned so close that his whisper tickled my ear. 'Be careful, Emmy,' he said. 'If he lays a finger on you, I will kill him.'

He was gone before I could react, which was just as well. Tom didn't need any more reason to feel unwelcome.

Inside the house, Hannah immediately came from the kitchen to greet us. Suddenly I felt awkward, and wished Mother had been there. 'Tom,' I said, 'here is Hannah, who looks after us and made your clothes. And Hannah, this is Tom.'

'Here you are then,' she said, briskly looking him up and down. 'There's not much meat on you. How Dr Murray thinks you'll be of any use around the house, I cannot tell. Can you chop wood? Milk a cow?'

'I can try,' he replied.

'Hannah,' I said. 'Tom has been ill. When he is fit and well I'm sure he will take his fair share of the chores.'

'Just as you do, you naughty girl,' said Hannah, wheezing a tiny laugh. She often teased me about my reluctance to help with any dull domestic tasks, but let me get away with it because I was the apple of her eye.

I showed Tom to his room. The bed and closet and chair were all jammed up against each other, and even with the door closed you could hear Hannah clattering her pans. I didn't think it very nice. I'd wanted him to have our spare bedroom – heaven knows, we never had any guests – but Mother said it was unsuitable, and this way he would have more privacy to wash and dress himself. The thought of a boy washing and dressing in our house made me blush, and I was annoyed at my girlish modesty.

He stood in the doorway looking in, but did not put one foot inside. I was worried that the room was not nice enough for him.

'Are you all right?' I asked. 'I'm sorry it's so small ... I could get another blanket ...'

'I cannot ... this cannot be for me.' He bit his fingernail, his forehead furrowed. 'It is too much,' he said.

'Mother thought you'd be more private here,' I said, and gently ushered him over the threshold.

He stood by the foot of the bed and laughed, a short, serious bark of astonishment. 'Thank you, Emmy.'

KEREN DAVID

I opened the door of the closet. 'Look, your clothes are here. More clothes for every day and a Sunday suit and a nightshirt ...'

Tom shook his head and laughed again, an infectious, gulping hiccup of a laugh, like a child. I laughed too, and suddenly I didn't feel so shy and awkward anymore.

'Come and see the rest of the house,' I told him.

I knew Hannah would disapprove if I took him upstairs to see the other bedrooms, so instead I showed him the kitchen and the living room where my mother's desk and many books were.

Then I took him outside to Hannah's herb and vegetable garden, and across to the shed where Myrtle our cow lived in the winter. I headed for the ladder at the far end. 'This is the storeroom,' I told him, as I climbed. He hesitated, then followed me up.

The ladder was high, and you had to sit on the edge of the storeroom floor and swing your legs up. I was so used to doing this that I did not think to warn Tom and before I knew it my foot had grazed the top his head. I squeaked, out of sheer embarrassment, but when I looked down he showed no sign that this uninvited physical contact had either hurt or surprised him.

Tom seemed impressed by our storeroom. I showed him the jars of preserves, the dried apples, the sacks of grain which Hannah had ready for the winter – she never trusted to luck. He picked up jars and examined them carefully, poked his finger at the sacks of grain and seemed reluctant to follow me back down the ladder.

Myrtle was in the field behind the house, and I pointed her out. Then we walked along to the coop where I kept my chickens, my beautiful Buff Orpingtons, with their bright eyes and glossy feathers. Because of the danger from wild animals, the chicken house was built from brick, and they lived behind the strongest chicken wire we could purchase.

Quite suddenly Tom sank to his knees, teeth chattering and great spasms shaking his body. He vomited into the grass, and I shrank back, horrified.

'Tom!' I exclaimed.

He struggled to recover himself, taking deep breaths, gulping at the air like a parched man drinking water. Finally he stood up, shakily, wiping his mouth with his forearm, and tried to brush the grass and mud from his new clothes.

I hurried to his side.

'Are you ill? Let me help you.'

'No. Leave me be.' He took several steps backwards, almost as though he were scared of me.

'Tom? I don't understand, what's the matter?'

He shook his head, looking down.

'Tom?' I tried again.

He would not answer.

The wind had turned cold, and I shivered as we walked

back to the house in silence. We were almost at the door when I reached out and grabbed his arm, making him turn towards me.

'Tom, talk to me! What have I done?'

He shrugged his shoulders. 'Nothing,' he said. 'You have done nothing wrong. All the wrong was my fault.'

'I don't understand. What did you do wrong?'

'Please, Emmy. Don't ask me again.' His voice was thick and harsh, quite unlike the boy I had come to know.

He turned and went inside. I watched him go, feeling both hurt and helpless, and the tears that stung my eyes were not from the bitter wind.

When I finally went to find him, Hannah was overseeing his attempts to sweep the yard while she headed to the storeroom. Left alone, I went into Tom's room, telling myself I was there to see if I could make things more comfortable for him; in truth, I was snooping – checking his clothes, his bedside locker – trying to uncover something, wanting to explain his mysteries, as if he were a puzzle I needed to solve.

I was about to give up when something caught my eye. Under his pillow I found a folded handkerchief. I shook it, and out tumbled a razor, the type men used to shave.

My finger tested the edge. It was sharp. Albert had taught him to shave, without mishap, and so I assumed he had worried that shaving would be both imperative and difficult in a house full of women. He could have taken it from the hospital. It might even be that Albert had trusted him with it.

But then Adam's words came back to me. 'If he lays a finger on you, I will kill him.'

CHAPTER TWELVE

1904

EMMY

On the first Sunday after Tom came to live with us, my mother was not able to attend church. Mrs John Trelawney had a fever, and Mother was doing all she could to save her life.

She'd left the house Saturday evening for the Trelawney residence, and she was not yet home, so it was left to Hannah to rouse Tom and me and instruct us to get ready for morning service.

I was not altogether sure that Tom would understand what was happening at church, but if he did not go Hannah would be scandalised and see it as proof of his ungodliness. As it was, when he came out of his room dressed in his ordinary clothes, she fussed around finding his new Sunday suit.

Tom did as he was told, but I could see he was struggling. He forgot all the table manners that I had been teaching him, plunging his fingers straight into the plate of preserves to pull out a plum, then licking them clean. Luckily, Hannah was still in the kitchen and did not notice. He saw me staring at him, and turned his head away.

At church, things became even more difficult. For most of the townsfolk, this was their first glimpse of the wild boy. Despite that, I feared that most people already had a fully formed opinion of him. It was widely believed that he had lived for months, possibly years in the forest, either with wolves or Indians; that he fought bears and ate insects – a Savage Pagan! To see him enter the chapel, meek and mild, clean and suited, with a prayer book in one hand and a hat in the other was a novelty indeed. Some grabbed their children and sat as far from us as possible. Every eye was upon us and the room buzzed with whispers.

I was never so grateful in my life to see Sadie's smiling face, followed by her parents and brothers, then Adam and the little ones: Susannah, Eben and Mary. When Adam saw us alone on our otherwise empty bench – Tom beside me, one hand on his heart, head bowed low to avoid meeting anyone's eyes; Hannah on his other side looked mortified – he led them all straight over to join us.

In front of us sat Mr Cuthbert Farmworth and his family.

Mr Farmworth was always keen to show off how well his lumber business was doing, and he did so by encouraging his wife and daughters to dress in showy fashions. Amelia wore a new dress, a vision of blue silk, puffed sleeves and a white lace collar. It set off her blonde ringlets to perfection, and made me all too conscious of my dull green dress, which had seemed like a good idea when I picked out the fabric – the green reminded me of the trees in the forest – but had proved a dismal mistake.

It wasn't that I wanted to be extravagant. I just wanted to find my own way of being, my own style if you like. Something that would stand out by virtue of being, simply, mine alone.

Amelia turned and stared at Tom, then smiled, showing all her tiny white teeth. He gazed back, blank and empty. I felt cross with him. I didn't want people to think he was an idiot as well as a monster.

The minister coughed loudly, and the congregation's mutters died down. Beside me, Tom sat very still and pale. I longed to reassure him, but I could not speak when all around me were silent.

'Let us pray.'

As the prayer started, I watched Tom. His eyes widened. I knew he could not read the book that Sadie had helpfully opened to the correct page, yet he seemed to join in. When I listened carefully I realised that he knew the rhythm of the words, rather than their meaning. He chanted along right

to the end, to the evident delight of Hannah, in whose esti-
mations he had clearly been raised after this performance.
'Forebberanebber-arr-men,' he jabbered, and came to a halt.

It was curious. Tom was familiar with these prayers, but
they brought him no clear comfort. His face was deathly
white and twisted in a dreadful grimace, and just for a
minute I allowed myself to wonder if there really *was* some
demon inside of him, fighting to survive as Tom spoke the
words of Christ. Hannah had raised me on these kinds of
stories. I shivered. Adam glanced at me, concerned.

Our minister had lately retired, and we had been trying
out new candidates. The latest was an earnest young man
straight out of Theology College. He took to the pulpit and
surveyed us from beneath furry brows.

'Lo, let us seek out the sinner in our midst,' he said.

I glanced at Tom, but he seemed lost in his own world.
He was now – or was it my imagination? – staring long-
ingly at the back of Amelia's head. Her every ringlet was
perfect, not a hair out of place. I looked at my plain braids
hanging limply on my shoulders. One ribbon was already
slipping off.

The minister's voice droned on, but I did not hear a word.
I was praying hard that Tom would not say or do anything
that would make people gossip or point or stare. But it was
not to be.

Tom reached forward and touched Amelia's shoulder,
stroking it gently. She screamed. Her sisters joined in,

jumping to their feet, shoving folk aside and stumbling over themselves in a rush to get away.

Tom, as much in shock as anyone, bolted for the door, trampling on feet and pushing past people as he went.

The door banged shut.

Amelia wailed and wept, brushed her dress and pretended to have palpitations.

Her father shouted angrily about an assault.

Her mother clutched a handkerchief to her lips.

The congregation was a-stir with excitement and confusion.

The hapless student minister banged his hand on the pulpit and appealed for calm.

I was struck dumb.

'Silence!' roared Jonathan Harkness.

Sadie's mother's sweet voice said, 'I do believe the child felt ill.' She rose, and made her way to the door, Sadie close behind her. I stood to follow, but Hannah grabbed my arm. 'Stay where you are!' she warned. 'I told your mother that he would disgrace us!'

Then Mr Wyngate Mitchell rose to his feet. His wife sat next to him, her face frozen into a mask of distaste.

'Ladies and gentlemen,' he said. 'I am not here to usurp our learned preacher. But I feel I should pass on a piece of wisdom that comes from our scriptures. Hebrews, Thirteen, Two. *Be not forgetful to entertain strangers, for thereby some have entertained angels unawares.*'

Some of the gentlemen laughed, and were hushed by their wives. Mr Mitchell was not finished. His eyes swept the room and found me. 'Emmy,' he said, quite gently. 'I think you should go and find Tom.'

The minister coughed. Mr Mitchell sat down again, and the service resumed with a hymn. I nudged my way past Jonathan and Adam, sensing inquisitive eyes upon me. I was glad to be able to escape, and even grateful to Mr Mitchell for making it possible.

I found Sadie and her mother in the porch. Of Tom, there was no sign.

'He ran off along the North Road,' said Mrs Harkness. 'I only hope he will come back soon.' She clicked her tongue against her teeth. 'What was your mother thinking of, Emmy, to let him come to church today? She should have known that he would be the centre of attention. No wonder the boy became confused. He can have no idea how to act in society.'

I explained Mother's absence and she said, 'Hannah should have known better. Why, the poor boy is hardly out of his hospital bed. Now the Farmworths will make trouble. I feel sorry for him, Emmy, truly I do. He needs a mother's care and a real family.'

I loved Mrs Harkness dearly. She had been very kind to me for many years, and had always treated me as part of her family. But she spoke as she found, and she and my mother were as different as a hen and a hawk.

'He *has* got a real family now,' I hissed. 'He has Mother and Hannah and me.'

'Emmy – Mother didn't mean—' said Sadie, but I was not listening.

'I will find him!' I declared, and I stepped off the porch and started running along the North Road.

I ran and ran, until I turned my ankle and was forced to stop and sit by the side of the road. Tom was nowhere to be seen. I half-hated him in that moment – for running away, for reaching out to Amelia Farmworth of all people. He was no different from most boys: dazzled by shiny hair, a pretty face and a party dress. I thought about giving up and going home. He had shown me scant respect. Why should I bother with him?

Then I wondered how I would get home, with my ankle hurting so, and my eyes filled with tears of pure self-pity. A shadow fell over me and I looked up, hoping, despite all, that it was Tom. But it was Mr Mitchell, his eyes wrinkled in amusement.

'No luck, Emmy?' he said. 'Maybe it is better for everyone if he disappears.'

'I have hurt my ankle, sir,' I said. I disliked his patronising tone. Mr Mitchell was reckoned good-looking, despite being at least as old as my mother, and he had that easy way about him that good-looking men so often have, as though they have no doubt that everyone finds them as fascinating as they think themselves.

'Let me give you a lift,' he said, indicating his horseless carriage. It is strange to think that Mr Mitchell was the first in Astor to drive a car powered by gasoline, when nowadays everyone has them, and the old roads and tracks all hum with traffic. He owned a Le Roy. It resembled a cart, but with no horse, large wheels, a curved dashboard and a hood which could be pulled up in case of rain. There was a near riot in Astor when he first drove it along the high street. I had never been driven in it, and despite my anxiety over Tom, I was secretly thrilled to take my seat beside Mr Mitchell. It truly felt like a taste of the future, and now, so many years later, I know that it was.

We drove along the bumpy road in silence, only broken by the chug of the engine. I was acutely aware that my hair was escaping its tight braids, and I must be red-faced and sweaty. I would not normally worry about the way I looked, but there was something about Mr Mitchell's interest that made me self-conscious.

Soon he started asking questions. Did I think that Tom was settling in to our home? Was I happy to have him there? How were my studies going? Did my mother still work such long hours? His tone invited confidence, but made me a little suspicious. I answered in blunt monosyllables – yes, yes, well, yes – keeping my eyes on the road and praying to see Tom appear.

The buggy trundled to a copse of spruce firs beyond which the stone road turned to a muddy pathway, used by the loggers when they went deep into the forest in the winter.

'I don't mean to be impertinent, Mr Mitchell,' I told him. 'But I know you are not really interested in Tom. You want a story for your paper.'

He shook his head, but his voice was mild and unperturbed. 'Why Emmy, you misjudge me. I am very interested in the welfare of young Tom, which is precisely why I want to bring his story to the attention of as many people as possible and find his true family. I am also very interested in your well-being, as a friend of the family.'

I ignored this last remark, which seemed to me simply his way of trying to gain favour.

'But you have tried that! No one has claimed him; he either has no family or they do not care.'

Mr Mitchell shrugged. I suddenly saw a way that I could turn this conversation to Tom's benefit.

'If he had a job in Astor, he would have good reason to stay. And he would not be so timid. Might you find a job for him at your office?'

Mr Mitchell's mouth twitched. 'The work of a newspaper is all about words, Emmy. How does that fit with a boy who cannot read?'

'I am teaching him,' I declared. 'And he is a fast learner.'

He considered this. 'Well, he has a good tutor. Carry on, and we will see. But let's find him first.'

We rode on through the forest.

'Tom reminds me of the story of Kasper Hauser,' he said.

I was paying little attention, but Mr Mitchell continued regardless.

'Kasper Hauser lived in Germany, oh, nearly one hundred years ago. Just like Tom, he came from nowhere. He presented himself with a letter asking to become a cavalryman. He said that he could remember nothing of his past life save his name and a few prayers. He was strong, though, and quick to learn.'

'What happened?' I said, interested now.

'After a few months, his memory returned to him. He told a very strange tale indeed. He said he had been kept prisoner in a tiny cell, fed on bread and water left by his bed whenever he woke. He had a bed of straw and a toy horse, carved from wood.'

I had nothing to say, imagining such a cell, such a life.

'He was almost certainly lying,' said Mr Mitchell.

'How do you know?'

'No one could live such a life. There were rumours that he was a prince, but those were never proven. And then the attacks started.'

I pulled my coat tight around me. It was cold in the forest, and the rustle of trees suddenly felt sinister.

'First, he was found bleeding from a head wound, and said he had been threatened by a man who told him he would die before he left the city of Nuremberg. Then a pistol went off in his room – an accident, he said.'

'How do you know so much about him?' I asked.

'I heard about it a long time ago, and looked it up when I visited the city recently,' he told me. 'It seemed very … pertinent.'

His story, and the forest canopy, had spooked me. And made me fear for Tom, too.

Suddenly Mr Mitchell hit the car's brakes, jerking both of us forward.

'There he is,' he said, pointing into the trees and inching the vehicle forward to get a better look. Tom was sitting with his back against a thick tree trunk. By his side lay an animal. But what an animal! At first sight, I thought it a wolf, but as we got closer I realised it was a huge dog.

Mr Mitchell turned off the car engine, which spluttered a little, and Tom looked up at us. His arm was resting on the dog's back I noticed and the creature seemed quite content by his side. It was certainly strange looking. A lean body atop long legs. A feathery tail. Shaggy grey fur. Yellow eyes and a mouth full of sharp teeth. It wouldn't win any beauty prizes, that's for sure, but the way it whined and wriggled to get closer to Tom spoke of loyal adoration.

'Tom! What happened? Why did you run off? I was worried to death!' My voice was shriller than usual, and it wobbled with the relief of seeing him safe.

Tom looked strangely calm and gave me a half smile.

'This animal is yours?' Mr Mitchell's voice behind me was deliberately light and unthreatening.

'He was with me. In the forest. His name is Wolf.'

'Emmy was very worried about you,' Mr Mitchell told Tom, stern as a judge, 'and you must not run off again without telling her where you are going. You would not want to cause her such concern, would you?'

'No, sir, I would not,' said Tom, just as I found I could breathe again without any danger of an unwanted sob emerging.

'And it is not just Emmy who worries about you,' Mr Mitchell continued. 'Why, Sadie Harkness was terribly distracted, and her mother had to stop her running after the two of you.'

'I know. Sir, I am sorry.' Tom's voice was all meekness.

'It is not considered polite behaviour to touch a girl's shoulder in church. If you want to admire a girl then you must seek her approval before you touch her, and possibly her father's approval as well.'

Tom shook his head. 'I did not mean to touch her ... It was the shiny stuff.'

'The shiny stuff? Do you mean her silk dress?'

'I remembered it ... '

'You have seen silk before?' I asked, quite astounded.

'I think so, yes.'

Mr Mitchell was interested now; the news hound in him wanted more. 'And where did you see such finery, Tom? Was it your mother, perhaps?'

Tom glanced sideways at him. 'A butterfly,' he said.

Mr Mitchell laughed uncertainly, and Tom looked down at his lap and would not say another word.

'Tom,' said Mr Mitchell. 'If you remember anything else, then we need to know.'

I bristled at his insincerity.

'A butterfly is a good description of Amelia,' said Mr Mitchell. 'Is Emmy here a butterfly, Tom?'

Tom shook his head. 'Emmy is a hawk. Her hair is like feathers.'

'Quite so,' said Mr Mitchell smugly, and I glared. He was a fine one to talk – if I was a hawk, he was a vulture, stripping meat from the dry bones of other lives. 'Come, Tom,' he said, indicating the rear of his runabout. 'You'll have to sit in the jump seat. No room for the dog, I'm afraid.'

Tom hesitated, but did as he was told. I followed on, hot stupid tears in my eyes – so much emotion over a boy I barely knew was both shameful and troubling. I was tired, my ankle was swollen and as eager as I was to be home, I was dreading having to face Hannah and my mother.

Mr Mitchell started the engine and we set off down the track. I glanced back and saw Tom's head turned, watching the ugly dog as he trailed along behind our vehicle.

'Is the dog following us?' asked Mr Mitchell. 'Perhaps it might provide a clue to Tom's provenance. Once seen, never forgotten, a brute like that.'

To change the subject I asked, 'So, what happened in

the end to Kasper Hauser, Mr Mitchell? The one you were telling me about before?'

Mr Mitchell shot me a smile – the smile of a man who knows he has succeeded in gaining an audience – and said, 'His death was just as much of a mystery as his beginnings. He was stabbed to death by an unknown assailant.'

I had not realised that I was holding my breath. I let it out in a sigh.

We were back on the road again, and I realised that we had not gone far into the forest at all.

CHAPTER THIRTEEN

1904

EMMY

It was Tom's greatest wish that Wolf should live with us, sharing his room and shadowing his every move. Mother and Hannah united to prevent this, agreeing that Wolf could sleep in the shed and that Tom would have to find food for him. Tom agreed, fashioning traps for rabbits with an ease that hinted at the life he had left behind. We looked for such clues all the time – they were there, for those who paid attention.

He washed his hands before he ate; but I had to teach him how to use a fork and knife.

He always took his boots off before coming indoors.

He knew how to launder clothes.

And – a great surprise, this – he knew how to make bread. Hannah watched him suspiciously while he mixed and worked the dough, convinced he might be planning to poison us all. But even she allowed that he was a competent baker and pronounced his loaves were 'edible'.

But the incident in church had made things worse for Tom, both at home and in town. Hannah was one among many who held that he had practically assaulted Amelia during her prayers; and what was worse, Amelia herself practically encouraged such stories spreading. When I saw her in the general store she talked loudly to her sister of how the dress had needed laundering, and how she 'hardly felt safe to walk outside her house' anymore. I ignored her, but others did not.

Tom could ignore the air of hostility towards him in the town, as he mostly kept to our house, but he was certainly well aware that Hannah made a habit of finding fault with almost everything about him. It made for a miserable atmosphere however hard Mother and I tried to improve things.

One day I came home from school to hear Hannah shouting quite loud, and I knew she must have caught him out in a misdemeanour. They were standing in the doorway of Tom's bedroom, and I could see by the expression on his face that whatever Hannah had accused him of was true.

'You'll bring vermin into the house!' she scolded. 'This won't do, boy!'

'What happened?' I asked.

Hannah turned her indignation on me. 'Look under his bed. Go on, look!'

I stooped and squinted underneath the bedframe. I could see little except a wooden box.

'What is it?' I asked.

Hannah pulled out the box. 'Now can you see?' she demanded. 'And when I tried to clean it up, he grabbed the broom from me!'

Behind the box sat two jars of preserves, a loaf of bread and a piece of cheese. The cheese was almost transparent with age and the loaf collapsed with a puff of green mould as she grabbed it. Tom moved as though to grab the remains, but thought better of it as Hannah rounded on him.

'Rats, we'll have, and the Lord knows what else, not to mention that mangy creature you've already brought to this house. You've been poking around in my storeroom and helping yourself. The winter is coming, and I must make sure that we can be fed. You're not to steal food!'

When Hannah got angry her breath came in short gasps, and I could see she was struggling.

'Oh, Hannah, he probably did not realise,' I said. Perhaps whoever he lived with before never gave him enough to eat. That, or he truly was a wild boy, who only knew how to scavenge for what he could get. 'Hannah, come and sit down. I can explain to Tom not to touch the food in the storeroom. He's obviously not used to living like this.'

Hannah reluctantly allowed herself to be guided to sit at the kitchen table. I patted her back to try to calm her down, aware of Tom stepping quietly into his bedroom.

She sighed. 'Dr Murray puts too much trust in him. Why, I found him upstairs in the middle of the night! Emmy, you must promise to latch your door. I swear, he will murder us in our beds.'

Tom was moving around again. I turned my head slightly to see him slip out the back door. Through the window I watched Wolf's rapturous reaction to seeing Tom again, and how Tom, sitting down to put on his boots, made a fuss of him, stroking his head and tickling under his chin. Boots on, the two of them disappeared. I felt absurdly excluded. How ridiculous, I told myself, to feel jealous of a dog.

I made Hannah a cup of tea and then offered to clean Tom's room for her. Her breath was easing. 'There's a good girl,' she said. 'I expect the boy will learn eventually, but sometimes ...'

I took the long broom from the scullery. I swept under his bed, finding in the process several hunks of stale bread and a stash of dried apple tied up in a handkerchief. Then I swept the cobwebs from his ceiling.

In contrast to his general housekeeping skills I saw how carefully he'd folded his clothes, how neatly he'd stacked the books we used for our lessons.

So far, our lessons were going well. He seemed to have a good appetite for both reading and writing. He could make out his letters almost immediately and I suspected that he had learned them before. He sounded out words with growing competence but their meaning often required explanation. He knew almost nothing of the world beyond our town – or so he claimed.

Hannah had finished her tea and announced her intention of heading for the storeroom to check what else Tom may have pilfered, so I laced my boots and went in search of him. He was nowhere to be found around the front of the house, and I knew he never went near the chicken coop, so I skirted the cow's field and walked along the edge of the little copse of birch trees that bordered our land and marked the beginning of the Harkness farm.

He was nowhere to be found. I prayed he had not run back to the forest. I was thinking about how I would break the news to my mother, when I felt something encircle my ankle.

I confess I screamed, as I tumbled down on to the ground.

'Tom!'

Tom let go and wriggled on his belly to lie at my side, smiling up at me. One of his rare smiles.

'Tom!' I said again, trying to be stern now. 'Why did you do that? It hurt!'

His smile disappeared. 'I am sorry, Emmy. I did not mean to hurt you. Where does it hurt?'

Well! What hurt was what Hannah called my sit-upon, and I could no more explain that to him than I could fly to the moon, so I laughed instead.

'What's so funny?' he asked, and I laughed all the more so that after a while he joined in. We lay there, side by side on the bare ground, hidden by trees and bushes, and I enjoyed a joke that could not be told.

The moment was broken by Wolf. He'd been sleeping by Tom's side and our mirth awoke him. He opened one eye, showed me one fang and growled very softly.

'He doesn't like me,' I said.

'He doesn't know you.'

'But he knows you.'

'We know each other.'

'Where from, Tom?'

'From the forest.' He'd said this before.

Wolf growled again and Tom patted his head and stroked his rough fur until the dog was persuaded to settle down again.

'Why did you take the food?' I asked gently, then.

'In case I should need it,' he said, as though it was the most obvious thing in the world. I explained to him about our stores for the winter and how we lived in good farming country and there was plenty of food for us all, and he said, 'Yes, but what if Hannah goes away?'

'Hannah isn't going to go away,' I said.

'Sometimes people go away,' he said. 'Your mother goes away.'

'She has to work.'

'Do you want to see what I found?' he asked.

115

'What?'

He opened his fist and I screamed. There was a big juicy spider, and as I shrieked as it made its way up Tom's sleeve. He did not seem worried or revolted in the slightest.

'You don't like them? They are so *clever*, Emmy. They spin silver ropes from their legs and they catch bugs and make the room clean from flies. They never give up. Even if their home is ripped to pieces they build it again.'

'Tom! Nobody likes spiders!'

'Spiders, yes! I forgot that was their name,' he said, dreamily, watching the spider which had crept back into his palm.

'It sounds like you've spent a lot of time observing them,' I said. 'Tell me.'

Tom was very still. His eyes still on the creepy-crawly, he was silent so long that I thought he was pretending not to have heard me.

'They helped me. It was good to have something to watch.'

'Watch?'

'When I was ... before here.'

'Tell me.'

'I cannot.'

His voice was all sadness, but there was coldness there too, and I felt rejected. He was utterly still, staring at the spider in his fist, and after a minute he said, 'I am sorry, Emmy. I do not mean to be rude.'

'I did not mean to pry,' I said. 'It is just that I thought it would help you to recover your memory.'

'Why do I need to? I never want to leave.'

How could I answer that? 'Perhaps there are people worrying about you. Perhaps you would be happier if you could remember.'

I would not be happier though. I realised it then.

He laughed. 'I do not think so. Do your memories make you happy, Emmy?'

I considered. 'Most of the time,' I said.

'Where are your memories?'

It was my turn to laugh. 'Why, in my head, of course. Where else should they be?'

He let the spider make its escape and he took my hand. I was too surprised to move. He pulled me towards him, and placed my fingers on his neck. I could feel his blood pulse under the skin, the rough hairs on his chin. It made me shiver, to be touching him.

'Can you feel that? Where it goes *t-t-t*.'

'Yes. That is your pulse. Where the blood pumps through the body.'

'When Dr Dupont treated me in the hospital, when I smelled his smell ... I felt a memory here, at my ... pulse.'

I thought of the pungent smell of cigar and whisky that hung around my mother's assistant. I felt Tom's pulse quicken. His breathing was shallower too and his face screwed up as if in pain.

'Tom?' I said, concerned, and he took my hand in his again.

'Did you feel it?' he asked.

'I think so. Your pulse was quicker.'

'Could that be a memory?'

'It could be,' I said. I was distracted by his physical proximity. I was wishing that I could have touched more of his face, not just his neck.

'Then I don't want any more. They aren't good feelings.'

'Tom,' I said, 'I hope you will not run away again. I hope you will stay.'

He looked me straight in the eye, with that clear, grey gaze.

'I will not run away,' he promised. 'I am staying.'

Later that night, alone in bed, those words thundered through my head.

I am staying.

I am staying.

I am staying.

CHAPTER FOURTEEN

1904

EMMY

Unlike Hannah, my mother had welcomed Tom into our household. She listened to Hannah's objections, then reminded her of the need to show Christian charity to waifs and strays. Hannah was not going to be outdone in religious duty, so she made more effort, while telling me her many fears and worries behind her back.

Tom slept a lot in the weeks after he came to live with us, and it was not unusual for him to be found curled up before the fire fast asleep, like a cat or a dog. Mother noted such behaviour in a leather-bound notebook, where she'd written the entire history of Tom's treatment in the hospital.

We sat together at the table while I worked on geometry

problems and she scribbled in her book until at last she put down her pen and I was able to ask her why she kept notes on our guest.

'I feel we have a truly unique opportunity here. You can help me, Emmy. Watch carefully how he responds to everyday life, and to the task of learning to read and write.'

'An opportunity for what?'

She suddenly became serious. 'For scientific observation, of course, and to understand why he is as he is. Here. See how he sleeps now.'

I looked at Tom, sprawled on the hearthrug, his head resting on his crossed forearms. My mother wanted my thoughts to be scientific – but I remembered lying by his side in the grass, laughing about spiders, and in truth my only wish was to be curled up at his side again.

'Does he not remind you of a dog?' she asked. 'The way a dog sleeps? See how his legs twitch, and his nostrils flare. What dreams does he have? What memories does he relive?'

I felt an urge to tell her about Tom's hints about bad memories, but an equally strong instinct to keep his secrets.

'He's not an experiment, he's a person,' I pointed out, but she was writing again and seemed not to hear me.

'There is great interest in this kind of case, Emmy,' she said, without looking up, 'among scientists and doctors. A boy with no memory, a boy who might have lived wild in the forest. It could bring recognition – even financial reward.'

'Tom is not a commodity to be sold,' I snapped. But Mother shook her head.

'You don't understand,' she said. 'The hospital is in sore need of more funds. All the things I should like to do – but there is no chance at the moment.'

At this point Tom cried out in his sleep, and she left the table to crouch by his side, listening intently for any sounds he might make. He woke, startled, and she patted him briskly on the head and asked, 'What were you thinking of just then?'

He shook his head, befuddled with sleep and murmured, 'I am sorry. I am sorry.'

'Sorry? Why, Tom?'

He was fully awake now and I could see his body tense at the question. 'I am sorry that I fell asleep on the floor. Hannah has told me that a Christian does not sleep like a dog. It is just the warmth of the fire, and the rug is very soft.' His hand stroked the soft pile, and I smiled because I used to do the same thing when I was smaller.

The rug was from India, a work of art in soft reds and blues, and was one of the few things my mother had brought with her from England, although her family owned an enormous town house packed from attic to basement with exotic treasures from the East. My mother was born in India, where her father was a colonial administrator, and sometimes she told me tales of tigers and elephants. As a child, she had loved the heat and colour of her birthplace, but not the disease and suffering she had witnessed afflict first the native people and then her mother. When fever finally stole her mother from her, she was sent away to cold, grey London and a stern grandmother. She was only reunited with her father three years later, by which time he was remarried with two baby sons.

I tried to explain the story of the rug to Tom, and I brought Mother's globe to the fireside to spin it from India to England and then trace her journey over the ocean to our little home, after she had studied to be a doctor. He was fascinated. He made her tell him about the ship she had sailed in when she came to Canada, and where it had started and stopped.

'You would not have enjoyed it,' she said. 'It was cold and I was very sick, and I was bored. I spent most of my time studying my books and planning how I would find employment when I disembarked.'

'But you also met Father,' I reminded her. It was not often that she talked about him, stolen from her by illness, and I had learned to seize on every opportunity to find out about him.

'I did indeed meet your father on the boat,' said Mother, 'and I was very glad to have found someone to talk to.'

Tom hugged his knees to his chest. 'Where is Emmy's father?' he asked.

'He died before I was born,' I told him. 'He was a teacher.

His name was William Murray, and he was a true gentleman and a scholar.'

'He is not here, living here?' asked Tom, and Mother said firmly, 'No, Tom, he died before Emmy was born. Do you understand what it means when someone dies?'

Tom narrowed his eyes and did not answer.

'Is it a difficult question to answer?' asked Mother, quietly.

He shook his head. 'Dead is dead. Like a rabbit. Dead meat. Gone away. Finished.'

'When we die we go to heaven, unlike rabbits,' I said. 'Or if we are bad, we go to the other place.'

'Where is heaven?' asked Tom.

'Tom, you came to church with me, and I heard you say your prayers. You know about heaven! Someone has taught you to pray!'

'I thought heaven was somewhere else,' he said. 'Some other land. Like England.' He traced Mother's journey on the globe. 'I didn't know it was for dead people.'

'For their souls,' I told him. 'Not their bodies.'

'Imagine heaven were a boat,' said Mother, 'a boat where you could feel entirely safe. You are floating far away from anything that could hurt you. Close your eyes and imagine that. Then perhaps you can tell us some more about what you remember.'

Tom's eyes remained open. 'I don't remember anything,' he said, firmly, meeting Mother's gaze with a touch of defiance.

She sighed. 'One day you will learn to trust us,' she told him. 'And then we can help you.'

I said nothing. But inside I wondered if what she said was true. Didn't she just want Tom's secrets to help herself?

'I do trust you,' said Tom. He scrambled to his feet. 'I have made something for you.'

He went into his room, and came out holding a small bundle in his hands, wrapped in newspaper. He presented it to Mother. 'It is for you. To thank you for giving me a home.'

She unwrapped the paper. Out fell something grey and soft. 'Oh!' she said. 'A rabbit!'

It was indeed a rabbit – or at least it had recently belonged to one. It was a rabbit's hide, perfectly prepared.

'I can make it into slippers, or a bag, whatever you want,' he said. 'I only need a needle and some thread. I was going to ask Hannah, but I thought I would give it to you first.'

Mother was turning the skin this way and that. 'It's lovely,' she said. 'I think I would like slippers. But how did you get this, Tom?'

'I trapped a rabbit.'

'And then what did you do?'

I thought of the razor I had found among his things. So this was why he needed it.

'I did what you need to do to make it into fur,' said Tom. 'Did I do something bad?'

'Not at all,' said Mother. 'But I have no idea how to make furs. Tell me.'

'First I caught the rabbit in a trap. Then I skinned it. I gave the meat to Wolf. Was that bad?'

'No, of course not.'

'Then I scraped the skin.' He made a brushing movement against the leather. 'To get away the meat. And then you split the head and take out the stuff inside.'

'The brain,' said Mother.

'You mash it and add water and spread it on,' explained Tom.

I felt a little nauseous. I had been stroking the soft fur, but now I put it down.

'But when did you learn how to do this?' asked Mother.

Tom shrugged. 'I just knew in my head and my hands.'

'Tom—' said Mother. But there was a knock at the door. This wasn't unusual, people ran to my mother at all times of the day and night, asking for her urgent help. I was used to waking up and finding her gone. She sighed, and went to open it.

'Why, Wyngate!' she said, and I stiffened. I knew she considered Mr Mitchell a friend, but it was strange to hear her so familiar with him.

'Good evening, Elizabeth. Good evening, Emmy and young Tom,' said Mr Mitchell, rubbing his hands as he strode to the fire. 'It's bitter cold out there.'

Mother poured him a whisky and took one for herself too. Tom sniffed the liquor scent and his mouth turned down. I wished I could put my hand on his neck, to feel

125

his pulse. I was sure that he had bad memories associated with alcohol.

'Cheers!' said Mr Mitchell. 'I am sorry to intrude so late, but I have just returned to town, and I have some news.'

'From the city?' asked Mother, and he nodded.

I had no interest in Mr Mitchell's news and I went back to my book. Tom took a step backwards, clearly hoping to escape.

'Don't go, young man, this affects you,' said Mr Mitchell. Tom froze.

'Why, what has happened?' asked Mother.

'I wanted to check it was true before I told you anything, but I think now is as good a time as any. Tom, we may have found your mother.'

I will never forget Tom's face at that moment. Suspicion and caution, puzzlement for a few moments, then utter, trusting, complete joy. A smile wide and unabashed, eyes almost closed, his arms hugging his chest.

'You remember her, I see,' said shrewd Mr Mitchell.

'She went away,' said Tom. 'I thought she would never come back, but you have found her. I . . . thank you.'

He fell to his knees, bowing his forehead to the ground.

CHAPTER FIFTEEN

1994

MEGAN

Dad's in Grandma Vera's kitchen, and he's on the phone. I sit and listen to him saying, 'Oh no,' and 'What can we do?' and I can tell it's bad news. I wonder what disaster has happened now, and whether it could be my fault.

He puts the phone down. 'Grammy's in the hospital,' he says. 'They think she's had a stroke.'

'Oh Wilf, that's terrible,' says Grandma Vera. 'How is she?'

'Betsy says she's semi-conscious but not making much sense. They're doing tests. Oh, Megan, don't cry love.'

'It's just ... she was okay until we went to see her.'

'But that's not what made this happen, if that's what you

mean,' says Grandma Vera. 'It could have happened at any time. When you're as old as Grammy . . . '

'Try not to worry, pumpkin,' says Dad. 'It's hard, I know.'

'Can we go and see her?' asks Grandma.

'Betsy's going to let us know. Not for a bit, she needs time to recover.'

The phone rings and I'm instantly braced for the worst, but no, it's Mom, and we all listen as Grandma breaks the news.

I really don't want to talk to her right now, but I take the phone from Grandma when it's offered. Dad's already halfway up the stairs. It's like he can't even bear to be in the room when I'm talking to Mom. I know that's crazy, they do actually talk to each other in an 'it's a very amicable separation' sort of way.

'Megan, darling,' she says. 'Are you okay?'

'I'm fine. Just worried. She could die.' I know I sound stupid and childish. Of course an old person could die. I mean, so could anyone.

'Let's hope that doesn't happen,' she says gently.

Mom never really understood Grammy. Mom was all about getting out of Astor. Grammy stayed. Mom had no interest in Grammy's stories about the old days – and she didn't want me to, either. Mom was about escaping. Grammy was about staying.

'How are you anyway, Mom? Having a good time with Fernando?' I ask. 'Or have you found someone else yet?' I know this is mean and unfair, but it makes me feel slightly better.

'Megan,' she sighs. But she doesn't take the bait. 'Well, I'm busy of course. Working hard.'

'As usual.'

'Yup, as usual! But we managed a weekend in Paris, and we're going to the theatre next week. I wish you could come with us, get to know him better.'

I don't begrudge Mom happiness, but she could do with a lesson in sensitivity at times.

'So when are you coming back to London?' she asks. 'I miss you.'

'There's no point. Everyone's away,' I say, shutting her down cold. I really can't seem to help myself.

'You could still do that volunteer project at the hospital in Cambodia.'

'I'm just going to stay here in Astor,' I tell her, thinking that if I went to some hospital in South East Asia people would probably start dying off in droves. I remember the counsellor at the hospital talking about irrational feelings of guilt. It didn't help then and it's not helping now.

'Oh, well. If it makes you happy.'

'You don't have a clue what makes me happy.'

'Maybe that's because you never talk to me, Megan.'

'Oh, right, well you always have so much time for talking ...'

Mom doesn't get a lot of vacation. I felt like I'd used up

my quota, what with the appointments at the clinic and the rest.

'You can talk to me now,' she says. 'I've got twenty minutes before my conference call.'

'I'm busy,' I say. 'Another time, Mom.'

'But—'

'I've got to go.'

I put the phone down, and go through to the kitchen to get myself a Coke. Grandma's in there. I don't know how much she heard.

'All right, darling?' she says. 'How's your mom?'

'She's okay,' I say. 'Having fun with Fernando.'

'It's hard for you, I know.'

'I'm fine. It's Grammy I'm worried about.'

'Grammy knows that every day is a gift,' says Grandma. 'And she knows that family life can be complicated and difficult. I know your mom has hurt you—'

'She's hurt Dad!'

'And you, Megan, darling—'

We're interrupted by a knock at the door. Grandma rushes to open it. 'Megan,' she calls. 'It's Ed!'

She's giving him an update on Grammy's health as I come to the door.

'Hey there, fancy a drive?'

I don't really, but I can't be bothered to think of an excuse, not with Grandma looking on. I grab a jacket and head out.

'Sorry to hear about Mrs Harkness,' he says as I climb into the car. 'I was hoping to talk more to her about the body they found. She's virtually an eye witness. They reckon the body dates from around a hundred or so years ago.'

Even by Ed's standards that's crass. At least he has the decency to look ashamed, when I glare at him.

'Sorry,' he says. 'Insensitivity goes with the territory sometimes. Not that I'm trying to excuse myself. My dad's always warning me about coming across as a jerk.'

Obviously he never listened to his dad. I wish I'd never got into the car. 'An eye witness of what, exactly? Elementary school?' I ask. 'She would have been pretty young.'

'Astor was a small place in those days. A woman going missing – it'd be noticed.'

'It's still a small place now,' I tell him. 'Where are we going anyway?'

'The police are having a press conference. I thought you'd want to come along.'

I'm taken aback. 'Really? Will they let me in?'

'Sure they will. I'll tell them you're shadowing me. Work experience. You want to be in the media, right? Everyone wants to be in the media.'

'I'm more interested in the science part – the forensics,' I tell him, but we're pulling up outside the police headquarters and I don't know if he heard me.

No one questions Ed when he signs me in for the press conference, and there are only around twenty people there anyway. A reporter and a cameraman from the local television station are checking the lighting, Ed greets some reporters from other local papers.

'Are you taking photos too?' I ask, but he says no, the paper is sending a photographer.

'Sam?' I ask, remembering the dark-eyed boy at the party.

'Could be. He's not bad. For a freelance.'

I turn and see him. Sam, laden with camera bag, assessing the room for the best spot. I wave at him and he smiles and ducks his head. *He's cute*, I think, but without conviction. Maybe I only think he's cute because the dark hair reminds me of . . .

Damn Ryo. How dare he make me fall in love with him and then run away to Tokyo? Not for the first time I ponder the option of flying out to Japan. Can you really get over someone when there's no chance to talk to them? I mean, I should be angry with him, but I'm not because I understand why he couldn't cope. If I could have run away, I probably would have done.

'Ladies and gentlemen, if we can begin,' says a policeman and we're off. An introduction, explaining where and how the body was found and then the police spokesman introduces Dr Mary Sweet, research fellow in forensic archaeology at Astor University.

She's brisk and competent. Her brown hair is tied back from her face. She's an impressive scientist, just like I want to be. She spends her whole life using modern technology to find out the secrets of old bones. I like her right away.

'The police asked for our help when they realised the age of the body,' she tells us. 'We have quite a few clues to help us piece together her story, and we're hoping that by sharing them with the public we can find out even more.

'We put her age at the time of death at anywhere between seventeen and thirty. Fully grown. She'd been pregnant in the past. We think she died between 1895 and 1905.

'We have a probable cause of death. Her skull is damaged, and we recovered this.' She holds up a small plastic bag. 'A bullet. Tests show it is from a pistol, of the sort commonly used in 1880. So we believe that this young woman was shot in the back of the head.'

She shows us a slide of the skull, pointing out the bullet hole. No one could survive that. I wonder if there was any warning, if she knew someone had a gun pointing at her back?

'We have fragments of her clothing. Some silk – from a dress, or underwear. And fur. A coat made from rabbit skins. Full length. Perhaps she had money, or maybe a benefactor.'

I imagine her, spinning around in her rustling dress, stroking the soft fur of her coat. 'Look how pretty I am!'

And then the shot rings out and she crumples to the ground. She might only have been my age.

'We have one more important piece of information,' says Dr Sweet. 'She had with her some papers. Most of them are degraded fragments, but one letter has survived pretty much intact.'

The audience stirs and mumbles as Dr Sweet changes the slide. Script-marks loop and curl across the screen.

'It's not the opening page,' she says. 'Some of the words are indistinct. But it's extraordinarily well preserved, considering the circumstances.'

I can't read the writing. The letters are so dense and busy they make my eyes hurt. But as Dr Sweet reads them out the words swim into focus.

'Miss P is kind enough to say that she will take you back, Mattie, despite all that has gone before. I hope you appreciate her generosity. However, there is no place for J here. Do you understand, Mattie? You must come alone or Miss P will not have you. Can you not—'

The letter stops in mid-sentence. Dr Sweet shows us the next page, stained and illegible. Only the signature is just about clear.

Ellen.

CHAPTER SIXTEEN

1994

MEGAN

'Interesting, huh?' says Ed to me. 'Mrs Harkness must remember someone like that. A fancy silk dress and a fur coat?'

'If she ever wakes up enough for us to ask,' I point out, wishing I could escape.

He waves Sam over to join us. Sam's in full-on grunge mode. Straight jeans, oversized jumper; a complete contrast to Ed's preppy chinos and sharply pressed button-down shirt. He's shorter than Ed, too. Ed ruffles Sam's hair and says, 'How's it going, boy?' Sam shrugs him off, clearly annoyed.

'Hey,' he says to me. 'You okay?'

'Fine, thanks, Sam.'

'I got to get some close ups of the letter,' he says. 'See you back at the office, Ed.'

'We're heading there now,' says Ed. 'You'll come, won't you Megan?'

'I'd just be in the way,' I say. 'I should be getting back anyway, check in on how Grammy's doing.'

'You can call from the office,' says Ed. 'And I could use your help with some research.'

'Sure thing,' I say. I glance back at Sam to catch his eye, to show that I'm irritated at the way Ed assumes I'm his unpaid helper. But Sam's busy taking pictures.

The *Astor Press* offices are in a brand new modern block on the south side of town. Lots of parking, no greenery, no shops or cafés around.

'Dad only moved us in here last year. I hate it,' says Ed as we pull into the parking lot. 'No character. I think it was a mistake.'

'Where were you before?' I ask.

'The original office – built way back in 1905. Full of history and personality. But Dad gets a great rent here, and he's having the old place converted into apartments. Maybe I'll move into one.'

'Sounds cool,' I say. 'I'd like to see it. Grammy used to work there. She's told me a few stories about how she used to write reports about church fetes and how Grandpa Jesse started out as a copy boy.'

'It's been gutted now, not much to see. But we've got loads of memorabilia here. I'll show you.'

When we get into the newsroom Ed takes a slight detour to show me what's been salvaged from the past. Old framed copies of front pages. A shining mahogany desk, which sits in the editor's office. A worn leather chair. The original wooden sign that hung on the wall outside.

The newsroom is quieter and emptier than I expected, although my entire experience of newspaper offices is via film and TV in which predominantly men (Lois Lane aside) type vigorously at desks scattered with piles of paper.

At the news desk, Ed dumps his backpack on to a chair. 'Hey, Ryan,' he says.

Ryan's a hefty guy in his thirties, with a McDonald's carton on his desk. He looks as though he's been frowning so hard for so long that a V shape has carved itself permanently into the space above his nose. 'You're late,' he tells Ed. 'And who's she?'

'This is Megan Harkness, my new research assistant,' says Ed, smooth as butter. 'Great-granddaughter of the famous Emmeline. Here visiting from London.'

Ryan nods his head to me. 'Well, good day to you, Megan. I take it Ed's paying you out of his own pocket?'

'I'm not—' I start, but Ed interrupts: 'No problem, Ryan, we'll be in the library.'

'I really do need to go soon,' I tell him, as he leads me down a corridor.

'I won't be long,' he says. 'And then I can drop you off at the hospital if you want. You can go and see Mrs Harkness for yourself. In the meantime, have a look at our library. A real link with the past.'

'Fifteen minutes,' I tell him. 'Then I'm getting a taxi.'

'Just look for our Fur Coat girl,' he says. 'Take your mind off things. Here we are.'

He opens the door to the library. It's full of shelves of files at one end and books the other.

'It's not as good as it used to be,' he says. 'We're archiving and it's a real mess. But maybe you can find something. Jack will help you, won't you, Jack? She needs to look at the issues from 1895 to 1905 or so. Looking for reports of a missing woman, or anything about a girl called Mattie coming to town. The body, you know. Found in Forest Heights.'

Jack's a short, slight guy about my age, his face dominated by huge black specs and a fringe of mousey hair. 'It's Zac, not Jack,' he says, as the door shuts behind Ed.

I laugh. 'Nice to meet you, Zac. You the librarian?'

'Just holiday cover. I'm studying history at the university. My cousin's the archivist, but she's off on annual leave. You're Bee's cousin, aren't you?'

'That's right.' I badly miss the anonymity of London.

'She's okay, Bee.' He's not smiling. 'Well, how about we start with where the body was found. No way it was part of Astor at the time. There were mineworks there earlier, but they'd have been closed down for maybe fifty years by then and pretty much forgotten. That cottage is an oddity. It would have stood miles into thick forest, alongside the old track the miners would've used. Maybe it was built for a miner, or just someone who didn't want to be near other folk. Jane Doe could have come from anywhere, and just been dumped at the side of the track by someone who knew their way.'

'Okay.'

'There's been a lot written about the town's expansion northwards into the forest over the years.'

He pulls a file off the shelf and hands it to me. It's labelled 'Forest Heights', and it's stuffed full of yellowing cuttings. 'How far back do these files go?' I ask him.

He shrugs. 'The paper was set up in 1890, so I guess as far back as then. It's hard to keep them up to date nowadays, though. They're cutting back on staff, putting everything on microfiche.'

'What's that?'

'Miniature film. If you want to read editions of the paper before 1950 you have to look it up on that viewer,' he says, pointing at a large TV-sized contraption. 'Kinda like looking at cells under a microscope? A shame, I think, you lose something not being able to feel the paper . . . but there you go, that's progress for you. According to my cousin, in the future we're going to be able to get every bit of information we need on our computers. Something called the interweb.'

'Can't wait,' I say, keen to finish this chat about library technology and start my research.

I begin sifting through the cuttings. It's mainly documents about building projects and protestors. But then I see an older cutting, from 1925, which catches my eye because it's out of chronological order. It isn't stuck on to a piece of paper, like the newer cuttings, and it's tattered round the edges and yellow as smokers' teeth.

It's about a planned new development 'to be built just half a mile to the east of Trader's Cottage, notorious as the site of the gruesome murder of Elijah Brown, less than twenty years ago.'

I pause.

'Hey, Zac, look at this.'

It's a murder, okay, but clearly not our girl. The writer is just a little bit vague on the date, though, and that's interesting.

Zac's intrigued. 'This is great. Mostly the reporters can't even be bothered to look at anything further back than a year or so ago.'

He pulls out a map of the area dated 1915 and unfolds it carefully on to a table at the back of the library. He points out Astor's oldest roads – including Harkness Street – and then some outlying farmsteads.

'That one there belonged to your great-grandfather.'

Then he traces North Road and shows me where it turned into a track. 'The development they're talking about must be around here ... ' His finger stabs a dense forest. 'And where the body was found.'

The door opens and someone comes in. Zac leaves me to it while he goes to see what they want. I can't see who it is, there are too many bookshelves in the way, but I recognise the voice of Sam the photographer.

'Hey, man,' he greets Zac. 'Jeez, Ed's getting worse by the day. Throwing his weight around like he's already in charge.'

Sam audibly hushes at that point – presumably Zac has gestured that they're not alone – but I smile to myself. *Couldn't agree more*, I think.

I look and look, but there's no trace of Trader's Cottage on the map. Elijah Brown's murder probably had nothing to do with the mysterious Mattie anyway. I'm about to get on and look at the old newspapers, when I notice something about half a centimetre from where Zac guessed Mattie's body was found: a faded ink-penned cross.

It's faint – almost invisible – and it's tiny ... but it's there.

CHAPTER SEVENTEEN

1994

Megan

The newspaper library is infuriating. No file for Elijah Brown, nothing on Trader's Cottage, and when I ask Zac if there's a file for 'Crimes' or 'Murders' he shakes his head apologetically.

'No, even somewhere like Astor, that'd be a pretty big file. I'll have a look at the bound copies from 1900.'

The older editions of the *Astor Press* are leather-bound in large formats, shelved and covered in dust. He pulls out a couple at random.

'We've pretty much microfiched everything from 1915 on, but these ones haven't been done yet. If any are missing they're probably off being processed.'

I get to work, turning the yellowing pages, but find no mention of Mattie. No news stories about a missing woman, nothing but small-town fodder – a farm burned down, a man killed at a lumber yard, the Harkness family donating money to help build a school, plans for a new hospital.

The hospital is fascinating to me and I'm transfixed by a photograph of Grammy's mother, Astor's first town doctor. *'We should value expert medical help, however it is dressed,'* says the editorial. *'Dr Murray is a welcome addition to our town.'*

I realise at once that Dr Murray was not welcome at all, and a glance at the letters page confirms it. I'm proud of her, glaring at the camera, not a hint of a smile on her face. She's defiantly plain, it seems to me, her light hair pulled back into a tight bun, eyes hidden behind glasses. Dr Murray means business. She wants to be taken seriously.

I think Dr Murray would be pleased to know her great-great-granddaughter has a place at university to study medicine. But I also bet she'd never let some boy break her heart – and she'd never be so stupid as to accidentally get pregnant.

I ask Zac if I can make a copy and he says he'll do it for tomorrow.

'Okay,' I say.

'Finished?' he asks.

'No, I'll keep looking.'

I soon lose all track of time, absorbed in the past as I

look through page upon page of advertisements for horses and liquor; story after story about the town's many new developments; about lumber, mining, the price of grain, the railway. An Indian chief killed by a rival, buried by his people. *'The old belief in spirits and witchcraft is slowly being defeated by education and the efforts of the Church.'* Canadian boys fighting for England and Empire in Africa, dying in battle far from home.

'Found anything?' someone says behind me.

I turn around to find Sam. 'Sorry to disturb you, you were miles away. I just thought, if you found anything, let me know and I can arrange a rag-out of the page.'

'A rag-out?'

'A copy of the page which looks like it's been freshly torn out of today's paper.' He smiles. 'It's what passes for artistic around here. Looks good next to copy.'

'Oh, right. But I haven't found anything.'

I go back to my research, thinking he'll leave. But he doesn't. I can smell him – soap and mint fresh despite his grungy clothes. I can see him out of the corner of my eye.

'Did you want something?' I ask.

'No ... it's just, look ... what I said about Ed ...'

'Oh, that? Don't worry.'

'It's just that Ed does have some power here, and I really need this work, so I'd appreciate it if you didn't say anything.'

I'm touched that he's bothered to ask and charmed by

the insecurity that clearly lies behind it. It makes me feel less embarrassed that he saw me crying at Grammy's party. He was kind to me then. And he is cute. It's not just the dark hair and brown eyes, he's got a sweet smile. He seems like a good person, an instinct I'm not used to.

'I'm not that friendly with Ed. I hardly know him,' I say, which is true.

'Thanks,' Sam smiles, 'I thought you'd be nice about it.'

I don't know why this cheers me up, but it does.

'I'd better get back to it,' I say. Sam stays by my side, looking over the newspaper with me.

'It must be strange for you, reading these. Almost every page is about your family.'

'I guess. But I don't see it like that. I'm me, Megan, not just a Harkness.'

'Fair enough,' he says. 'I understand that. And it's not like you grew up here. You've lived all over the world, I'm told.'

'Sounds so glamorous when you put it like that,' I say. 'Even so, my roots are here. How come we never met before? I know most people.'

'I think we did meet actually, back when my mom died,' he says. 'Your grandma helped us out.'

'Oh,' I say. 'I'm sorry.'

'You don't remember. No worries,' he says.

I think back. A vague memory of sitting in the car while Grandma dropped off some food at a run-down house.

'I'm sorry about Mrs Harkness,' he says, as if he can read my thoughts. 'She came to talk at our school once. Told us about the town's history. I sat there, and the way she told it, it was like I'd gone back in time.'

'I wish I'd asked her more questions. I wish I'd listened more.' I check my watch. 'And I need to go and see her, or at least find out how she's doing. Can you help me get a taxi? If I wait for Ed I'll be here forever.'

'Sure,' he says. Then I turn the page of the volume in front of me. A new front page, from March 1904.

Wild Boy Found on North Road.

Chaos in Town Hospital.

Did He Live with Wolves?

Below the headline is a photograph. A dark-haired boy, with a straight nose and a big mouth. Light-coloured eyes, slanted eyebrows, a heart-shaped face.

'Oh!' I say out loud, startled. Sam looks over my shoulder. He sees it right away.

'Wow,' he says. 'He looks just like you.'

CHAPTER EIGHTEEN

1904

EMMY

It's fair to say that by the time we made the trip to Toronto, everyone involved was out of sorts.

Mr Mitchell and Mother were frustrated that Tom couldn't or wouldn't talk about his memories of his mother. Every question they asked was met with a vague, 'I don't know' or 'I don't remember', and it was clear that was not entirely true.

Tom himself had grown largely quiet and seemed anxious. I never caught him consumed by a spontaneous moment of joy, or playfulness, as I had done in the early days. In the evenings he avoided our company, staying in his room, and having to be coaxed to eat. After taking a few spoonfuls of food he would make an excuse to leave the table, and go outside to be with Wolf. I felt rejected and shut out. Half of me wanted him to have his happy reunion, and leave us; but a small, selfish corner of my heart wished that this Mrs McNaughton had never seen the news item about Tom, and that he would stay with us for ever.

During the train journey, Tom and I gazed out of our separate windows, while Mr Mitchell and Mother talked about the hospital and the newspaper. No mention was made of the frosty encounter with Mrs Mitchell, who had accompanied her husband to the station, gripping his arm possessively and glaring furiously at the rest of us and as she bade him farewell.

I watched Mother, so easy and relaxed in conversation. It was a strange friendship, I thought. She was – necessarily – so guarded about her work, and he was so open, so irreverent, so, well, if he had been a woman he would have been called a gossip. He told us stories of his time as a reporter in Toronto and some of them were so extraordinary – the man who slaughtered his entire family, the woman who went crazy and ran through the streets stark naked – that I swear he invented them.

Later in life, I thought back to this trip to Toronto and wondered at my innocence. My lack of suspicion. My acceptance that Mother could be friendly with a man – a married man – and that there was nothing to it. But I took it all at face value. After all, a child trusts its parent.

I know my children have always trusted me. But did I deserve that trust? It is for you to judge.

When we arrived, Mr Mitchell led us swiftly through the hustle and bustle of the station to the Queen's Hotel where, once inside, Tom and I gawped at the ornate carved furniture, the damask drapes and hand-blocked wallpaper.

'It is so grand!' I said, knowing as the words passed my lips that I sounded like a country bumpkin.

'Not as grand as it once was,' said Mr Mitchell. 'In years gone by, presidents and foreign dignitaries all came to dine at the Queen's when they were in town. But now it has more competition, it's beginning to fade a little. What do you think, Tom?'

Tom was still staring around, fascinated, shaking his head and blinking. I touched his hand. 'Are you all right?' I asked.

'The music . . . ' he said.

There was the faint sound of someone playing the piano.

'It's coming from the Grand Salon,' said Mr Mitchell, 'where you can take tea.'

'Is that where we will meet her?'

'No, Tom, I have taken a private room for the purpose. Come now, we must hurry, we only have an hour to prepare.'

It was arranged that Mr Mitchell and I would meet Mrs McNaughton first, while Mother waited with Tom until I was sent to collect them for the formal introductions. I had wanted to wait with Tom, but it was not to be. He was fidgety with nerves, and Mother had to tell him to stop biting his fingernails.

We identified her easily upon entering the salon. Mrs McNaughton was a small-boned, fine-featured woman. Her eyes were bluer than Tom's, and her hair a lighter shade of brown, threaded with grey.

She was not an old woman, but her forehead bore lines, criss-crossed like the train tracks we'd seen approaching the city. The skin on her hands was red and raw, her nails stained yellow with tobacco. They never stopped moving, fussing and fidgeting in her lap.

'It's so cold,' she said. 'April, and yet it's trying to snow. Are you going back to Astor tonight?'

'We plan to, ma'am, yes,' I said. *Tom included*, I added, silently.

Mr Mitchell confirmed that she was Margaret McNaughton, thirty-six years old, a washerwoman here in Toronto. She had been born on the Isle of Mull and emigrated fourteen years earlier.

'So, Mrs McNaughton. What's your claim to the lost boy from the forest?'

'He is the right age to be my Andrew. He has the same face ... the eyes ... He is my boy, I am sure. And look, he's the image of my nephew,' she told him. 'Look, here he is.'

She pulled a creased photograph from her pocket. The boy did look a little like Tom, but there were many differences. The nephew's mouth was wider, his ears stuck out, he had wavy hair, while Tom's was straight.

'Where is this boy?' asked Mr Mitchell, studying the photograph. 'Can we compare the two?'

She shook her head. 'He is back in Scotland with the rest of my family. Once my husband died I was all alone, just me and my sweet wee boy.' Her voice trailed away. Her hands kept up their motion, twisting and turning as though she were kneading dough. I longed to reach out and make her hold them still, partly from sympathy and partly because her anxiety fed mine, that she was telling the truth and my Tom truly was her son.

'What happened to Andrew?' asked Mr Mitchell. His voice was kind and somehow fatherly. Anyone would want to confide in a man with such a voice.

Her hands were momentarily still. 'He was taken. One night. I was working; I know, I should not have left him, I should not have, but I did. He was asleep, I know he was asleep and I told the woman downstairs to listen for him. He slept well, my boy, he never stirred. And I needed the money to feed him. None of it was for me, just for my boy. They looked for him. He was in the newspapers. But they said that there were no clues, nothing, and he could have been taken away on a train, or in a wagon. I never went back to Scotland, because I never gave up hope that he would be found. And then this boy ... this lost boy ... he is the right age ... and he looks so like Andrew.'

'You have a photograph?' asked Mr Mitchell.

'No.' She looked at her hands. 'I lost it years ago. I only have the one of my nephew. I would know my son, though. I would know him in an instant.'

'Ah yes, but will he know you?' said Mr Mitchell.

'I hope so,' she said. 'But he was so young.'

Mr Mitchell asked more about her husband – was he tall or short, what did he die of? Her answers were vague and there was none of the fervour that came into her voice when she spoke of Andrew.

'Have you a birth certificate for Andrew?'

She did. She pulled it from her bag, smoothed it out. We peered at it. The date of birth – 1890 – would make Andrew sixteen years old. I thought Tom was older – but only by maybe a year. Her husband was tall, she had said. It did fit.

'Emmy,' said Mr Mitchell at last, 'perhaps you should ask Tom to come into the room.'

I did not want to. Now that I had met her, my heart had softened towards Mrs McNaughton. I wanted her little boy to be alive and reunited with his heartbroken mother, but still I hoped it was not Tom. Not my Tom. For if he was, there was no chance at all that she would ever let him leave her side again.

CHAPTER NINETEEN

1904

EMMY

I found Mother and Tom in the public salon. The piano was closed and silent, but Tom's gaze was fixed on it.

'It is time,' I said. 'She seems nice.'

We were silent as we walked up the stairs, but I could sense Tom's excitement. There was a spring in his step, and his arms swung freely at his side. It made me realise how tense his body usually was, how his shoulders hunched. *He has a right to a family*, I told myself. *Do not feel sad that he is happy.*

The instant Tom walked into the room, Margaret McNaughton made a sound something between a sob and a gasp, but in that same moment I knew that she was not the mother he himself had expected to find. He exhaled, and I watched as all his giddy anticipation disappeared.

'Tom,' said Mr Mitchell, 'I know you say you have no memory at all of anything that happened to you before you came to our town. But this lady says she is your mother. Do you remember her at all?'

Margaret McNaughton was sobbing into her handkerchief.

Tom shook his head. 'No, sir,' he said.

'Does the name Andrew mean anything to you? Andrew McNaughton?'

'No, sir.'

Margaret McNaughton was overcome with emotion. 'Andrew!' she said. 'Andrew, it's me, your mother! You remember me, I know you do.'

He looked her at her then, really looked. He took in her poor cracked hands, her down-turned mouth, her wispy hair. I saw only pity in his eyes.

'No, ma'am. I don't remember you at all. I am sorry.'

She whimpered in distress, and he looked away, as though it hurt him to see her pain.

Mr Mitchell was displeased, I could tell. His great story, the reunion of mother and son, was collapsing because Tom would not cooperate.

'Maybe if we take Tom back to your home?' he suggested. 'It might bring back memories.'

'It was pulled down,' she said, dismally. 'They said

it weren't sanitary. It wasn't much anyway, just a room. Andrew, don't you remember? You and me and Mrs McGinty downstairs, and the French girl, Jeanne. You used to play ball with the McGinty boys. You had . . . '

She fumbled with her bag.

'Here!' She thrust a stuffed toy at him. A ragged dog, grey and worn as her clothes. 'This was yours. You must remember it!'

He took it from her, turned it over and over in his hands. His long fingers stroked its ears. He held it to his nose and breathed in its scent. His eyes blinked, once, twice. Then he spoke.

'How did you lose your son?'

She tried to take his hand, but he stepped away. 'Someone took you. They took you from your bed. Do you remember your little bed? You had a red blanket and—'

'Did you see who took him?' he asked.

'I . . . I wasn't there. I left him – you – to go and work.'

'Why do you say it was me? How do you know?' He thrust the ragged dog back to her. 'You don't know anything. I don't remember anything about you. You lost your son but it's too late to get him back.'

Mr Mitchell was looking again at the birth certificate that Mrs McNaughton had handed him.

'This is a copy,' he said. 'It's not the original document.'

She was twisting and turning the toy dog in those hands now. 'Yes, it is a copy. I couldn't find the certificate. Maybe it was mislaid, we had moved a few times. Rooms were hard to find, and the landlords ... You wouldn't believe it now, but I was reckoned to be pretty, and sometimes that meant we had to move ... quickly ... '

'So, the certificate?'

'I sent back to Scotland for a replacement. I needed to prove that he'd ever existed. See? Sometimes the years play tricks on your mind.'

Mr Mitchell looked impatient, though he was trying to hide it.

'Anyone can get a copy of a birth certificate,' he said. 'We need proof, woman, not copied documents and instinct. What about witnesses – anyone who knew your Andrew?'

'You don't understand what it was like in those days! Everyone was new to town. Mrs McGinty was kind, but she died and so many others died, and people were hard to keep track of.'

Tom turned away. He seemed detached, but his hand was shaking.

'Please, Andrew – come back to me. Just spend some time with me and you will remember, I know you will.'

Tom shook his head. 'I am sorry, ma'am. But no. I have a place to live and work to do. And I have Emmy, and Emmy's mother.'

Warmth spread from my tingling toes to the top of my head. Joy danced in me. And Mrs Margaret McNaughton saw.

She looked from Tom to me and back again.

She bundled the toy and the certificate back into her bag. She jumped to her feet and almost ran to the door.

And there she paused. I thought she would make one more appeal to Tom, but it was to me that she addressed these words.

'My son was stolen,' she said quietly, 'and now you have taken him away again. Please find it in your heart to give him back to me.'

I did not know what to say, but Tom said it for me. He looked different, I realised, less haunted. He spoke confidently.

'Emmy hasn't done anything to you. There's no one here for you. Go away and leave us alone.'

No amount of pleading on Mrs McNaughton's part could move Tom. In the end, she departed in tears.

Mr Mitchell said he thought she was motivated by the promise of the financial reward offered by the *Astor Press*.

Mother said she believed that she'd come in search of her child; 'she will probably spend her life believing that she has lost him a second time, poor woman.'

They both questioned Tom about how he was able to be so certain.

Tom was morose and silent, taking refuge in his usual shrugs and monosyllabic answers.

As for me, I still tingled with joy that Tom had made it so clear that he wanted to stay in our house.

*

Later that afternoon, Mother went out to see about supplies for the hospital and, somewhat to my surprise, announced that Mr Mitchell would accompany her. Tom and I were left to our own devices. We walked around the city a little. Tom seemed at ease in the noisy traffic and crowded streets and I began to wonder if he had lived here before, or in some other city at least.

'It's so different from Astor,' I said. 'Do you like it?'

'I prefer Astor,' he replied.

'There's more here, more people, more things to do.'

'I don't want more,' he said. And then, 'Do you think Wolf will be all right without me?'

'Why wouldn't he?'

Tom shrugged. 'I don't want him to run off.'

'He won't, he loves you too much.'

'He's not even mine,' he said.

'Who does he belong to then?'

'No one,' he replied. 'No one at all.' Then he seized my hand, and said, 'We're in the big city! Like London!' and we forgot our troubles in looking at shops and cars and people.

It was growing colder. Our breath froze on the air and by late afternoon we were glad to return to the warmth of the hotel, where we ordered hot chocolate in the Grand Salon. The piano was being played now, and yet again Tom was transfixed.

I dared to reach forward, to touch his hand. 'You remember a place like this, don't you, Tom? I am your friend. You can trust me. I *know* you remember your mother. Earlier, you knew who you were hoping to see – and you were so disappointed to find a perfect stranger instead.'

He looked at me.

'You will not tell anyone?'

'I promise.'

He seemed to reach a decision.

'All right. But not here, let's find somewhere private.'

He grasped my hand, and we searched the hotel until we found a quiet room, hung with heavy velvet drapes. There was a window seat behind one set of curtains, the perfect place to hide.

'Here,' said Tom, putting his arm around me to help me on to the seat. Never mind that we had to sit very close together. It was thrilling, to feel his breath against my cheek, to smell his hair and his skin, to rest my head on his shoulder.

'You can tell me,' I told him. 'You can trust me.'

His hand stroked my shoulder.

'I cannot remember it all,' he said. 'Just her. And a place like this, but different. Noisier. A resort.'

And then Tom told me his story.

CHAPTER TWENTY

1904

EMMY

How can I tell you Tom's story? He remembered some things in great detail and others hardly at all. He lacked the words to describe much of what he did recall, but he used everything that he had learned, talking and reading with me, to illustrate his story. The love he felt for his mother shone through every sentence. But that's no surprise. Love is the strongest memory of all, and it lives well beyond the grave.

That's why I'm telling you this, after all.

'My ma was beautiful,' he said. 'Nothing like the lady this morning. She wore silk dresses, and her hair was dark and shiny. She had pink on her cheeks and her lips, and she smelled of roses.'

'You remember her well,' I said, surprised.

'I think so,' he agreed. 'She was all I had to remember for a long time.'

His earliest memories were all confusion. Dark rooms, babies crying, bad smells. He did not think his mother lived there with him all the time. Later on – much later – I realised that he had probably been trusted to a 'baby farm', run by one of those women who looks after many children, and charge their mothers plenty for it. I've read descriptions of those places which make me shudder. I think Tom was lucky to survive this start in life, and it seems his mother thought so too, because he told me of a quarrel, of raised voices, and angry words, and of being grabbed out of one woman's arms by his ma, and of her running down a steep staircase and out into the cold, dark night, running and running with her tears falling like sea spray on to his upturned face.

And then they arrived at a house – 'a big, warm, house full of music' – and there was more shouting, and a woman telling her to get out. 'She could not have a child there. That's what I remember.'

'What happened? Where did you go?' I breathed, and he thought for a while and said he had no idea.

He didn't know when and he couldn't tell me how, but they ended up in another big house – the 'resort' – because his ma's friend Ellen worked there. The 'boss lady' was called Peggy, and Tom had to hide from her, because

Peggy had said that she would let them stay, but she didn't want to be bothered with the child. 'Ma said it was only for a while, but I think it was a long time, because at first I would hide in the closet in her room, but later I got too big to sleep there.'

Tom made the house sound like a palace, 'like the one in your book, Emmy,' and I knew he meant the Tudor court in *The Prince and the Pauper*. It smelled of perfume and beeswax, and there were always flowers in silver vases. There was a staircase down the middle that went round and round, and sparkling jewels hanging from the ceilings. There were huge mirrors with gold frames on the walls, and a bright blue bird called Freddie, who could speak. He would say, 'Welcome! Welcome!'

'Was it a hotel, like this?' I asked, and Tom just shook his head. I realised he was embarrassed, but I didn't quite know why. You will think I was slow on the uptake, and very innocent besides, but it took time to fully appreciate exactly the nature of the place he was describing. There were a lot of pretty girls there, he said, and there were gentlemen visitors, and there was dancing and drinking and so much smoking that the rooms stank of tobacco.

Still I did not understand. So – carefully, gently – he explained.

'The girls were there for the men. They gave them money. They gave them gifts too, sometimes. Ma got candy and flowers and jewellery for her ears and her neck. She looked pretty. I know this was a bad place, Emmy, I know that people in Astor would call it . . . would call her . . . bad names. I am not stupid. But she was not a bad person. She was only trying to make some money so that we could have a home of our own one day.'

I was shocked, I must admit. We had once had a preacher from the United States, who had talked to us about the plight of Fallen Girls, dragged into Dens of Iniquity, and subjected to Utter Depravity. At the time, I had no idea what he was talking about. Now I realised that Tom's ma had been one of these Fallen Girls, that the resort he described was a Den of Iniquity and that Utter Depravity was less complicated than I had imagined. But I was determined that I would not say or do anything to make Tom feel uncomfortable about telling me his story. I told him that his ma sounded very brave, which indeed she did.

Tom had to stay in the closet at night, and stay quiet, no matter what. Sometimes he heard rustling noises, and thought they were mice or rats. He had nightmares, which made him cry out, so Peggy ordered that he should have a cloth tied around his mouth. He heard noises sometimes, men shouting, his ma crying. But he knew not to try and escape.

One night he woke up and everything was quiet, and when he tried the door it opened. So he thought it was morning. His ma wasn't there, so he went to look for her. And when he went downstairs it was all noise and smoke and movement, ladies dancing and men drinking. And he remembered everything going quiet. Everyone turning to look at him. And Peggy running up the stairs and chasing him back to the wardrobe. Locking him in. And for once, he was scared and angry and tried to get free, banging and kicking at the door until his ma opened it, begging him to be quiet. He saw that she had been crying. And he saw a red mark on the side of her face.

He didn't remember much after that. Just that he wasn't allowed to sleep in his mother's room anymore. He was given a bed in an outhouse, where it was cold and dirty and there were rats. But it wasn't all bad, living there. The other women were nice to him, and gave him chocolate and one, Ellen, began teaching him his letters. And he loved the music from the piano, and sometimes, if Peggy was away, he would try to play music himself. Ellen taught him that as well.

'She told me that Ma should send me away, to her folks,' he said. 'But Ma said she never would do that. That they were cruel to her and would be worse to me. So Ellen said she should go away with me, and find some other life. But Ma wanted to stay at Peggy's. She needed her.'

I asked him why, and he shook his head. 'I really can't remember. It was a long time ago, Emmy, and my head is full of holes. But I think, maybe, Peggy gave her something that she needed. Not money, but medicine perhaps? That's just an idea I have.'

We left it there, but later – much, much later – I read something which suggested that women like Peggy, women who exploited young girls for profit, gave them opiates to keep them loyal and addicted and docile. So maybe that was the answer.

'But your mother left eventually, didn't she?' I asked. I desperately wanted Tom's ma to have shown enough gumption to rescue herself and her son from this wicked place.

I felt his breath on my neck.

'She had to,' he said. 'We had no choice. There was a man in Ma's bed one morning, and his throat had been cut.'

CHAPTER TWENTY-ONE

1904

EMMY

I could hardly breathe, but then Tom paused.

'What's that?' he whispered.

I could hear the faint sound of a hand bell ringing and someone running. Then I heard shouting, but could not make out the words.

I was about to speak when there was a tremendous thumping at our door and a man's voice bellowed, 'Fire! Fire!'

'Come on!' I said, seizing Tom's hand. We ran to the door. People were streaming down the main staircase, and we followed them. It was chaos in the vestibule, a crowd of people, all shouting and crying. I could not understand why no one was evacuating the hotel. The air smelled of smoke, and behind the hubbub I could hear the roar and crack of flames.

'Form a chain, form a chain!'

A line of people began to form. I looked around for Mother and Mr Mitchell, but could not see them, so Tom and I joined the fire-fighting efforts, passing heavy buckets of water along the line.

'What happened?' I gasped to the woman next to me. 'Where is the fire brigade? Why aren't they helping?'

Her face was red with effort and heat, her hair wet with perspiration. 'You don't understand,' she said. 'The whole city is alight.'

'The whole city?' I repeated, stupidly, but before I could answer I saw Mr Mitchell, and cried out in relief. I did not dare vacate my place in the chain though, so I just shouted, 'Mr Mitchell! Over here!'

'Emmy, thank God!' he said. 'And Tom! Keep working. The whole of the business district is alight. The fire brigade are doing their best, but it's an inferno out there.'

'What if the hotel burns down?' I panted. The heat in the hotel lobby was becoming unbearable. Sweat ran down my forehead like water.

'Heaven help us all,' Mr Mitchell said sombrely.

'Where's Mother?'

'They have set up a first aid station down the road, she is helping there. I had to come and find you, make sure you were safe.'

'We are both safe,' I gasped, although I was not sure how long that would be true.

'I must go. They're calling for men to fill the buckets.' He hesitated, as though there was something else he wanted to say. Then he stepped towards me and, before I knew what he was doing, landed a kiss on my clammy forehead. 'Stay safe, Emmy,' he said. And he was gone.

After that, I lost track of time. All I could think about was the ache that started in my wrists and went up to my neck and back. The blisters on my palms from the buckets of water. The ever-intensifying heat, the sheer *noise* of the fire, the smoke that made my eyes itch and my mouth dry and my lungs raw. I was coughing and gasping, but I went on swinging the buckets from one hand to the other, passing them to Tom, whose pale face glowed in the gloom.

It was dawn before a fireman shouted for us to stop, and announced that we could stand down.

'Ladies and gentlemen, you have saved the hotel,' he said. 'Thank you.'

Tom and I followed the crowds out to the street. Where the grand buildings had stood earlier, now there was nothing but ruins. The air was acrid, making me gulp painfully at the smoke around me.

I am not ashamed to say that I sobbed, then, and cried out for Tom. I was so scared to lose him in the confusion. Then I felt someone take my hand, and all at once I was held in an embrace so tight that all I knew was the brush of his bristled cheek against mine.

'Emmy!' I looked up and I saw his pale eyes gleam from his dirty face, and I remembered the very first time I saw him, in the middle of the forest and what seemed a lifetime ago.

'Tom, oh, Tom, I thought we would die,' I sobbed, and we clung to each other as the snow fell through the smoky April sky, like a blanket to put out the remaining flames, dusting our heads and shoulders with soft, sharp flakes.

CHAPTER TWENTY-TWO

1994

MEGAN

'Well, found anything? You've been here long enough.'

Ed's voice booms across the library. Sam and I glance at each other, and move away from the open volume.

'Nothing at all about a woman going missing,' I tell him. 'But we've only got to 1904, loads more to look at.'

Go away, I urge him silently. I want him to leave us to find out more about Elijah Brown and the photograph of the boy who looks like me ... the Wild Boy – or Tom, as the paper goes on to name him. Sam and I have been reading and the whole thing's making my skin tingle. And Grammy is involved. She and her mother, Dr Murray, are all over these pages. I've just got to something called the

Second Great Fire of Toronto and I'm desperate to read about it.

But Ed doesn't go away.

'That's okay. Story's written, page is laid out.' He rounds on Sam who's moving away quietly. 'Phil's looking for you. I think he's got a few jobs to throw your way.'

'Oh, great,' says Sam, without enthusiasm.

'So, Megan, you coming? I can drop you at your grandma's.'

'Oh, right, okay,' I say. I'm reluctant to stop, but for some reason I really don't want Ed to know that I've stumbled on something that interests me, before I've worked out exactly what the story is and why I feel that I care so much. I want to keep it to myself.

Sam follows us out into the corridor. I'm trying to think of a way to ask him to keep quiet about the story, about the wild boy. But maybe it's common knowledge around here.

'So, are you coming to the gig tonight?' I ask him.

'Yeah,' said Sam. 'I'm the resident photographer at the venue. I'll be pretty busy, but I'll look out for you.'

Ed's already in the lift, holding it for me. I turn away from him and back to Sam, and quickly put my finger to my lips, hoping that he understands me. He nods, then turns and plods towards the newsroom.

'Sorry about that,' says Ed. 'Was it boring looking through the old papers?'

'No, it was okay,' I tell him. 'I might even come back

another day, go on looking. She's got to be there somewhere, don't you think?'

'The filing system is terrible. I think a lot of files got
dumped at some point.'

'How come?'

'No idea. It was a bit of a shambles when my grandpop
took over. Mrs Harkness didn't pay a load of attention to it.'

'Grammy?'

'Yeah, when she was in charge. Before she sold it to my
grandpop. She had enough on her hands, with her children
and all.'

Ugh, he's so patronising. Maybe I shouldn't go to the gig
tonight, but on the other hand, I don't want to be sitting in,
brooding about Grammy and Ryo and stuff.

'Hey, Ed, if she hadn't sold to your grandpop, *I'd* be the
one giving *you* a lift. You'd be the humble researcher. Twist
of fate and all that.'

He rolls his eyes. 'I don't think so. Talent will out. And
besides, you're a foreigner. And you're going to be a medical
student.' He smiles, flashing those dazzling teeth. 'Very
impressive.'

'Well, thank you.' What else can I say?

'You can take my temperature later,' he says as he stops at
Grandma's door, but doesn't stop to hear my cutting reply.

Grandma Vera insists that I go out for the evening;
there's been no change in Grammy's condition and I can
go and visit her tomorrow. It doesn't take me long to get

ready for the gig. I wash my hair, apply some mascara and a slick of lip gloss, change into jeans and a black T-shirt. Grandma Vera makes me a sandwich. 'It's nice to see you enjoying yourself,' she says.

'Oh, well, I don't know what this band is like. They might be terrible.'

'You go and have fun.'

'I'll try.' I hesitate. 'Grandma, did you ever hear the name Elijah Brown? He was murdered, here in Astor – about ninety years ago. Grammy was about my age then.'

She thinks, then shakes her head. 'I don't think I ever heard that name. Has he any connection with the body they just discovered?'

'That's what I don't know,' I say. 'Or rather, that's what I'd like to know.'

'Your father's the one to talk to. He's all over the family history right now.'

'I don't want to encourage him, Grandma,' I sigh. 'I'm worried about him. It feels like he's just living in the past. He's not doing anything, you know, proactive – about living life here and now.'

'I know, darling. But don't worry. He's a grown man. He just needs to adjust to building a life without Sandra.'

My dad was always the stay-at-home parent. The trailing spouse, they call them in the expat world. Mom was off on business trips, staying in hotels, calling us at bedtime from her office. Dad read to us, cooked supper, picked us up after gymnastics and basketball. He never had much of a chance to figure out what he wanted to do in life.

'Poor Dad.'

'They had a good long time to make it work,' says Grandma. 'And you know, I was always surprised that Sandra married Wilf in the first place. She was such an ambitious girl. She couldn't wait to leave Astor. Who'd have thought that she'd have married a hometown boy?' She sighed. 'Still. They've raised two children together. Now they both need time to work out what they want.'

She's right. I suppose I may have been a bit unfair, being angry at them for not staying together. I know its selfish, only thinking of myself and not their happiness. Still, I think they could have handled things better – for all of our sakes. It's hard living in a family where nobody talks about the things that really matter.

The gig is not at all bad. I'd been kind of worried that the Canadian music scene would begin and end with Celine Dion, but turns out they're as into grunge as anyone else. I suppose the flannel shirt lumberjack look fits right in with the culture. Afterwards, we all go to a bar, where Bee and Ed start dissecting the sludgy sound of the guitars. Bee knows her music, and Ed finally seems to get the message that I'm not interested, because he hardly gives me a second glance. Bee's looking good, hair newly dyed scarlet and lipstick to match. I reckon she'll see through Ed's charm as quickly as I did.

Sam comes into the bar about twenty minutes later, camera bag hanging off his shoulder, SLR slung around his neck. He's changed into a dark red T-shirt and black jeans and he's done something to his hair. He looks different, more confident, more open. He's got what Grandma would call an honest face. His eyes are too serious to lie about important things. I like him, I realise.

Sam smiles at me and sits down with a beer.

'So . . . I kept on looking at the files after you left,' he says.

It's so noisy in the bar that I have to put my head right close to him to hear. I can smell the shampoo he's used. 'And?'

'Very annoying. The next volume is missing.'

'What?'

'Zac says it might have been sent away to be copied for microfiche, but he checked the log and it wasn't signed out. So either there's been an error or it's gone missing.'

'It must be an error.'

Sam shrugs. 'Who knows? It's had years to get lost.'

'But it's so huge! How would you lose a thing that size?'

'Maybe someone took it home? I don't know, Megan. Big things go missing all the time.'

'I know. It's just so frustrating! Are there any other copies, do you think?'

'We could try the town library.'

I like the way he says 'we', like we've got a joint homework project or something.

'Why are you so interested?' I ask him.

Sam leans in, so I can hear him clearly without him having to shout over the noise of the bar.

'He was someone new to this town, a stranger. I've been in that position. It's not easy.'

I know what that's like. I've been the new girl again and again. You feel disorientated when you start somewhere new. You don't have your friends, you don't know your way around. I nod. 'Yeah, me too.'

'And he came from the forest. You know, we keep on cutting down trees and clearing land. We try and control the wildness that's all around us. We think we can control everything. But, we can't. Not really. And maybe we shouldn't.'

I lost control of my own body. And then I took that control right back again. I almost tell him everything, right now. But we're in a crowded bar. It's not the place.

'Maybe the wild boy was someone to be scared of,' I say. 'Maybe he was connected with the murder of Elijah Brown. Or maybe he killed the woman whose body they've just found. Mattie.'

'What's that?' Ed's leaning across the table. 'What about Mattie?'

Sam's immediately wary. 'Nothing. Just talking about the pictures I took earlier.'

'You said someone killed Mattie. You got a lead that you're planning to sell to the Toronto papers?' Ed's teasing.

Sam shakes his head. 'If only,' he says.

'Come on, you can tell me. What did you find in the archive?'

'It was all Sunday School picnics and golden weddings. Typical small town.'

God, I really know how to make myself popular. The second the words are out of my mouth, I sense the whole group withdrawing from me. Ed turns back to Bee. Several of my cousins wander off.

All except Sam.

'Good job,' he says. 'So ... I thought you were seeing Ed?'

'No, I am not,' I sound suitably emphatic.

'Oh, okay. Well, how about we meet up tomorrow?' He ducks his head. 'Not as a date or anything, just to try and find out more. We could go to the library.'

I suppress a smile. He's the polar opposite of arrogant Ed, or even Ryo who wasn't exactly big-headed but who did sort of exist in his own bubble, expecting me to make the arrangements about when we'd meet up. I used to think that I was the practical one, and he was the artistic dreamer. Now I'm reframing my memories, and wondering if he just couldn't be bothered. Ugh, Megan, what an idiot.

'I'm going to see Grammy at the hospital. Maybe we could meet outside at about two?'

He's about to reply when there's a disturbance at the bar. A stocky man, shouting at the staff. Banging his fist on the counter.

'Don't speak to me like that,' he bellows.

'Sam,' says Ed, jerking his head towards the noise.

Sam glances over, and jumps to his feet. Without saying goodbye to me, he walks swiftly to the bar and grabs the man's flailing arm, deflecting it from the barman and getting swiped in the face himself.

'Sam!' I stand up, but hesitate – I don't want to get involved in a fight. 'Ed, he needs help!'

Sam's nose is bleeding, but he's undaunted, pulling the man's arm to get him to leave. People watch in silence, as the door slams behind them. Then the bartender yells, 'Show's over, folks,' and the normal buzz of conversation starts again.

I sit down uncertainly. 'What was that? Poor Sam!'

'It's his stepdad,' says Bee. 'Lucky Sam was here, really. Meant they didn't have to call the police.'

'But Sam got hit – I mean his nose was bleeding. Is he going to be okay?' Sam's dad was about twice his size, in height and breadth. He wasn't making much sense either.

'Nothing he hasn't had to deal with before,' says Bee. 'Honest, Megan, you don't want to get involved.'

There's no point protesting, so I shrug and say, 'Seems a shame,' and sip my drink. Then I realise that Sam's left his camera bag behind.

'What's his number?' I ask Ed. 'I could call him.'

Ed frowns. 'Don't worry about that. I'll give it back to him.'

'But . . .'

Ed's got a smug, knowing expression on his face. He leans over, and says, 'Be careful around Sam. There's bad blood in that family.'

CHAPTER TWENTY-THREE

1994

MEGAN

Grandma thinks that it's a good idea for me to visit Grammy.

'I hope so,' I say, nervously. 'What if I upset her?'

'Now, why would you think that? We just need to let her know that we're with her, sweetheart. The hardest thing is to feel alone.'

'Thanks, Grandma,' I say, as she drops me off by the hospital. As I find my way to the ward and Grammy's room, I think about how lonely *she* must feel, now that Grandpa is dead. It makes me wonder whether life is nothing but loss and emptiness, failure and sadness. I shake my head, annoyed with myself. *Get a grip, Megan!* I'm not even a little bit alone. Sam's meeting me after I've finished at the hospital, and Bee wants to see a movie tonight.

Aunt Betsy is sitting at her bedside, but leaps up when I arrive. 'She's conscious, but a little confused,' she whispers. 'Don't worry, Megan. Just chat a while.' She bustles around, finding her handbag. 'I'll just have a short break,' she says. 'I've been here all day. It's so kind of you to take over for a while.'

'I've got to go at two,' I say, feeling bad that I can't stay longer. 'It's only half an hour.'

'That's long enough, darling,' she says. 'I've got to go and breathe some fresh air.'

Left alone with Grammy, I sit down and take her hand. Her eyes flicker open, but she gives no sign of recognising me. 'It's me, Megan,' I say, and her eyes close again.

I mumble a few lines about being very sorry she's not well, and hoping she'll feel better soon. Then, I think I might as well try.

'I've been reading the old copies of the *Astor Press*,' I tell her. 'They've got a library, with files and cuttings.'

Her eyes open again. I swear she's listening.

'I found you in a story, Grammy. You and someone called Sadie. You found a wild boy.'

She's struggling to speak, but she can't make her voice work. I stroke her gnarled hand, the skin as soft as a peach and wait, hopeful. But her mouth closes, and then her eyes flicker closed.

'I wish I'd known about him before. I felt a sort of ... interest in him. Sort of a connection with him. You know? He looks like me, Grammy.'

As I say it, I feel doubtful. Am I just imagining the connection? Maybe I just see my own face everywhere because I'm mourning someone who I'll never know? Someone who might have grown up into, well, anything. Anyone. I can't afford to let my thoughts go there.

Honestly, I'm getting completely over-dramatic. It was a mistake to come to Canada. I was only a few weeks pregnant, I should have gone travelling, moved on. Been more like Ryo – concentrated on my education, my future, instead of looking back to the past, trying to find myself in a crumbling newspaper. Idiot.

But Sam saw the likeness too. He was the one who commented on it. And I want to know more.

Grammy's head moves, just a tiny amount on the pillow. Nothing like a nod, but a gesture in that direction, maybe?

'You better hurry up and get well, Grammy, because I want to hear all about him. How you found him and what happened to him. There are a lot of papers missing.'

She opens her mouth again, and I lean forward to hear what she's trying to say. It's hard to make out, more of a sigh than a word, but if I had to guess I think what she says is: 'fire'.

'Fire, yes. The fire in Toronto? I read about that too.' But she's still and silent again.

'I don't know why I care so much about this boy,' I tell her. 'He must be very old by now, if he's even still alive.' That's tactless, considering her age, so I add, 'Of course, being old doesn't mean no one cares. It's just ... oh, you know ...'

Then I remember how anxious Grammy was about the body that was found. How she thought it was her fault.

'You never forget, do you?' I whisper. 'No matter how many years go by. You never forget. People say it gets easier, but I don't think it will. It won't, will it?'

I know Grammy has no idea what I'm talking about. But she feels like the right person to talk to. I think it won't do any harm to tell her. And something tells me she will understand.

'The thing is, Grammy, I was pregnant, back in London. Me and my boyfriend. We were careless, I suppose, and well ... it just happened. It couldn't have worked out. He didn't want a baby. Nor did I, really. I'm going to medical school. I didn't have any choice ...'

I check her face for signs of comprehension – of disapproval even. But she seems quite peaceful. Maybe she can't even hear me.

'There's no way I could have coped, but it's hard, you know? With a baby. I keep on thinking about it now. Well ... it's difficult. I know I did the right thing, but knowing that doesn't seem to make it easier.'

Grammy's eyes blink open. She gazes at me, as though

she's trying to work out who I am. Then she croaks a few words. I strain to hear her.

'You ...' she tries again. 'You have to make the best of things.'

'Oh, Grammy.'

To my surprise she goes on.

'Tom,' she says. 'Tom loved me. She hated me. And now I know why. It wasn't my fault.'

'Grammy?'

'What's done is done. I'll never forgive myself.'

'Grammy, I don't understand. What happened?'

But she shuts her eyes again, and her breathing deepens, and then she falls asleep until Aunt Betsy arrives back in the room, armed with grapes and magazines and three paperback romances.

'How's she been?' she asks, and I tell her that Grammy was awake and talking, and only a little bit confused.

'That's wonderful news!' she exclaims. 'She'll outlive us all, I swear.'

'Aunt Betsy, has Grammy ever talked to you about finding a wild boy who'd come from the forest? I found a story in an old newspaper ... he came to live in her house.'

Aunt Betsy nods. 'I do know about him. My father talked about him once or twice, but Mother never did. There is a gravestone in the cemetery for someone called Tom Murray, and Mother lays flowers there once a year. I think that was him. He became her adopted brother . . . the wild boy who came from nowhere.'

I feel strangely deflated, as though I'm expecting the boy to walk through the door.

'How did he die?'

'I truly have no idea. If he was around the same age as Grammy, then it's likely he'd have fought in the Great War. So many young Canadian men died over in Europe. Thousands were wiped out, a whole generation. Maybe Tom was a soldier and they erected the gravestone later on when he never came home. My own father fought in France, we were so lucky that he survived – poor Grammy though, left with two children to raise while he was away.'

My eyes sting with tears. I stand up, so she won't notice.

'I'm really sorry, Aunt Betsy,' I say. 'I have to go now. I'm meeting someone.'

'Of course.' She smiles at me. 'Thank you, darling. I needed a break.'

It's hard to leave Grammy, even though she hardly spoke. Talking to her has stirred something in me . . . a need to find out the truth. What happened with Tom? Who does Grammy think that she hurt?

Sam's waiting for me outside the hospital, sitting on a wall, reading the *Astor Press*. He rolls it up and puts it in his camera bag when he sees me.

'Oh, you got it back!' I say, and he nods, looking

awkward. There's a bruise on his face, blue and purple. It makes me wince.

'How is Mrs Harkness?' he asks.

'She's much better. We could even talk for a bit.'

'That's great.' He hesitates. 'Megan, I owe you an explanation.'

'Oh, no, it's okay ... it looked like you were having a difficult time.'

'Not so difficult. Nothing that hasn't happened before.'

'Oh, right.'

'Kevin is my mother's partner, that is, he was before she died. He and she ... they ...'

'Sam, it's okay, you don't have to—'

'They were in a car wreck. She died. He was injured – head injuries – and he's never been the same since.'

'Oh, I'm so sorry.'

'I was thirteen when it happened, so pretty much grown up. Lexi was only four. She's my sister. Kevin's daughter. He couldn't look after her for a long while. Couldn't look after himself. So I stuck around to look after the both of them.'

'But he ... that's how he thanks you? By hitting you?'

Sam shrugs. 'He can't help it. Brain injuries. He's on a short fuse the whole time. Better he lets it out on me than Lexi.'

'Oh, Sam.'

'He's got a sister. Alice. She lives down in Saskatoon. She offered to take Lexi when it happened. She offered to take Kevin too, but he didn't want to leave home – where he knew people and stuff was familiar and all that. And he didn't want to dump me in some children's home. So we stayed. It's not been easy, but we cope.'

'I wish I could do something.'

'Nothing you can do about it,' he says, trying to smile. 'But your grandma was one of the ladies who helped us out after the crash. She used to bring food and stuff. You came with her once.'

'It's a shame we weren't friends then,' I say. I feel incredibly awkward.

'Yeah. Well. Anyway,' says Sam, 'what did you and Mrs Harkness talk about?'

So I tell him, and then what Aunt Betsy said, that the wild boy probably died in the First World War.

'Easy to find out,' he says.

'How?'

He points across the road, at a stone cross set on a patch of green. 'Let's see if his name is on the war memorial.'

We cross over and contemplate the list of names on the base of the cross. Goodfellow features. So does Harkness – Ebenezer, my great-uncle. But Tom Murray's name is not there at all.

CHAPTER TWENTY-FOUR

1904

EMMY

Back in Astor, after the fire, we were the talk of the town. Mr Mitchell wrote a story about our ordeal during the Second Great Fire of Toronto and published it in the *Astor Press* with great drama. Our work in helping to save the hotel was lauded, and for a while the gossip around Tom subsided.

I asked him to carry on with his story – in particular the dead man in his mother's bed – but he was not forthcoming.

'I don't know what happened after that,' he said, vaguely, and, 'It's all mixed up in my head.' I worried that if I pressed him too hard on the question, he would not talk to me at all.

But I did think about it a great deal. In church the following Sunday, as the congregation listened to the sermon, transfixed, I thought a lot about sin and guilt, and Tom's mother, and wondered if she was an evil woman who had murdered a man and abandoned her child, or a victim of terrible circumstances. I felt dizzy, trying to stretch my imagination to its limits. And thinking about men and women, and all the things they might do together, that was quite new to me. At least, it was quite new to be thinking of these things and applying them to myself and Tom, and remembering how close we were. It was a good thing that no one could hear my thoughts, because they were not suitable for church at all. And it was a good thing that Tom had stayed at home with Wolf because I was finding it difficult to know how to behave around him. I only wanted to be in his arms again.

Mr Cuthbert Farmworth, built like a walrus, complete with tusk-like teeth, bristling whiskers and a sagging waistline, shuffled up to my mother after the service.

'I'm here to tell you that I'll take the boy off your hands,' said Mr Farmworth in his deliberate way, letting each word hiss out through the gap between his teeth, with a little bit of spit to help them on their way. 'I'm looking for a new lad to help out. I'll overlook his behaviour towards my daughter, on account of his heroics in the fire.'

Mr Farmworth owned a lumber and grain mill, which consumed an extraordinary number of young boys and men, thanks to the dangers of the work, his slapdash approach to maintenance and his reluctance to waste money on medical fees should his employees fall sick or injured. His neglect – which made him a small fortune – was never challenged, partly because he chaired the town board and additionally because few of the lads had families or friends who cared one jot for them, at least not on this continent. The ones who were maimed were the lucky ones. Few of the others even got a headstone in the cemetery. A lost boy like Tom was his perfect recruit.

'He is most certainly not strong enough,' snapped Mother. That the conversation was taking place at church was enough to put her in a bad temper. Mother hated being lectured and she believed in science more than any God. She recognised the need to be seen in the congregation on occasion, but it did not make her any happier about it.

Mr Farmworth rubbed his hands together. 'I have heard that he is well able to chop wood and dig potatoes, and he fought the fire in Toronto. He sounds plenty strong enough. I will attend your home at the end of the week for him to sign an apprenticeship. You wouldn't want him to miss this opportunity. I'll soon curb any anti-social tendencies that he has.'

'So, you'd be prepared to pay his bill for the care received from the hospital?' said my mother shrewdly. 'Not to mention the sum outstanding for the last boy that came to me from your yard. What was his name? Eric Adams?'

Poor Eric Adams was crushed by rolling timber under Farmworth's watch. He'd been rushed to hospital before Mr Farmworth could prevent it, but he died three days later, never having regained consciousness. Mr Farmworth was still disputing the bill.

He was shameless though. 'Why, that should be no problem,' he spluttered. 'I'll be up to the hospital tomorrow.'

'Ah, no need, Bertie, no need.' It was Mr Mitchell's smooth voice. I turned to see him and his wife on his arm, her face pale as candlewax. Mr Mitchell continued. 'You are, alas, too late.'

Mother raised her eyebrow.

'What do you mean, too late?' Mr Farmworth asked.

'I mean that the response from our readers to his story has been most generous. His medical bills are more than taken care of.'

'That is most welcome news, Mr Mitchell,' Mother said, meeting his eye without a glimmer of a smile.

'Excellent!' said Mr Farmworth, rubbing his plump hands.

'Furthermore,' Mr Mitchell continued, 'I have already prepared his apprenticeship papers. Dr Murray and I have agreed that he will work at the *Astor Press*. I was impressed by Tom's courage and industry, fighting the fire in Toronto. I feel I owe the lad a chance. And printing is a fine profession.'

I was surprised that Mother had not mentioned this

to me, or to Tom in my hearing. Had they kept it a secret from me?

Mrs Mitchell's mouth twisted into a grimace. '*Must* we stand around discussing business on a Sunday?' she complained. 'Is it truly safe to employ the boy? What if he runs berserk? And how can he work in the composing room? Does he even know his letters? Is he not retarded in intelligence?'

'He is far better suited to my line of work,' said Mr Farmworth. 'And I doubt Angus will take kindly to a boy who can hardly speak, let alone master his letters.'

'I have been teaching him his letters,' I burst out. 'He has learned very quickly and is on the sixth reader now.'

'Emmy has been an excellent teacher,' said my mother.

'I'm sure she has,' agreed Mr Mitchell. 'So that settles the matter.' I felt embarrassed all of a sudden, and hurried away to meet Sadie and Adam, leaving Mother to sort out the details of Tom's employment.

On the way home I quizzed her. Yes, in Toronto they had discussed the possibility of Tom being apprenticed as a printer. No, she had not mentioned it to Tom. She had wanted to test his reading first. 'I have done so and been very impressed, Emmy. You will make a good teacher one day.'

'I don't know if I want to be a teacher,' I told her.

She paused. 'School is over,' she said. 'Perhaps there is another job you can do before you go to college.'

'At the hospital?' I asked, dubiously. 'Because I don't think

I am really a good nurse. Looking after Tom was different.'

'You like Tom, don't you?'

Mother never asked me questions like that. She and I had lived together all those years, perfectly contented, but like two ships side by side in the ocean. Together, but apart. Close, but with distance. I did not query it at all, it was all that I knew. It was only later, when I had children of my own, that I realised it did not have to be like that.

But I know now that Mother had her secrets. So did I, which is why I am telling you this story. Perhaps I kept my secrets too long.

Anyway, later we broke the news to Tom. 'Printing is a good trade,' said Mother, 'and Wyngate Mitchell a good employer. He will pay you, Tom and you will learn how to put letters together to make a book or a paper. Would you like that?'

'I think so,' said Tom. 'How much money will I make?'

She told him, and he looked pleased enough. Money was important to Tom. Mother paid him a small sum for the rabbits he caught, and he saved his earnings carefully in a wooden box which he kept locked in a drawer. I had seen him open it up and count his money painstakingly. We sometimes went to the general stores together, and he always asked me what everything cost. Then he would come back and count up his money again, but never spend any of it. Sometimes I feared he was saving up to run away.

Much to my surprise, Mr Mitchell came to see us on

the Friday evening before Tom was due to start work. My mother welcomed him warmly and he accepted a drink and came and sat at our table where we were eating.

First he talked to Tom a little about his new job, and gave him his apprenticeship papers to sign. Then he turned his attention to me.

'I have a proposition to make,' he said. 'Emmy, why don't you come and work for me while you are waiting to go to college? There is much that needs doing and it would interest you, I am sure.'

'Emmy needs to prepare for college,' said Mother.

'There's no better preparation for life than a newspaper office,' said Mr Mitchell. 'Emmy, you're a bright girl. You might perhaps find this trade of mine quite interesting. More interesting than teaching, anyhow.'

'I think I am a good teacher,' I said, with some force.

'That's true,' said Mr Mitchell, lazily. 'But from what I hear, Tom is a joy to teach. Teaching a pupil like Tom, just you and he, is a very different task from keeping order in a crowded classroom.'

He was right, as usual. He knew the aspect of life as a schoolteacher that I anticipated would be the hardest. The thought of standing at the front of a room filled with rowdy boys and giggling girls – well, it didn't exactly scare me, but I felt weary at the prospect.

I looked at Mother, who nodded, as if to say it was my choice.

'I will think about it,' I told him. 'Thank you.'

'Come along with Tom on Monday,' he said. 'I'll show you the ropes.'

Mr Mitchell, I still believed, was likely unscrupulous and not to be trusted. I had better keep a close eye on him if Tom was to work there. I also had to admit finding life at home dull, and I hated housework. Now that school was over – I could hardly believe that I would never again sit on those long benches where I had started out as a little girl making her letters on a slate – I felt restless and unsettled. What is more, I could save money for college life in Toronto. Here I was, worried about Tom running away, when that's exactly what I was planning to do myself. What in heaven's name would he do here in Astor, without me helping him?

And what would I do without him?

Could Tom come with Sadie and me to Toronto? Not if he were an apprentice printer in Astor. I decided to take the job. I wanted to spend as much time with Tom as possible before I left for Toronto.

Though I did not like Mr Mitchell's manner, I soon found that I enjoyed his trade far more than I had expected. Life in a newspaper office was as stimulating and ever-changing as a hospital, but without the blood and gore.

I had various jobs. To take notes when Mr Mitchell conducted interviews. To make the tea. To take the copy down to the composing room, and to bring back the page proofs that Angus McFarland, the head of the print room, printed out for me. Mr Mitchell would check the page proofs and then I would take them back for Angus and Tom to make the changes. It was nice to see Tom hard at work, and I was impressed by the way his nimble fingers fitted the letters together. His hands were black with ink. The noise of the presses was terrible when they rolled, but that was only one day a week.

The composing room was on the ground floor of the building, with the presses down in the basement. The letters, which Angus called 'sorts', sat in cases under the desks on which sat the frames where the pages were put together. I really doubted that Tom would be able to do the work, because it involved finding the right letters again and again, but he learned remarkably fast. The other compositors were not exactly friendly, but they were not overtly hostile either, and Angus, once he saw how keen and hard-working Tom was, went out of his way to teach him how to use the new Linotype machine which set the text into columns. He even allowed Wolf to stay in a corner of the room if it rained, although mostly Tom's dog waited for him on the pavement outside.

My desk was upstairs in the editorial department. Sometimes Mr Mitchell allowed me to write reports myself, or prepare the pages of village news that came in with every post. There was little to do besides typing them out – I soon mastered the typewriter – and tidying the spelling and grammar, but occasionally I found myself rewording some phrases. The office was busier and busier until press day – Wednesday – when I was running from office to print room all day long.

Then the pace slowed down for another week. On Thursday when the paper came out, I had to go through it with scissor and glue, cutting out stories and placing them in files for the small cuttings library up on the second floor. My filing was a little haphazard, and Mr Mitchell said he would soon have to employ a full-time librarian, but in the meantime I would have to do.

As I cut and pasted I looked at the *Astor Press* with a surprising amount of pride. It seemed quite magical the way that the scraps of paper that flew from the typewriters of Mr Mitchell and his two reporters turned into a newspaper by the end of the week. And I liked Mr Mitchell better for the care he took over his reports and editorials, and for his kindness in giving Tom a job. I wondered if I had been a little unfair to him in the past.

The older reporter was Walt McDonagh, who was wrinkled and grizzled and stank of whisky at ten in the morning. By 4 p.m. his fingers could not find the correct keys and sometimes he had to dictate his copy to me. 'I should sack him, but he writes like an angel,' Mr Mitchell told me. The other was young Billy Thompson, a spotty boy a few years older than me, who was usually quiet and morose, unless he could write for the sports pages. Luckily for him, neither Mr Mitchell nor Old Walt had any interest in football or hockey, so Billy had a free rein.

At the end of the day Tom and I would walk home together. Wolf accompanied us there and back, of course. He was friendlier to me by then, having worked out, I think, that I was no threat to Tom. I treasured this time together, although sometimes, as we walked along the high street, I'd notice the way people looked at Tom and Wolf. People were still wary. But the newness and the strangeness had worn off a little. I dared to hope that one day they would accept him.

Not Amelia Farmworth, though. She made a big point of avoiding us whenever we came across her in the town. And one day, when I was walking alone for once, she rushed up to me, all false concern. 'How do you bear it, poor Emmy?' she said, tucking her arm in mine. 'That awful dog! Aren't you scared?'

'Of course not,' I said, scornfully.

She wrinkled her little snub nose. 'Of course, I suppose you are pretty safe with the halfwit,' she said. 'I mean, there must be advantages in being . . . you know . . . homely.'

Homely? I wanted to box her ears!

Instead, I bit my tongue. 'Must there?' I said, demure as I could. 'I wouldn't know.'

Then I pulled my arm from hers, and pretended to have an urgent need to visit the draper's shop.

Another day we were in the office when we heard a

woman's shrill screams. We rushed to the window – no worries about being curious in a newspaper office – and saw a woman clutching her bawling child.

'Emmy, go and see,' said Mr Mitchell, and I ran downstairs, just as Tom emerged from the print works.

'Your dog bit my little boy! He's a menace!' the mother shouted at him.

Tom applied himself to calming Wolf, and I tried to make sense of what had happened. It turned out that the child had approached Wolf and pulled his ears. The child was scared, not injured, so I assumed the dog had just snapped at him.

'What do you expect to happen?' I asked the mother. 'You should take more care.'

'That animal is a wild beast, and your boy is no better!' she retorted. 'It's a disgrace that your mother allows you to spend time with him, Emmy Murray. I don't know what she's thinking of!'

'I don't know what you're thinking of!' I told her. 'Any mother should keep her child away from dogs!'

'That dog should be on a chain,' she said. 'Put *that* in your newspaper.'

That evening I suggested to Tom that Wolf should stay at home while we were working but he had already asked Angus if Wolf could be in his own corner of the print works every day, and Angus had agreed. I was pleased, but still uneasy. It seemed to me that Wolf reminded people of Tom's origins, and made it less possible for him to be accepted.

Still, I enjoyed my work. Often I would read the page proofs over myself and sometimes I would find mistakes that Mr Mitchell had missed. I pointed them out to him, triumphantly, and he never seemed to mind. 'Bravo, Emmy!' he would say. And once, 'You're a chip off the old block!'

I was pleased that he thought that I was as professional and competent as my mother, even if I was proving myself in a different sphere.

In fact, I was as happy as I had ever been, until the day I heard the name Elijah Brown.

CHAPTER TWENTY-FIVE

1904

EMMY

Opening the letters sent to the editor was one of my jobs. I was tasked with reading each one and sorting them into piles: those suitable for publication, those that could lead to a news story and those to be thrown away. There was always a pile of mail waiting for me: a sign, according to Mr Mitchell, of a successful newspaper. He even liked the letters that complained about his reports and disagreed with his editorials. 'Controversy is the lifeblood of journalism,' he would say. 'We want to make our readers desperate to express their views.'

I enjoyed reading the letters, all except for those which concerned Tom. There were several each day to contend with and I felt that they all contained the potential to take him away from us – from me. Some were obvious ploys, submitted in hopes of picking up the cash reward that Mr Mitchell had offered. Others were angry rants, complaining that 'the savage' was roaming free around our town, accompanied by a vicious dog, accusing him of stealing and staring at girls, threatening vengeance if he put a foot wrong. These letters scared me, and I marked them for Mr Mitchell's attention.

But nothing arrived that gave any clue to where Tom had come from, and I grew complacent that none would. So I was not prepared for the letter that I opened one morning in early June. It came from a fur trader who had visited Astor a few weeks before Tom emerged from the forest. His favourite boots had sprung a leak, he wrote, and he had left them to be repaired by our local cobbler, Mr Addison. A few weeks ago, they had been delivered to his home, just outside Toronto, but only opened recently as he had been away, visiting suppliers.

The boots were stuffed with newspaper, and for curiosity's sake I flattened out the pages, to see what the news was in your good town. I was astounded to see the story of the wild boy and the reward offered for information, as I am as certain as I can be that I have seen this boy before.

My heart sank. I cursed the trader for his aimless curiosity, and blameless Mr Addison for choosing the wrong edition of the *Astor Press* to pack his blessed boots.

I believe him to be a servant boy, working for Elijah Brown, a fur trader living in a secluded cottage outside Astor. Mr Brown is more or less a hermit who does not prattle about his affairs, but whenever I have bought hides and furs from Mr Brown, the boy has helped to carry the furs to my canoe. I had thought him to be a mute. He certainly bears a strong resemblance to the photograph in your newspaper.

Mr Elijah Brown can be found at Trader's Cottage, north of the town of Astor. If I qualify for your reward, it can be sent to the address above.

I remain, yours truly, James Norris.

My first thought was to throw the letter in the garbage. Or should I try and burn it? I did not want Tom claimed by some mysterious hermit, who had clearly mistreated him. But what if James Norris wrote again, demanding his reward? Could I somehow find the money to pay him off?

'Is there a problem, Emmy?' asked Mr Mitchell, startling me.

'No, no problem at all.'

'Your face is a picture,' he said thoughtfully. Before I

could move, he leaned across and plucked the letter from my hand.

'Is this letter upsetting you?'

In vain I tried to retrieve it. 'No ... it is nothing ... please let me have it back.'

His sharp eyes scanned the page.

'Interesting,' he said. 'Should we ask Tom?'

'It's probably just a fake,' I said. 'Just an attempt to get the reward money.'

'Oh, most probably you are right. You've got a wise head on your shoulders, young Emmy. But still, interesting, wouldn't you say?'

'Don't tell Tom,' I blurted. 'He can't have ... this man ... not good ... '

'I agree with you, that we shouldn't tell Tom anything. We don't want him running off again.'

I breathed a sigh of silent relief.

'But we should investigate. Let us find out what sort of a man this Mr Brown is.'

'Tom shouldn't go back there,' I said, quite fiercely.

'We will probably find that he has no claim over Tom at all. Then he will be free to live his life as he pleases.' His voice softened. 'Tom's situation needs to be resolved. And if Elijah Brown was that concerned, then surely he would have claimed the reward – and the boy – himself?'

I felt sick. There were so many things that could go wrong.

'Will you come with me, Emmy? If we take a drive into the forest to find this cottage?'

'Yes, I will come with you,' I said. Perhaps if Elijah Brown did lay claim to Tom, I could somehow persuade him not to pursue him. I could not leave this task to Mr Mitchell alone. There was a danger that his preference for a happy reunion story would trump any concern for Tom's welfare.

'Let me make some enquiries,' said Mr Mitchell. 'We'll leave here at three.'

I had no choice but to nod, and he said, 'Don't look so worried, Emmy. If Elijah Brown was concerned about losing Tom, he'd have come looking for him in Astor. He cannot be all that worried. This could be the best news possible.'

'I hope so,' I said, and I bent my head to the pile of letters in front of me.

'Did you find anything out about Elijah Brown?' I asked, as Mr Mitchell and I drove along the North Road.

'I've asked around a little. Not so much as to draw attention, but enough to gather some facts. The house was built by one Ian Cameron, for his family – this was just as the town was being settled. He and his wife tried to farm the land but everything they did was blighted, and their crops failed year after year. They soon fell into despair, Mrs Cameron died in childbirth and their two children died soon after, half-starved and neglected. Ian Cameron just abandoned his house after that and it fell into rack and ruin. All the land he had cleared became overgrown. Some thirty or so years later, along comes this Elijah Brown, claims it for his own and lives there, eschewing all company. Once or twice a year he goes to Toronto to trade furs and buy provisions. Maybe once in the last ten years he's been into town, to trade with Mr Johnson at the general store.'

'But how does he live?'

'Ach, as many do. He hunts, he grows things, he prefers the company of dogs and horses to men and women. No doubt he deals with the Indians to get furs to trade; perhaps he has an Indian woman too. There are more like him than you'd imagine, Emmy. An empty land like ours attracts those who shun other men's company.'

'I cannot imagine wanting to live like that,' I told him.

'No, me neither,' he said, with a smile. 'Though some would envy him. My wife, for example, or perhaps your mother.'

'My mother could not live without people to cure,' I said.

'True. But how much does she want to be with those of us who are whole and healthy? She's at ease in her own company, in a way that I would never be. I do, very much, admire that trait in her.'

'Hmm.' Once again, I was disconcerted by Mr Mitchell.

He swung the cart off the main road and on to a forest track.

'How do you know this is the right way?' I asked.

'Well, I am guessing. My mother-in-law, Mrs Mortimer,

she thinks she remembers the Cameron family living along here. Past the McManus farmhouse, about two miles along the road and then maybe five miles ... She was at school with the Cameron daughter. Says she was a nice girl.'

Old Mrs Mortimer was as sour-faced as her daughter. She wouldn't give most people the time of day.

'It seems strange to think of Mrs Mortimer being a schoolgirl,' I said.

He laughed. 'It does indeed. But that's one trick you need to learn, Emmy, if you are to get people to trust you. Inside all of us is the child we once were. Most children aren't unfriendly, although some learn bad ways early on. Get through the reserve and harm of adulthood, reach out to the child, and people will tell you just what you want them to.'

I was silent, thinking of Tom and how I wished he would confide in me again.

'This must be it,' he said.

It was hard to see in the gloom of the forest, but there was undoubtedly a house, although the great swags of ivy hanging off it were as good a disguise as a soldier in camouflage. The house had been solidly built from timber, but was now in bad repair. I could see that much of the wood was rotten, and the paint so faded and blistered that one could only guess at its original colour.

Mr Mitchell stopped the cart and tied up the horse. He

held out his hand for me to jump down. 'Come on, Emmy, we'll make a reporter of you. What do you see?'

'Just a house,' I told him. 'There are no signs of anyone living here.'

'What signs would you look for?'

'Well, smoke from the chimney, and noise. The yard is overgrown and the house is in a bad state. There's a hole in the roof. It's the middle of the day, but no one has pulled the drapes.'

'Good girl,' he said. 'Well observed. But yet there are drapes. I think that someone has been living here, at least.'

He stepped up on to the porch and I followed him. My nose twitched. Something smelled bad.

There was an eerie feel to the old place, and I did not like it. 'There is no one here,' I said. 'We should go back.'

'Come on, Emmy. Has Tom never said anything to you about his former life? You don't have to tell me what he has said exactly, just whether he mentioned living with anyone; someone who might possibly be Elijah Brown.'

I could not bring myself to reply, but my silence weighed on my shoulders. I lowered my head. Tears prickled my eyes. 'No,' I said, 'nothing like that.'

'Come on, Emmy. You can tell me.' Mr Mitchell's voice was coaxing and kind. 'I've been awfully impressed with how you've taken to the work. Maybe we can solve this mystery together.'

'Only if it is good for Tom,' I said.

'Of course. Tom is my employee and it is my duty to protect him.'

'I am scared that we will find this man. Someone has been cruel to Tom in the past, and now he will be again.'

Mr Mitchell's face softened. He patted my hand.

'Emmy, I will not allow that to happen. Trust me. Now let's see what we can find. Perhaps we can unlock Tom's memory and find some happier times.'

I doubted it. But I followed him as he approached the house.

CHAPTER TWENTY-SIX

1904

EMMY

First Mr Mitchell banged at the front door, but achieved nothing except further damage to the paintwork, which splintered at his touch, like tattered silk. Then he tapped on the window. No response.

'It's empty,' I said. 'There's no one there.'

The smell was stronger on the porch, the sickly-sweet stench of decay. I felt nauseous and giddy. I wanted to run home through the forest, away from this place.

'There's something dead here,' I told Mr Mitchell, as he peered into the front room to no avail, because the drapes were dark and thick and thoroughly drawn.

'An animal, perhaps,' he agreed.

We walked around to the back of the house. The yard was littered with cages, large and small. They all seemed to be empty – the doors flapped open on their hinges – but animals had lived there; you could tell from the smell of dried urine and dung and decay. We walked around from cage to cage, looking for the dead beast, but even the chicken run was empty.

There was a small outhouse at the far end of the yard and when we looked inside we thought we had found the source of the stench: the walls were hung with animal hides – a bear, rabbits, several wolves. They had been skilfully cut, but still smelled vile. I let out my breath and stepped backwards into the fresh air.

'Was that it?' I asked, and Mr Mitchell said, 'I hope so. But let's see if we can take a look inside.'

We approached the back door of the house, and Mr Mitchell banged it hard. When there was no response, he tried the handle. To our surprise, the door opened.

The smell was even worse inside, although the kitchen where we stood was scrupulously clean, grey and sparse in its furnishings. I could hear a buzzing noise. Mr Mitchell's nose wrinkled. 'Perhaps you should wait outside, Emmy.'

I desperately wanted to escape but I shook my head. Worse than the thought of what we might discover here was the thought of waiting outside alone ... What if he never emerged? I summoned all my courage. 'I am not as chicken-hearted as you think,' I told him, and he chuckled and said, 'Good girl.'

He opened the kitchen door, walked forward into the parlour, and then stopped dead in his tracks. 'Emmy! Get back, get back!'

Mr Mitchell was transformed. His suave confidence vanished and he was white and shaking, gripped by horror. I could not help myself. I pushed past him.

A room full of books, was my first impression. Soft rugs and finer furniture than one would expect in a hovel in the woods. A fine mahogany desk. And before it a chair with a man sitting in it.

A man's shape, anyhow. But there was precious little flesh left on the bones that I could see, and he had no head. No complete head anyway. Dried blood and brains spilled out on the desk before him. And a buzzing cloud of flies was all around.

I shall remember the sight all my days, although I only stood and gawped for a few seconds. Sometimes at night I close my eyes and I see it again. Then I cannot sleep, and have to get up and come downstairs and read to distract myself and try to forget.

He had a silver-topped cane by his side and a sharp knife on the table beside him. His split head lay on a leather-bound book, and a pen was at his side. He was wearing a dark suit, and the collar of his white shirt was dark brown with gore.

I thought for a moment I would faint. The flies seemed to

make for me, speckled in front of my eyes, buzzing louder and louder as though they were inside my head, circling round and round. Then I felt my stomach heave and I ran, past Mr Mitchell, out through the door and into the overgrown yard where I fell to my knees and vomited.

Mr Mitchell was hard on my heels, rubbing my shoulders. 'Oh, Emmy, I'm so sorry. So sorry you had to see that. So sorry, my dear girl. I wouldn't have had you see that for the world.'

I waited until the retching stopped, wiped my mouth with his handkerchief. 'We must tell the police,' I said, shakily. 'Do you think he was murdered?'

'He was shot at close range, judging by the damage to his head,' said Mr Mitchell. 'It was most probably a suicide.'

He was shot. All I could think of was the gun Tom held as he came towards Sadie and me that day near the forest. I would never betray Tom and besides . . . surely, surely he could never have killed someone. Could he?

'How long had he been like that? Can you tell?'

'The coroner will have to mount an investigation. Your mother may have some idea. But judging by the state of deterioration – a not inconsiderable time, I would say. Perhaps six months?'

Tom had appeared on the North Road almost exactly five months previously. I retched one more time, hoping Mr Mitchell would not make any connection.

He helped me to my feet. I resisted the desire to hold his

hand once I was standing, although I was still trembling from head to toe, and gulping mouthfuls of air.

We started the journey back through the forest. I kept glancing behind me. I don't know what I expected to see, but I was grateful when we trundled out of the trees into the light out on the main road towards home.

Only then did I break the silence. 'Mr Mitchell,' I said, trying to keep my voice steady. 'If that was Elijah Brown ... well, there is nothing, no proof of a link between him and Tom.'

'Nothing except the letter. But Tom ... '

'Elijah Brown committed suicide, as you said, or was robbed.'

'Or perhaps he had traded with fur trappers who felt he had not been square with them. Perhaps he had enemies. There might be any number of explanations.'

'And Tom ... if Tom was his servant ... but there is no reason to think ... '

'It is complete conjecture. Unless you know something that you are not telling me, Emmy.'

'No, nothing,' I lied. My soul would shrivel away before I would tell him about the pistol.

'Well, if Tom has any links to this house, it is quite possible that he might have come home and found Elijah Brown murdered. Such a shock could turn someone crazy. It might well wipe his memory. It is a completely plausible explanation.'

It was, and silently I added to that the idea that Tom had, in his shock, scooped up the murder weapon discarded by the murderers, and taken it with him, only to fling it aside in horror when I challenged him. Of course he was innocent!

'What will we do?'

'We must tell the police.'

'What about Tom?'

'They may wish to talk to him.'

I knew exactly what the Mounties would do. They would take Tom back to that place of blood and death and flies, to see how he responded when confronted with the scene of the crime.

'So what would it do . . . to Tom . . . to go back there?' My voice was smaller than usual.

'I am no doctor, Emmy, just a reporter. I have observed human behaviour but never studied it. You would do better to ask your mother.'

'But what do you think?'

'Pray hard, Emmy, that he has the strength to survive it,' said Mr Mitchell, grim-faced, as he drew up right outside the office of the chief of police.

CHAPTER TWENTY-SEVEN

1994

MEGAN

Sam calls me the next day, says he's free and asks me if I want to go for a coffee, all in that soft voice. I say yes. I'm warming to Sam, I admit. He's had troubles of his own. He understands how it feels to be in pain.

Maybe if we get to know each other better, he could be someone to trust.

But all Sam wants to talk about is the Wild Boy, his possible connection to Mattie and the murder of the mysterious Elijah Brown.

We talk about it for a while. 'I wonder how far back the police records go,' he says. 'Maybe they have a file on Elijah Brown. We can find out – the regional headquarters is in New Elgin. I had to go there once to check out some archive material.'

'Can we go there now?'

Sam looks at his watch. 'I'm sorry. It's a bit of a drive to New Elgin. I've got to pick Lexi up from school in half an hour, and I'm working tomorrow.'

'What if I came to pick her up with you now, could we take her with us?'

He looks dubious. 'She'll be tired but I suppose so.'

I feel bad. 'We don't have to. I mean, maybe they'll laugh at us.'

'Asking about a ninety-year-old case? Yeah, I guess they will.'

'So . . . is it worth it?'

'We can only try.'

We drive to Lexi's school. It's on the outskirts of town, near where the new mall is being built. The school backs on to the forest and the kids are just starting to stream from the building as we arrive and join the waiting moms out front. It hits me how young Lexi is to have no mother.

She shoots out of her classroom like a racehorse from its stall. She's a small, dark girl with a tangle of curls and Sam's big, brown eyes. She grabs him around the middle for a fierce hug, then frowns at me.

'Who's she?'

Sam laughs.

'Don't be rude, Lexi. *She's* Megan and *she's* my friend. I'm allowed to have friends,' he says, smiling.

'Only if I like them.'

'You'll like Megan. She's come all the way from London.'

'Why?' demands Lexi.

'Well, because my dad's here ... and my grandma,' I tell her. 'I wanted a bit of peace and quiet.'

'Me and Sam are going to go to London when I'm older,' she tells me. 'London and Montreal and New York and Sydney and everywhere.'

'Only if your dad's okay,' says Sam.

'He'll be okay,' she says. 'My dad got hit on the head in a car crash,' she informs me.

'Oh. That's awful.'

'Yeah. It gives him bad moods. He's a shouty monster then.'

'Come and get in the truck,' says Sam. 'I've got a sandwich and an apple for you. Then you're going to come with us for a while, so Megan and I can do some work.'

Lexi eats her sandwich, silent and solemn, and I can see her shrug off the school day and relax again. She bombards me with questions: what's London like, how long am I staying, do I like to dance?

'Lexi likes dancing,' Sam explains.

'But we can't afford lessons anymore,' says Lexi, mournfully.

'What sort of dancing?' I ask. I can imagine her as a

ballerina; she's got a certain grace about the way she holds her head.

'Jazz and tap. But any, really. Sam's saving up, aren't you, Sam? And I had a yard sale of my old toys.'

Sam pulls up in front of an office block. 'Here we go. Thought about what we're going to say, Megan?'

'Not really.'

'Let's busk it.'

I let him do the talking at the front desk. He explains that we're from the *Astor Press*. We're doing a piece on crime in the past. He asks if there's an archivist, whether we can access old files. And he mentions the name Elijah Brown.

A bored receptionist writes it all down and disappears into the back office.

We sit and wait. And wait. And wait. Lexi soon gets restless and starts dancing. Sam watches her, a frown on his face.

'She's great,' I whisper to him. 'She can really dance.'

He shrugs. 'I'm letting her down. I just can't stretch to fund her classes.'

'Surely that's her dad's responsibility, not yours?'

'Kevin can't do much. Not since his accident. He was a cab driver, you know, but he gets blackouts now so he can't get a licence.'

So he goes out and gets drunk instead, I think.

'What can he do then, for work?'

'He's a good handyman. Just, sometimes he doesn't give a good impression. A lot of the time he needs to rest.'

'That can't be easy.'

'No.' He runs his hand through his hair. 'It's certainly not easy.'

The receptionist comes back and hands a piece of paper to Sam. 'There you go.'

Sam reads: 'Case open. Files sealed.'

'Can we challenge this?' he asks her. 'The case was ninety years ago.'

She hands us a form to fill in, which we do, and tells us we'll hear in a few weeks, but we're all deflated when we get back into the truck, even Lexi.

'It's ridiculous,' says Sam.

'It's like someone's trying to hide the facts from us,' I say.

They drop me at Grandma's. I watch them go, Lexi chattering to Sam about her day. It makes me feel lonely somehow, and miss my big brother Rob. I trudge up the step to the front door, fumble for the key. But the door opens before I find it.

'Megan!' says my dad. 'Thank God you're home.'

'Why? What's happened?'

'It's Grammy, pumpkin. She died.'

CHAPTER TWENTY-EIGHT

1994

MEGAN

It's the morning of Grammy's funeral. It's a hot, dry, dusty day, the house is crammed with cousins and we've been cutting sandwiches for hours. My dad's surrounded by family, but Mom's at some summit in Geneva, and I feel weirdly alone.

The strangest thing about someone very old dying is how shocking it is. It's like you expected them to live forever.

Then there's a knock on the door and Grandma glances at her watch. 'Can you answer that one, Megan, darling?' The tall scruffy, bearded guy standing on the doorstep with a massive rucksack isn't just any guy; it's my big brother, Rob. I gasp with surprise, and then he grabs me

KEREN DAVID

in a massive hug, squeezing so tight I think my ribs might crack.

'Surprise! Or did you guess?'

'I never thought for one moment that you'd have time.'

'That's where you're wrong. Grammy always had time for me and I always had time for her, and still do.'

'I'd better tell Grandma that you've turned up, she'll be so excited.'

'She knows, noodle head, we decided to surprise you.'

'Oh! That's kind of sweet.'

'We thought so,' he says, all smug and pleased with himself, and I mock-punch him, because I'm so happy he's here.

I lead him into the house. Grandma's delighted to hear that the surprise worked. Dad was in on the secret as well, it turns out. Rob goes all around the aunts and cousins, kissing and hugging and shaking hands. It takes ages but finally he comes back and we sit in a corner, far enough away from the nearest bunch of relatives so we can talk without anyone hearing.

'So, how're you doing?' Rob's not sure how to broach the subject. 'You know, after the—'

I interrupt before he can say whatever euphemism he was stumbling towards. 'It's okay. All over. Probably best that way.'

'I told you Ryo was a jerk.'

'No, you didn't! And no, he isn't.'

Rob scratches his head. 'I didn't? Probably assumed you wouldn't listen. Well, I definitely thought it anyway, and I know I told Katie and she agrees. You're better off without him.'

Katie is Rob's girlfriend. She's from New Zealand. I've met her twice.

'Why did you think he was such a jerk?' I'm desperate to hear something that might poison my mind against Ryo, even now.

'Terrible guitar player,' said Rob, whose idea of good music is loud, with a lot of bass and black leather. 'Too interested in himself and no one else. Not good enough for you.'

'Rob!'

'It's okay, sis. If I can't tease you, who can?'

I'm not sure whether to laugh or cry, so I have a go at laughing. It comes out a little too loud, and attracts a few stares.

'Now look what you've done. I'm going to get told off for being disrespectful.'

'I'll tell them you're hysterical in your grief. Tell you what, let's go and sit outside. I bet Grandma will give us something to eat, I'm famished.'

'Grandma's too busy to run around after you,' I tell him. 'Stop being such a manipulator! Go and sit outside, I'll get you some sandwiches.'

We sit on the dry grass, and Rob applies himself to

a huge pile of roast beef, pickles and bread. I've lost my appetite.

'What's wrong? You've got all skinny.'

I can't really believe he said that. I don't even credit him with an answer. I just look at him, until he figures it out.

'What? What did I say? Oh. I didn't mean ... But Megan, it's over now. And it wasn't like – I mean, Mom said you caught it in the very early stages. You didn't really think about keeping it – did you? I mean, university and all that, it's got to be for the best ...'

His voice trails off. He shakes his head.

'I'm a clod. Sorry, Megan. I didn't mean to make you cry.'

'I'm not crying,' I say, furiously struggling for that to be true. 'I'm not. It's just, if it hadn't ... Ryo might have ... everything might have been different.'

'I know. It's sad, Megan, but – tough as it was and is – it just wasn't meant to be. You can't rewind the past. What happened, happened. Now it's over. Time to move on.'

I blow my nose and nod, trying to smile.

'Come on,' he says, encouragingly. 'It's a funeral after all, can't have anyone thinking you're upset or crying or anything.'

'I miss you, God knows why.'

He ruffles my hair, which he knows I hate. 'I miss you too. Come and stay with me in Boston some time?'

'Yeah, okay, might do that.'

He glances at his watch. 'If this is the right time, we'd

better get ready. Grammy wouldn't approve of us turning up to her funeral in jeans.'

'I doubt Grammy would have cared what we were wearing,' I tell him.

'You're right. She wouldn't have cared. But Grandma will.'

Later, at the church, Rob's almost unrecognisable in his dark suit – particularly as he decided to shave off the beard in Grammy's honour. I've got a navy-blue dress on, and I'm wearing a silver locket that Grammy gave me when I turned fourteen. I used to keep a tiny pearl inside that Ryo gave me – a black pearl from Japan – but now it's loose in my jewellery box. It started life as a piece of grit in an oyster shell, and now it's a piece of grit in my life, niggling and irritating me every time I see it. I will never be able to transform my memories of this summer into anything as beautiful as a pearl, that's for sure.

The funeral is long and slow and dull, and my heart aches for Grammy because no one remembers her when she was a kid, no one here knew her when she was my age, even. She was fifty or sixty before most of the people in the room were born. It strikes me then how lonely she must have been. The minister talks about heaven. I've never thought much about religion – we go to church once a year on Christmas Eve, but now I can see the attraction of heaven, with angels and everyone you love waiting for you. Maybe Grammy wasn't so lonely now. Maybe she was reunited with her husband, with my grandpa Jesse, with her other children, Aunt Sarah, Uncle Ebenezer, Aunt Marianne. Her friends, her mother . . .

And Tom, the Wild Boy. Was he in heaven?

Maybe one day I'd meet my baby . . . except it never was a baby, I never knew if it was a girl or boy, so . . . And heaven probably doesn't exist either. And would I even get there, after I'd done what I did? Some people would say not.

Heaven holds no comfort. Grammy's just dead. I'm going to hell. A tear runs down my nose. I grope in my pocket for a handkerchief.

Aunt Betsy walks to the front of the church and steps up to the lectern. I'm so glad she decided to speak. This morning Grandma told me that Betsy wasn't sure if she could go ahead with it. Her large hands are shaking.

'Well,' she said. 'Well. Here we all are. Do you know, I had begun to believe that my mother would outlive us all.'

There's a ripple of approval.

'It's tempting to see her life as being all about her last years. Her final years. Her strength of body and mind. The way she survived so many losses – her mother, her husband, all of her children except me. But Mother had a long life before she grew old, and although she never went far from Astor, she had her share of adventures.'

Aunt Betsy talks about Grammy, her happy marriage, her hard-working life on the farm. How she'd been a working mother when the children were slightly older after inheriting the local newspaper from her stepfather, Mr Wyngate Mitchell.

She goes on, telling us how Grammy was a link to the past, to the people who'd established Astor as it is today and turned it into a fine town. How Grammy had written editorials, grown the paper into a thriving business before selling it to her old colleague Billy Thompson, so she could care for Grandad Adam when he was sick.

'Most of all I will miss her stories,' Aunt Betsy tells us. 'Stories from her mother's hospital. Stories about her schooldays here in Astor, when the entire school could fit into one classroom. Stories about her days as a journalist, running the *Press*.'

Aunt Betsy moves on to tales of fires and storms, of births and marriages and Grammy flying to Paris for her sixtieth birthday. There is nothing about the Wild Boy, the story I want to hear.

Later, in the churchyard, Ed's at my side. 'Hey, stranger,' he says.

'Hey, Ed. How's it going?'

'It's going fine. Not working today. Representing the family at the funeral. But don't you worry, we're giving her a good spread, front page and inside.'

I'm not sure what to say. 'Oh, uh, thanks.' Typical Ed and his thick skin.

Ed nods towards Sam, who definitely is working,

photographing the crowd of mourners at a respectful distance. 'So, you're seeing snapper boy, I gather?'

'Not seeing him, exactly,' I say, irritated. 'We're friends.'

'I did warn you. Met the family yet? You're safer keeping away. Poor old Sam's a bit of a punch bag. Just have to hope he hasn't picked up bad habits from his old man.'

'Look, that's none of our business. And I'm not seeing Sam.'

'Glad to hear it. You're obviously too clever to go for the victim type. So, when can I take you to dinner?'

I'm about to tell him to get lost, when Bee comes over. She's been working on a cartoon strip forever, and Ed's agreed to show it to the art director at the paper – he has got a nice side after all, underneath all that pomposity. I leave them to talk and go to find my brother.

'You all right, Megan?' he asks when I finally locate him.

'I'm fine. Let's go back to the house.'

'Sure. We can walk it, can't we? I don't really want to ride in one of those big cars.'

'Yeah, come on.'

I don't even say goodbye to Ed as Rob and I make our way through the graves to the gate at the far end of the churchyard, reading the inscriptions as we go.

'*Harkness. Harkness. Dr Elizabeth Mitchell* – that must be our great-great-grandmother.' We pause by her headstone. She's buried beside her husband (*'died 1930'*) and next to him is his first wife – *'Mrs Isabella Mitchell, 20 August 1904'*.

'A woman of worth, who can find, her price is above rubies'.
'Esteemed by her neighbours, mourned by her husband'.

'Come on, we need to get back to the house,' says Rob, but I keep looking along the line of graves. I just have a feeling that there's something here.

I find my grandpa Jesse. I find my great-aunt Sadie, her husband and their son. And then I see what I've been looking for all along. A flat stone, grey as a London sky. I crouch down and read:

'In Memory of Tom Murray, died 20 August 1904. His innocence will be judged in the highest court. "Be not forgetful to entertain strangers, for thereby some have entertained angels unawares." Hebrews, 13:2.'

I feel as though I've been punched in my stomach.

'What is it?'

I point, wordless, knowing that Rob won't understand.

'It's just a grave, Megan. Like all the others. Sad, sure, but this dude died ninety years ago.'

'It's Tom ... 20 August 1904, the same day as Isabella Mitchell from before, remember? *"His innocence will be judged in the highest court."* It sounds like they thought he was guilty of something.'

'I don't have the first clue what you are on about. Come on, sis, we've got to get back to Grandma's.'

'I have to show this to someone.'

I look for Sam in the crowd, but I can't see him. Maybe he's left already.

Tom and Mrs Isabella Mitchell died on the same day. What could have happened – a shooting? An accident? Wild ideas tumble though my mind.

The sun is burning down and I feel a little giddy, light-headed, numb. It reminds me of the day I looked at a little blue line on a white stick, and threw up with the shock of it. It reminds me of the nurse telling me, 'It'll be a little bit uncomfortable when you wake up.'

Rob's shaking my arm. 'Megan, are you all right?'

And then Sam's there too. I point wordlessly at the stone and he wraps his arms around me in a silent hug. For a minute or two all I can hear is his heartbeat and all I can feel is his breath. I feel safe and cared for, and a little thought sneaks into my head. *Ryo never held me like this. Ryo never comforted me.*

Neither of us had enough for each other when we needed it.

And another little thought: I like being this close to Sam.

But we're at a funeral, in front of a ton of relatives and strangers, and even thinking about being attracted to someone (and I am thinking about it) is wildly inappropriate and wrong. How screwed up *am* I?

I take a step backwards, trying not to step on an ancient grave. Breathe, Megan. Talk about something else. Talk about something neutral.

'Well, I guess you two are all right,' says Rob. 'I'll see you by the church gate, Megan.'

'I'm sorry,' I say. 'I guess the funeral, and then seeing that Tom died . . . And he died on the same day as Isabella Mitchell – the newspaper editor's first wife. I mean, could that be a coincidence? Or did something awful happen? And look – the editor married Grammy's mother, about a year and a half later . . . I mean it's all connected, isn't it? Tom and everyone else.'

'Poor guy,' says Sam.

'I didn't mean to . . . ' I start, just as he says, 'I'm sorry if . . . ' Then we both fall silent.

'Megan—' says Sam, but then someone shouts for him, across the nearly empty graveyard, and he turns. It's Ed, of course, striding towards us.

'Can you hurry up?' he says. 'We need to get your pictures developed, if we're going to make the first edition. Sorry to spoil the moment, Megan, with all due respect, but Sam's here to work.'

'I'd better go,' Sam whispers to me.

'That's fine. I need to get back to Grandma's anyway.'

He's gone.

CHAPTER TWENTY-NINE

1904

EMMY

The police heard our story. Mr Mitchell made no mention of Tom at all. As soon as we were free to leave, he said, 'To work, Emmy! This calls for a special edition. Are you up to it?'

My thoughts were all of Tom. He was back at the office – I imagined giving him the news, first-hand. I'd see in his reaction whether or not it meant anything to him at all.

'Yes, of course.' I did not want to be alone, anyway. Every time I closed my eyes, the horror was there. I wondered if I would ever sleep again.

As we drew near to the office, I summoned up my courage. 'Mr Mitchell? Why didn't you tell the police about the letter we received?'

He looked at me, and for the first time I felt that I saw the real man behind the smooth professional. There was more kindness and understanding in his face than I had expected.

'Tom does not need more trouble in his life,' he said. 'And I know how much he means to you. I think that while I brief the staff you should go and find Tom, and take him away from the print room, and tell him what we have found.'

'And then?'

'It is his choice, and yours, but if you need my help, then feel free to ask.'

'Why would you help us?'

His eyes met mine. 'You can always come to me. Please remember that, Emmy.'

So, when we returned to the office, I went and found Tom in the print room. 'Come with me,' I said. 'Angus, Mr Mitchell says it is all right for Tom to leave now.'

Outside the office, I seized Tom's hand. 'Come on,' I said. 'We need to talk.'

We ran together along North Road to the edge of the forest. Wolf bounded along at his side. 'Here,' I said, near the spot where I first saw him. 'Stop. No one will see us here.'

We sat at the foot of a tree, the ground dry underneath us.

'Tom,' I began. 'You must tell me now. Your whole story. Everything you remember.'

He started to shake his head, and I grabbed his arm. I brought my face right up to his. 'Tom! This is urgent!'

'Why are you scared? You are trembling.'

I closed my eyes, then opened them again because all I could see was that cloud of buzzing flies.

'Tom, talk to me. Tell me everything, from the time that there was a dead man in your ma's bed. There is no use telling me that you cannot remember anything.'

Don't ask me who moved forward first. I only know that when we kissed, it was tender and beautiful and somehow, despite everything that had happened that day, it made me feel a happiness like nothing I had ever felt before.

I wanted to keep kissing him, sink into the feeling, forget all else. But it was impossible. I had to tell him what had happened – and I needed to hear his story. So, I pulled away. I touched his face. 'Tell me,' I said. 'Tell me.'

So we sat down on the ground, the tree behind us. And he told me the rest of his story. There were fewer hesitations this time, less uncertainty. His memory had returned, but as he spoke I understood why he had tried to wipe it clean.

'There are only three things that I remember about the dead man,' he told me. 'He had no shirt or pants, but he still had his boots on. He had ginger whiskers all over his face. And elsewhere too. There was a knife on the bed next to him. A black-handled knife, like you use to skin animals. I saw these things about the man and then Ellen covered him up with a sheet. She couldn't cover the blood though, because it was everywhere. On the bed and on the floor and speckled all over the wall.

'There was blood all over my ma. In her pretty hair. Splashed on her face. All over her hands and her shift, and it was like she was naked because the material was so wet with his blood that it clung to her body. She was screaming, but Ellen slapped her face and told her to hush and go wash herself.'

Listening, I felt sick. But I forced myself to stay calm and not react. How many horrors could one day contain?

He told me how his ma had not even said one word to him but was taken away by one of the other girls. Then Ellen pulled him close. 'Her breath smelled of liquorice and she gripped my shoulders hard. Her fingernails were so sharp – like Freddie the talking bird digging his claws into me.' She growled at him to forget what he had seen, and she took him to the kitchen for bread and hot chocolate. Later on – he wasn't sure how long – he went back to the room, and everything was clean and fresh and new.

'There was no blood,' he told me. 'It disappeared like magic.'

His mother was asleep in the bed, and she was also clean and fresh. He was allowed to sleep in the bed with her, although she never stirred. But he lay awake all night, listening to the sound of music and men, breathing in the smell of perfume and paint.

'And the next day we left that place for ever.

'Ellen took us to a place where they prayed all the time. They had a home for people like Ma. They called it the Mission for Fallen Women.

'It was a big enterprise. They'd pray for the souls of all the girls in all the resorts and they'd promise all kinds of things if only they left the bad houses. They took us in, all right, and fed us and gave us a place to stay.'

'That sounds good,' I said, encouragingly, as Tom had fallen silent.

'It wasn't good. They fed us and they taught me my letters, and they prayed a lot. But they kept on at Ma, all about sin and evil and hellfire, and Ma was sad all the time. She felt bad. And they told her that I was better off without her.'

The next part of his story was difficult to make sense of, because, I realised, Tom didn't want to say anything that would make me think badly of his mother. But I gathered that she started to leave him more and more, for days on end. And when she came back, she would cry and say that she wanted to have him to live with her, but the time wasn't right. He wouldn't speculate about what she was doing, or where she was living, but I've had a long time to think about this, and I've concluded that she returned to her old life. The poor woman was, most probably, addicted to the opiates that she'd been fed. And she didn't seem to have many advantages apart from her pretty face.

Tom was taken in by a Reverend and his wife. They had fourteen children there already. Five of their own and the rest fostered, like Tom. There were four to a bed, top and tailed, and there was never enough to eat.

The Reverend Mister, Tom called him, took a dislike to the new boy. Or maybe he treated all the new children the same. He beat Tom, saying it was for the good of his soul. Tom's anger grew, but he was still young – maybe seven years old, he estimated – and there was nothing he could do.

'Then one day, one of the Reverend's kids started ordering me around. Just for fun, telling me to lace his boots and lick them clean. He had all his cronies around, laughing at me. I just hit him once, just enough to show he couldn't treat me like that. But he squealed for his pa, and when the Reverend came, he wasn't interested in a word I had to say. Took off his belt and thrashed me near to death.'

So Tom ran away, back to the only place he knew, to the resort, the fancy house. And his ma was there – of course, I thought, of course she was – but she looked thin and pale and the make-up on her face was smudged and too bright. She told Tom he had to go back, and he refused, and Ellen told her to take him back to her parents. But Ma shook her head and said she'd rather die.

'And so I had to go back to the Reverend, and say I was sorry for what I'd done. After that I fought the Reverend and I fought the other children and I wouldn't say my prayers. They said I was the child of the devil, and I was proud. I laughed. I said I was happy and proud to be the devil's child because then maybe they'd treat me with respect. I didn't know what I was saying. But it's hard, Emmy, when someone tells you that you are bad. You believe it. I didn't understand it, but I believed it.'

He worked hard at his reading and writing, hoping that somehow it might mean he could escape from that place. How, I wondered, had he forgotten his education so thoroughly? When I started to read to him, I could swear he didn't even know what letters were. Had he been lying to me, even then? Time went by, and Tom never saw his mother. But then, one day she turned up, transformed. She was as beautiful as before, dressed in silks and furs, and riding in a carriage.

'Right by her side was my pa. I'd never seen him before. He had a huge thick bushy beard, and his brows stuck out from his face and he carried a big stick with a silver top.

'Mr and Mrs Reverend, they told Ma to go away, I was their son now, but I started hollering. I pulled off my shirt to show what the Reverend had done, and Ma was shouting bad words at him. Pa just stood there, grim-faced and silent, but then the youngest child asked, "Is that the devil?" and Pa started to laugh.

'Then he got his pistol and pointed it at the Reverend. "Why yes, I am the devil himself, come to liberate this child," he told the little boy. They all fell silent and trembled with fear, and I laughed out loud.

'He told me to get up into his carriage. No one said a

thing, so I did as he said. He and Ma got in, and we drove off.

'Once we were in the carriage, Pa and Ma were happy and laughing, and I joined in. We were laughing and cheering and whooping, and I was so happy to be back with Ma, and to have a pa as well – because that's what he said he would be. But I was wrong. He said he was the devil, and he was.'

CHAPTER THIRTY

1904

EMMY

Tom and his ma and new pa took a train north. The laughter and the joking soon came to an end – as soon as the motion of the train and the unaccustomed rich food that they'd given him for supper and breakfast combined to make the child sick. Tom's breakfast ended up all over his pa's newspaper, and the man forced liquor down his throat as a punishment.

When his ma protested, the man told her to be silent. And at that point two things were clear to Tom, although he was only eight years old. His pa was not a good man. And his ma was not going to be able to protect him.

After the train they stayed in a city, and then bought a

cart and horses to travel to Pa's house. It was buried deep in the trees, and there were no other houses around. Tom had never seen anything like it. That first night his ma and pa drank whisky and he laughed and she giggled and after a while they were chasing each other around the room, and they disappeared somewhere. Tom didn't follow because he knew that would make his pa angry. He huddled by the fire, and Wolf – 'my pa's dog, he bought him with the horses' – came and huddled with him. When Tom told me that I felt bad for all the times that I had resented his love for Wolf. And I wondered that he still loved his mother so much, although she had let him down so often.

But I did not say that to Tom. I knew better.

And soon Tom's ma never laughed at all. Everything about the forest scared her and she was convinced that she would be mauled by animals if she stepped foot outside. They knew there was a small town just miles away, but they were forbidden from going there. She talked about going to meet the townsfolk and take Tom to school, but his pa just laughed at her and told her that the people would sneer at her. 'They'll know what you are and what you have been and they will reject you as a sinner,' he said.

'They wouldn't have,' I told Tom, but there was doubt in my voice, and even now, years later, I cannot decide. Would Astor have been kind to a young woman like her? Would Tom have been accepted among the children at our school? We were a town of incomers, but maybe that made us more rigid, less accepting, less generous? We were all strangers, but we never wanted to acknowledge it.

She was sad and tired and she couldn't do the chores that were expected of her. She didn't clean or cook. So gradually, Tom started doing more and more. His pa taught him to make bread, to cook meat, to skin rabbits and cure their hides. And his ma got thinner and sadder and spoke less and less.

'She stayed maybe three months,' he said. 'Three months of shouting and slaps and drinking. She wasn't so pretty no more after three months. She had bruises on her face, her dresses were grey and torn, and they hung loose on her front.'

One day she showed Tom her coat. A warm fur coat his pa had given her. She'd sewn things into the lining, her jewellery, some money. She said she was showing him, so he'd know where everything was if anything happened to her.

He begged her not to leave him behind. And she swore she never would. With tears in her eyes, she hugged him to her, and said she would take him with her, of course she would.

'And did you believe her?' I demanded, and then wanted to bite my tongue, because he looked so hurt that anyone could question his mother's love.

'I know she would have taken me,' he replied. 'It was only Pa that would have stopped her.'

So I didn't say anything when he told me about waking up and discovering that she had gone. And how Pa had been unusually sympathetic, and dried his tears, and promised that she would come back. 'So, you see, Emmy, I could never leave. I knew she would come back one day.'

His pa's kindness did not last. His treatment of Tom became worse and worse. It was not just the physical abuse – and there was plenty of that. But he played games with the boy's mind. He told him that he was stupid and evil, and that he could never learn anything. When Tom tried to read his books, his pa beat him. He told him that the whole world would hate him, and see how evil he was, and hang him for it. The only person in the world that Tom could trust was his pa. He would have to serve him with complete obedience, just for the chance to see his mother again.

'Why did you stay?' I asked him then, and he shrugged, with no words to explain. But now I have seen evil in the world, and I think I understand. When you are small and weak, and there is someone stronger and bigger, then you believe what they say. When there is only one person in the world who notices you, then if they say that they can see into your soul and it is rotten, then you have no way of contradicting them.

There are people in the world so warped that they can only feel strong by exercising power over the weak. I think that Tom's pa had so little in his life to entertain him, that

243

he took joy from building a prison for a child, by making him utterly dependent on him.

You took me to Toronto once, and we saw *The Tempest*, do you remember? And I watched Prospero, all puffed up with his own importance, and I saw him abuse his monster, Caliban. And I cried, and you did not understand why.

I could not – would not – explain then, although I should have. But one week later, I started to make this record for you. Because this is your story, too.

CHAPTER THIRTY-ONE

1904

EMMY

I never asked Tom if he knew his pa's name. I didn't want to hear my fears confirmed, that this was Elijah Brown. I clung to the hope that this was some other man, some other house. But as he continued, I knew it could not be.

Tom's pa made his living trapping and hunting animals, then skinning them for their furs. The smell of death was always present. He would capture animals and keep them in cages. And sometimes – for sport or punishment – he would lock Tom in those cages too.

Tom was ashamed to tell me this. He could not look me in the eye. Gently, I took his hand. 'It was not your fault,' I told him. 'He was sick. He was inhumane.'

'I didn't even remember my own name,' he said. 'I was nothing. Not even worth as much to him as an animal. Then he could have killed me and skinned me and got money. I was just useless.'

'This is what he told you?'

He didn't answer. I understood that there was little difference by the end, in what he was told and what he thought to be true.

'How did you survive?' I asked. 'How did you keep living?'

'I was waiting for Ma to come back, I couldn't let her come back and only find him. I worry now ...'

'You worry now?'

'If she went back – and I wasn't there – she'd come to Astor, wouldn't she?'

I thought only of my own hurt feelings. 'Is that why you stayed?' I blurted out.

This time he did look straight at me.

'At first, yes. But then, later, I stayed for you, Emmy. You know that. You know that I trust you, that I ... that you have given me so much ...'

'Tell me the end of the story,' I said. I felt warm, inside and out, when he looked at me like that.

'As I got older, he got ill. He hated that. He didn't like the idea that I was getting big and strong, and he was weak. So he put me in the cages more. And one time, he took me out to the meat store, and showed me the hooks on the ceiling, and threw up a rope and looped it around my neck.

'The rope felt rough against my skin. He pulled it tight, so I was choking and coughing, and the blood thundered in my ears.'

'Oh, Tom,' I said, helplessly.

'I knew why he did it. To warn me what would happen if I ran to the town. But I was too . . . too trapped to do that. Too scared.'

'Anyone would be.'

'I wish . . . ' he said, and fell silent. I squeezed his hand. 'I wish too,' I said.

'Sometimes men would come to our house to trade. Then I had to serve them, but I was not allowed to speak. I carried furs to their boats, or their carts, but I never said one word. Sometimes they tried to talk to me, but mostly they did not bother. I don't know what he told them about me, but I do know what he would have done to me if I had tried to ask for help.'

I remembered the letter from the fur trader. There was no room for doubt now.

'Tom,' I said. 'Today I went with Mr Mitchell to the house where your pa kept you. We found him. Mr Mitchell has told the police what we found. You know, don't you? You know he is dead.'

Slowly he nodded. He let out a long breath.

'I remember it all now. I know what I did.'

CHAPTER THIRTY-TWO

1904

EMMY

Somehow I believed that if he didn't say it, it wouldn't be true.

'Shush,' I said. 'I don't want to hear any more. I don't want to know.'

Tom shook his head. 'You don't want to know?'

'I don't want to have to lie to the police.'

'I don't want to leave you, Emmy. You are everything to me.'

'Then don't leave. Lie to them! I don't know what happened, and I don't want to . . . just make up a story!'

I was near hysterical, and he put his arms around me to calm me down.

'You are the only person I will tell,' he said. 'I can hide the true story.'

'But Tom—'

'He always told me that if I came to the town, and if I spoke to other people, that I would be hunted and killed. But, that did not happen. People were mostly kind.'

'Not everyone—'

'Do you want me to stay?'

I was crying. 'Of course I do.'

'Then I will. Come on now. We must go back to the office.'

It was the bravest thing I have ever witnessed. Tom walked right back into the print room, and typeset the story of the man who had treated him as a slave. And we lived with the shared secret of his story.

Elijah Brown was shot by robbers, I told myself. If Tom had a gun, then it was to defend himself.

He could not be a murderer.

He could not.

And the days went on. The man was identified as Elijah Brown by William Masters, the owner of the general store who had occasionally served him.

'He weren't a regular customer, that I can tell you. Came here maybe once in a year to buy provisions and liquor. Not a talker, neither. Just barked out his orders and got on his way.'

My mother was asked to assist the coroner with the post-mortem examination, which took place at the hospital.

She came home afterwards, her face white with weariness. I hurried to get her a cup of tea and some pound cake. I'd made it myself from Sadie's great-grandmother's recipe and I was quite proud of the way it had turned out.

At last my mother put down her cup and said, abruptly, 'I am sorry you had to see the corpse, Emmy. That was not a pretty sight.'

'Oh, well,' I said. 'I only got a very quick glimpse.' I did not tell her that every time I closed my eyes I saw the man's slumped body, the cloud of flies. What was the point? There was nothing she could do about it.

'He had been dead for some time. He was shot in the head at close range. No signs of a struggle. He was not a well man, his body was riddled with tumours. I would have had no hesitation in calling it suicide, but the coroner has ruled that out.'

'Why?'

'There was no weapon at the scene.'

'No weapon?'

'No gun.'

'But ... it still could be. It could! What if someone took the gun? A thief or someone ... someone ...'

'Without the knowledge of how he was killed, the coroner cannot make a finding of suicide,' she explained. 'It also makes the police investigation more difficult. They are searching the land around the house now. Maybe they will find it.'

I swallowed, but tried not to let my nervousness show.

'What do they think happened?'

'I do not know.' She lowered her voice. 'I think they will want to question Tom. Apparently they found clothes, boots, too small to be Elijah Brown's.'

'But ... that could be anyone! There is no proof that it is Tom.'

'Emmy. Look at me.'

I found it hard to look at her. I felt too full of secrets.

'Tom cannot live here anymore.'

I gasped. 'Why? He has done nothing! This is his home!'

'It is too dangerous. It can only be a matter of time before people point the finger at him.'

'He would never hurt us! And if we turn him out, then people will assume we think he is ... that he is a killer.'

'Emmy. Some people – some ignorant, bad people – may want to hurt him.'

I was fighting back tears. 'But where will he go? And how can he be safe?'

'Mr Mitchell says he can sleep at the office, there's a room near the presses. He'll set a guard outside.'

'But I don't—'

'It is the best thing.'

'What will the police do? There is nothing to link Tom to the cottage.'

'Mr Mitchell says they are bringing an expert from the city. Someone who has made a study of the science of fingerprints.'

'Fingerprints?'

'There is growing use of fingerprint analysis as a means of identification,' she tells me. 'We all have different prints, and no two hands are the same. So they can be used in identifying criminals.'

I looked at the lines and whorls on my fingers. Who could ever check that no one else had the same pattern?

'Why, Emmy, your favourite writer, Mr Mark Twain, wrote a book twenty years ago using fingerprinting to identify a murderer.'

'Well, I never read that book,' I said.

'Fingerprinting is not valid evidence in court, to be sure, but if Tom's prints were found at the house, it would be difficult to fail to link him with the killing.'

'He would not hurt anyone!'

'If they could find the firearm, that would be proof enough,' said Mother.

I prayed that Sadie had forgotten ever seeing the gun that Tom brought with him that first day.

We were interrupted by Tom himself, coming indoors. He had been chopping wood and his face was rosy with exertion.

'Tom,' said Mother, 'come and sit with us.'

She told him what she had told me.

'You can come back here when all this is over,' I told him.

'That is very kind,' he replied, his voice very steady.

'Tom, the police will want to talk to you,' said Mother.

He nodded and said, 'Should I go to them?'

'Have you anything to tell them?'

I waited for him to deny any knowledge of Elijah Brown, but he sat very still, keeping his eyes averted from Mother's direct gaze.

'What will they do to the person who killed him?'

'If they were found guilty of murder then they would be hanged,' said Mother. 'If found guilty of a lesser charge – accidental killing, for example – then they would serve life imprisonment.'

Tom still said nothing.

'Tom?' Mother's voice was unusually soft, almost fearful.

'What can I do,' he said, 'when I don't remember?'

'Sometimes memory loss can be restored,' said Mother, slowly. 'Often just by revisiting a place where a traumatic event occurred. I have seen it happen. Annie Sowerby, she lost her memory altogether when she found her father hanged in his outhouse. She was only eight years old. But when they took her back there, it all came back to her.'

Annie Sowerby was an unmarried woman of more than thirty who lived with her mother in a cottage on the edge of Astor. She was well known to be touched in the head. I could not bear the comparison.

'That's nothing to do with you,' I told him.

'I will go there,' he said. 'I should see it for myself.'

CHAPTER THIRTY-THREE

1904

EMMY

Adam Harkness was waiting for me the next day as I came out of church. I greeted him as usual, but he reached out and gently took my arm.

'Emmy, I must talk to you.'

'I need to get home,' I told him. Neither my mother nor Tom had come with me this morning, so I alone had suffered the whispers, the stares, the pointed fingers of all the people who'd decided that Tom must be guilty of murder, on the basis of no evidence whatsoever.

Except the blood. The blood that covered his body when he came out of the forest.

'I will walk with you,' Adam said, firmly.

'But the rest of your family—'

'My father will drive them. Please, Emmy?'

I nodded reluctantly. Was this the moment that I would have to admit to Adam that I could never be his sweetheart? Or was he going to tell me that he no longer thought of me in the same way? I was suddenly aware of how much I had taken his devotion for granted all those years. But I had no choice. I was too distracted, too involved with Tom, his welfare and his heart. Even though Tom might chop my heart in two, ruin my life, condemn me to pain and misery, scandal and anguish, I was bound to him.

We walked away from the church, away from the crowds, until all we could hear was the rustle of the wind in the trees. The air smelled of grass, a bumblebee buzzed lazily among the meadow flowers.

Adam spoke first. 'Emmy,' he said, 'the word in town is that they are going to arrest Tom for the murder of Elijah Brown.'

I hid my alarm.

'They have no proof against him. They cannot arrest him with no proof.'

'They are bringing in a fingerprint expert,' said Adam.

'So what?' I said, stubbornly. 'Even if his prints are found, they can't use that in court.'

'Emmy, be careful. You don't want people to gossip, and you mustn't put yourself in danger. You should not associate with Tom. Not until his name is cleared.'

'Shame on you, Adam Harkness. Tom needs his friends all the more, right now.'

'You don't really know him. You don't, Emmy. You need to separate from him, until the truth – the whole truth – is known.'

'You think he will hang?' The word made me feel sick to my stomach.

'Emmy, I am sure they will never hang an innocent man. But Tom, he is like someone from a fairy tale, a mystery. Really, anything could be true of him.'

'I know a lot about him,' I said, although I was not going to tell Adam how much. 'He is clever, he learned his letters very fast. He is gentle with his dog, and with people too. He wants to learn all the time, about everything. He is interested in other people. He is—'

'He is new and exciting and mysterious and very fascinating to be sure,' said Adam. 'I prefer people that I have known all my life, and their families as well.'

I could read his mind as well as my own. I knew he wanted me to put my hand over his and say, 'That's what I prefer as well,' but I could not do it.

'Not everyone is as lucky as you, Adam Harkness. Not everyone has a mother and father and grandparents and uncles and aunts and cousins, all living in the same town and they all love and care for one another. Some of us don't have much of a family at all.'

I should not have said that. The next thing I knew,

Adam had seized me by the shoulders, and was kissing me with a passion that I had never thought was in him. I had no chance to react. I could hardly even breathe, until he released me.

'Adam!' My voice squeaked, much to my annoyance. I was so uncertain what to do, that I couldn't find anything to say.

'I'm sorry, Emmy. I should not have done that, but you must know how I feel. You must!'

'You could have asked me!'

'I could,' he said, 'but I didn't know what you would say.'

I looked at Adam, so tall and handsome, so reliable and open. He had no secrets. He had no past.

'I don't know what to say,' I said at last, speaking the honest truth.

We walked on in silence a little while. All I could hear was the blood rushing in my ears, my heart thudding. Then he stopped suddenly. 'This is the place,' he said.

'What place?' We were a little way along from the spot where I had first seen Tom.

He took my hand. 'Emmy, I have something for you.' I looked down at the ground, hot and clammy with embarrassment. Surely Adam could not be about to propose?

'Adam ... I am sorry—' I started, but stumbled to a halt when he reached down and pulled something from among the tree roots that was definitely not an engagement ring.

'I removed the ammunition,' he said, 'but it is up to you

what should be done with this. Whether you hand it to the police, and whether you tell them where it came from.'

There was no point in dissembling. Adam knew the gun was Tom's. He or Sadie – or maybe the two of them together – must have hidden it all those months before.

'I – I do not see that the police would be helped if I handed it over,' I said. 'There is no real proof, Adam.'

'No real proof,' he agreed. 'But I saw him as well as you did, Emmy. He was covered in blood, old dried blood, but his wound was not so great. If the blood had been all his, well, I do not see how he survived. Your mother must know it too. And Sadie – she saw this gun, Emmy. She hasn't said anything because she loves you, and she is fond of Tom. She trusts him, as you do.'

I felt ashamed then, because I had never talked to Sadie about the gun, or about my feelings for Tom, and I knew I had neglected our friendship in the past few months. I'd been avoiding her because I feared her reaction, if she realised I loved Tom and not Adam. And now Adam had proved himself so loving, so good . . . or was he testing me? Could I really trust him?

'If you think he is guilty why did you say nothing about this? Why didn't you run to the police?' I tried to keep my voice steady, but I am not sure that I succeeded.

'Why do you think, Emmy? Because I care so much for you and your happiness. And if Tom were hanged you would never be happy again.' He smiled at me, that sweet smile that I knew so well, a smile that stretched from his chin to his forehead. 'Now, you must make your choice as to what happens next. If Tom is innocent, he has nothing to fear.'

CHAPTER THIRTY-FOUR

1994

MEGAN

When Grandma leaves for the station with Rob I make Betsy a cup of tea. She's lost all her noise and energy, and sits on the sofa looking exhausted.

'I'm so sorry,' I tell her and she smiles and says, 'It's hard losing your mother at any age, you know, Megan? Even an old woman like me feels it.'

I feel like I've already lost my mother, I think, surprising myself by the sudden wave of sadness that overcomes me. I remember how hard Mom worked at being our mother when she had time off work. How she used to arrange playdates for me, but join in with whatever my friend and I were doing, because she felt she ought to be a super-mom whenever she wasn't at work. And what happened? I felt smothered and spied on, and by the time I was about eleven was actively trying to avoid her. And when something bad happened, when I needed her, I'd forgotten how to talk to her.

And I'd thought that distance was all her fault. But it wasn't really.

'Let's look at some photos,' I say. There's an old photograph album sitting on the coffee table in front of us. Dad produced a pile of them earlier, so that people could see Grammy when she was young and strong.

I open it. Straight away I see Grammy, wearing a dark dress and an apron, cradling a small girl in her arms. Her expression might be happy or it might be something more thoughtful.

I turn more pages, but I can't see her.

'Tell me who the people are,' I ask Betsy.

'Oh, it's me. Me and my family.' She counts them on her fingers. 'Sarah ... Ebenezer ... Marianne and me.'

The photographs are black and white, old-fashioned. It's quite hard to imagine Betsy and her brothers and sisters as young people.

'Where's Jesse?' I ask, interested to see my grandfather as a young man. I remember him as old, bearded, stout and serious.

Betsy turns the pages. 'There's one somewhere. Here we are. All together.'

Sarah, Ebenezer, Marianne and Betsy, tall and fair-haired, sturdy and laughing. Jesse is shorter, wiry with darker hair and eyes. He frowns out of the picture as though he's trying to tell me something.

'You know I've been doing some research at the newspaper?' I say. 'I found a story about a wild boy coming from the forest. Grammy and her friend Sadie discovered him. Did she ever talk about him?'

Betsy shakes her head. 'Not Mother. She hardly ever talked about him. Just that he was burnt to death in a fire, a terrible accident. And he was like a brother to her. She taught him to read and write. I think his death made her very sad, so much that she couldn't discuss it.'

'What about your dad? Did he know him?'

'My father knew him – he was the one who told us about him. He said I should remember Tom, just in case Mother ever did want to talk about him. But she never did.' Betsy's eyes fill with tears, expelled by a brisk flick of a tissue and a thorough blow of her nose.

'What else did your dad say about Tom?' I said, trying not to sound too much like an investigative journalist.

'He told me how scared his sister Sadie was when the wild boy came out of the forest, but that Mother was fearless. She only cared about his welfare. The boy was naked and dirty and he could barely speak. But trouble followed him like a cat stalks a mouse. People wouldn't trust him, they blamed him for anything that went wrong.'

'And what else did he say?' I try and imagine my great-grandfather Adam, who died years ago, before I was born, telling the story. I hardly know anything about Adam, except what Grammy told me, once or twice, that he was good and loving and gentle and strong.

'He said that Grammy and Sadie were convinced that Tom was innocent of every crime that they accused him of. Oh, and he did say one more thing.'

'What's that?'

'He said that he'd had all the luck.'

I must have looked confused, because Betsy explains, 'He had all the luck, because he lived and he married and he had a family. And Tom had none of those things.

'He said, "Sometimes I feel guilty because I have so much and he had so little."

'He said, "I don't know what I did to be so lucky."'

CHAPTER THIRTY-FIVE

1994

MEGAN

Mom calls and asks about the funeral. She sounds really concerned and actually upset, and I try my best to answer, to communicate, but the phone crackles and I can hear people in the background, and it's too difficult to explain all the emotions that I'm feeling.

'Megan, talk to me, honey. I'm sorry I couldn't be there.'

'Don't worry about it, Mom.'

'Megan . . .' she says. 'I know you must be hurting.'

I can't bear to tell her how much. 'I'm okay,' I say. 'How's Fernando?'

'He's good,' she says. 'You'd like him if you gave him a chance.'

'Maybe.'

'When you come back to the UK we can spend time together.'

'I'm not coming back.' I say it without thinking it through, but as soon as it's out of my mouth I know it's the truth. I'm never going back. I don't want any reminders of Ryo or the baby or our London home. 'I'm going to live here in Astor with Dad, and maybe I'll go to university right here in town, or maybe I won't bother.'

'Megan?' she says. 'We need to talk about this,' but I've got nothing more to say.

'Mom, I have to go. Betsy's cooked for us,' I lie. 'I'll talk to you later.' I put down the phone and sit on the stairs, breathing in and out and trying not to think about the weeks that have passed since the termination. I'd be huge by now. Feeling the baby moving inside me. Buying little sleepsuits and toys and stuff. My eyes blur over. I could've done it. Even without Ryo, maybe I could've done it.

'Megan? Are you okay?' Bee's carrying a tray of tea cups to the kitchen. She puts the tray down on the floor and comes to sit next to me.

'Shift up,' she says, and puts her arm around me. I put my head on her shoulder and let the tears come.

'It's okay, we're all sad,' she says. 'We all loved her. I sort of thought she'd never die.'

I don't tell her that I'm not crying for Grammy.

'Look, why don't I call Sam? I know you like him, I saw you together earlier. He's a sweet guy. I'll give him a call.'

I start to tell her not to bother, but she's grabbed the phone already. 'Megan's very upset ... yes ... could you? I think she'd like that.'

Listening, I feel hot and cold with shame, because I'm being dishonest with them all, and I still don't know how to tell the truth.

She hangs up and comes back over. 'He's on his way. Here, take a tissue. You might want to go and splash some water on your face before he turns up.'

'I'm going to go and get changed,' I tell her, just to have an excuse to get away. Upstairs I pull on jeans and a T-shirt, and I splash cold water on my face until I look ... well ... what do I care, anyway?

Sam's waiting in the living room when I come back down, making awkward conversation with Bee. I see immediately that he's acquired a red mark on his cheekbone since the morning and that he's embarrassed, trying to hide it but drawing attention to it in the process. I want to hug him. Sam's got so much going on, his home life is so difficult, yet he still has time for me.

'Hi, Sam.' I try and put on a smile for him. 'It's good to see you.'

'You too,' he says, smiling back. 'Want to come for a drive?' he asks.

'Yeah, that would be nice,' I say. The house feels hot and stuffy and unbearable; it will be good to get out.

'Where shall we go?' he asks as I climb into the truck. 'I'm free now, the paper's gone to press and Lexi's gone to a friend's house.'

'Get good pictures of Grammy's funeral?' I ask, knowing the minute it comes out of my mouth that it's a mean question. He pulls a wry smile. 'It's my job, Megan. Sorry if it offends you.'

'No, I'm sorry. That came out wrong.'

'It's okay. I always feel bad, taking pictures at a funeral. We did have permission,' he says.

'I understand. And you were really respectful.'

There's a slightly awkward pause, in which I'm sure we're both thinking about our cemetery hug. 'I always try to be respectful,' he says, glancing sideways at me, and I have to look out of the window to stop myself blushing.

'After all, your grammy used to own that newspaper,' he adds. 'I'm sure she covered a good few funerals in her time.'

A thought crosses my mind, then. All those files about Tom and Elijah Brown that should have been in the newspaper library but aren't. What if Grammy destroyed them?

I almost tell Sam, and then decide against it. I'm sick of theories with no hard facts. The past has hidden the truth about Astor's wild boy and everyone who knew him. The only secret we have managed to uncover, the woman with her fur coat and silk dress, she was probably nothing to do with him.

'Let's go to the forest,' I tell Sam. 'I could do with a walk.'

CHAPTER THIRTY-SIX

1904

EMMY

The police came looking for Tom pretty early on in their investigation. They questioned him, and he stuck to the story which I now know to be lies. No, he could not remember anything of his life before he came out of the forest. No, he had no knowledge of a house and a man, cages and animal hides.

And no, he had no objection to the police taking him to see the scene of the crime.

I was not permitted to go with him. All day I worked and worried and thought of him. I had no idea if he had been detained at the jailhouse, or allowed to return to his little room in the upper floor of the print works, a backroom formerly used as an office, hastily cleared of papers and swept clean. There was no bed, just a straw-filled mattress. Tom had a table and a chair. He had to wash himself in the outhouse. The room smelled of damp and petroleum, wax and ink and dust. It was no place to live.

But it was better than a prison cell.

I worked late, after all the journalists had finished, and promised Mr Mitchell that I would lock up when I left. I think he understood how worried I was, because he did not make any objection, nor warn me to stay away from Tom, as most people had. 'Take care of yourself, Emmy,' he said, as he left.

I barely dared to hope that there would be an answer when I knocked softly at Tom's door. My heart leapt as I heard his voice. 'Yes? Who's there?'

'Tom!' I almost ran into the room.

There he was, standing to greet me. I flung my arms around him. I couldn't bear to hear what had happened that day. All I wanted was to feel close to him, his skin, his bones, his breath and his heart.

Eventually, we broke apart.

'They took you to that place,' I said. 'What happened? How did you . . . what did you . . . '

'Remember?'

'Did you?'

'I told them I did not. I told them I remembered noth-ing. But there were marks on the wall, and they said that they were my fingerprints. They said it proved that I was there.'

'But they can't use that in evidence!'

'I said I might have been there, I did not remember. I said it again and again. And in the end they let me go.'

'What was it like? It must have been horrible to go back there.'

He shook his head. 'It was strange to be there, without him. I felt his power – all the control he had over me – it was gone. I felt like my true self again. It was bad to lie, I know, but I want my freedom, Emmy. I don't want his words to come true.'

'So what will happen?'

'The lawyer man that Mr Mitchell brought from the city, he said that they could not charge me. There are no witnesses, no weapon, nothing to say what happened.'

'So you are free?'

He nodded, but there was no happiness in his face.

'But Tom, this is good news! You can live your life again!'

'Mr Mitchell said . . . he told he that I must leave.'

'What?'

'He said I would never be safe here.' Tom's voice shook. 'He said that people would take justice into their own hands.'

I was furious. 'How dare he! I will talk to him!'

But Tom shook his head.

'He is wise. And he loves you too much to let me hurt you.'

'What do you mean?' He shook his head.

'He loves you very much, Emmy. You and your mother. I can see it. And he is right. I should leave.'

'No,' I said. I was more angry than I had ever been. 'No! You are wrong! He does not care about us! He is nothing to us! He can't tell us what to do!'

'He said he would help me.'

'I will help you!' Tears were streaming down my face, and he put his arms around me.

'I can't have a normal life, Emmy. I never did and now I never will.'

'You could not be a murderer!'

I waited for him to reassure me. But he turned his face away.

'Anyone could be. Talk to Mr Mitchell. He has seen things – men killing men over a drink spilled—'

'Not you. Not you, Tom.'

I felt him shiver. I was scared that he would once again become that wild, lost boy who came out of the forest.

So I drew him closer to me.

'Tom, I trust you,' I told him. 'This will all be over and then we can be together for ever.' My mouth met his and we kissed – a sweet kiss, that became something more urgent, unfinished, something overwhelming.

'I love you,' I told him, and he repeated it back to me. 'I love you. I love you. I love you.'

I cannot talk about what happened next.

It is the 1980s now. I am so much older, and I see how the young are all meant to be open and unafraid. I envy them, I really do. I look at the freedom that they have and I wonder – but even if I could talk as freely, as casually, as they do, I would not. For this was a private moment between Tom and me. Something removed from the rest of our lives.

All that you need to know was that it was mutual, and wanted, and wonderful.

'Everything will be all right,' I told him as we lay together afterwards.

He laughed then, but his laugh was bitter. 'No one here will never trust me, and why should they?'

'I trust you. That is all that matters.'

He gazed at my face as though to memorise every freckle.

'You know I love you. I want to spend every minute of every day with you. Nothing else matters to me.'

'Or me!' I said. 'We will be together, always.'

'But I cannot lie to you,' he said, softly. 'I did kill Elijah Brown.'

CHAPTER THIRTY-SEVEN

1994

MEGAN

The forest around Astor is beautiful. I've done these hikes before, when I was a kid, but never in September when the trees glow orange and yellow and red, leaves sizzling like flames in the wind.

We'd parked Sam's van in the car park and got ourselves a map of the route.

'It's all marked out anyway,' he tells me as we walk along. 'No room for getting lost.'

'I used to want to just go anywhere, when I was a kid,' I told him. 'I thought it would be romantic to be lost in the wood. Like a Disney movie.'

'Yeah, sometimes I think I'd quite like to get lost. Just wander and see where I end up.'

'Would you? Really?'

He shrugs. 'Got to be better than the way I'm living my life now.'

'What happened? I can see you've been in a fight. Was it Kevin?' I gently touch his face. His skin is soft, and I realise that I'd actually like to find out what it would be like to kiss Sam.

'Just standard stuff,' he says. 'Nothing to worry about.' But his voice is sadder than his words.

'It's not standard, if he hits you. It's actually abuse.'

'He can't help it.' He changes the subject so abruptly that I back off. 'So, that was your brother at the funeral?'

'Yeah, Rob. He's at Harvard.'

Sam whistles. 'Impressive. And where will you go? Harvard as well?'

I shake my head. 'No. I have a place at Edinburgh University if I want it. I'm meant to start in a year's time. But I'm going to reject it. I'm going to stay here.'

I thought he would be pleased, but he looks horrified. I'm taken aback. Have I completely misjudged the situation? Maybe Sam doesn't like me at all.

'Stay in Astor?' he says. 'Have you gone mad?'

'Why wouldn't I?'

'Why would you?'

It's almost as though he *wants* me to go.

I could tell him how raw I feel, and why I need to be somewhere that makes me feel safe and loved, not just some stranger passing through. I could tell him I need family and roots and history to anchor me and help me recover from everything that's happened.

I could even tell him how I want him to be a part of that.

But I'd have to explain exactly what's happened, and I'm not sure how to do that. And I'm hurt by the baffled look on his face.

'Why are *you* still here if you feel like that?' I demand.

'I ask myself that every day,' he says. 'I mean, people judge us all the time. We're a disaster as a family. Mom's dead and Kevin's lost all the sense he ever had, and I'm stuck looking after Lexi. People here despise us. They think we're trash and they ask me all the time why I stay here with this. Why do you live with someone who beats the crap out of you all the time? Why do you take the beating?'

'Sam, I didn't mean—'

'But you know what, he doesn't mean to do it. It's not his fault. I stay because Lexi and I are all he's got. I stay because I love him for who he used to be, and I have to believe that man's still in there, somewhere; and I stay because I'm sure as hell not leaving Lexi alone with him.'

'Sam—'

'But you, Megan. You could go anywhere. Do anything. If I were you I'd be travelling, seeing the world, taking my pick of places to study. Why would you choose to stay here?

This is a nothing sort of place. Small town, small minds.'
He picks up a stick and lashes the bushes at the side of the
path. The forest is darker here, the trees closer together. It's
eerily quiet and the path has narrowed, nearly to a single
track.

'You know why I stay?' he says. 'For Mom. Because she
believed in us as a family. Kevin took her in when she was
a single parent, and she was so happy, she truly was. She
could've got rid of me when she found herself pregnant at
seventeen, had a convenient termination. She could've got
rid of Lexi too, because we sure didn't have the money for
another kid. But she didn't because he wanted to have a
family. Now I'm trying to do that for her.'

Something inside me snaps. All of the grief and anger
that I've been holding inside me, come shrieking out of my
mouth at lovely Sam, who I'd just moments ago wanted to
kiss.

'You don't know!' I shout at him. 'You can't say things
like that! Who are you to judge?'

He blinks, shocked, and then I see him working out what
I mean, what must have happened . . . And the thought of
his sympathy, his curiosity, is too much to bear.

I run, blind and wild, away from him, into the forest,
dodging trees and kicking through undergrowth, not
thinking about where I am going, just wanting to be far
away from everyone in the world.

CHAPTER THIRTY-EIGHT

1904

EMMY

I remember his words to this day. Every single one of them. I've carried them with me for all these years. It was the least I could do.

He sat upright on the mattress, and looked into the distance as he told me his story. I kept very still and very quiet. I did not want to disturb him at all.

'You cannot wipe away memories, however much you want to. That is what I have learned,' he said. 'At first, when I came from the forest, my mind was as blank as a field of new snow. I did not lie when I told you that I knew nothing of where I came from. But gradually my past came back to me, just as snow melts and exposes the dirt and mud beneath.

'Things changed when Pa got ill. He needed me more, but he loved me less. He was scared of me, even though I never did anything bad to him.

'He didn't like that I'd got taller, nearly as tall as him. He didn't like that my voice was deeper, more like his. He was angry to see that I was changing and growing and he said it was a sign of my evil and I needed to be controlled and caged.

'So he caged me. Most of the time I slept in an old shed in the backyard. It was cold, and it smelled of blood and tanned hides and my own dirt. He put chicken wire all around, so I could only get out if he let me.

'I must have lived like that for about a year. Pa had stopped trusting me. He let me out to do the chores, but he kept his shotgun on me the whole time. I never had a free moment out of his sight.

'Sometimes I thought I would be better if I let him shoot me. There was nothing worth living for. I could hardly remember Ma anymore. There was only me and him, and he was thinner and paler and older, and never said one word to me, just kept his gun on me, till he locked me in again.

'Sometimes I thought that I was strong enough to tear down the wire. I could tell him that I didn't want to sleep out in the cold, in the dirt. I could even put him to sleep in those cages.

'But I never did anything. I didn't want to let the

evil in me come out. I accepted that place was where I belonged. There's more than one way to imprison someone. Pa built his walls round my heart and my soul. I was nothing without him. I had no name. He was all that I had.

'I watched Pa get weaker and paler. I listened to him raving and shouting. I saw him full of pain, hardly able to lift his gun to threaten me.

'And I said to him, "Don't lock me away. I can care for you. You are sick, and I will look after you."

'He groaned and said I was bad and evil and lying and not to be trusted. I could have destroyed him then. But I feared that I would be nothing without him.

'I was nothing.

'So he did not lock me away. And I washed him and cooked for him. I fed him soup, spoon by spoon. I dressed him and held a cold cloth to his head when he had a fever, and held his hand when he cried with pain.

'When he could no longer walk, when there was no danger of him seeing what I was doing, I went to the yard and let out all the animals from their cages. Rabbits and foxes. I let them run free into the forest. I could have gone with them, but I did not.

'I could not leave my pa. I guess I loved him, in a way.

'He was angry with himself that he had never taught me to read. "I was a fool to myself," he said. "You could have read to me, these long, full days."

'"You could still teach me now," I told him, hopeful. But he shook his head. "It is too late for you. You will never learn to read. You would not be capable."

'So, you see, Emmy, when you taught me to read, how important that was. You didn't just open my mind to books and newspapers and everything else in the world; you showed me that Pa was wrong. If he was wrong about reading, he could be wrong about everything.

'I never understood that before.

'Anyway, I could not read to him, so I would sit and listen while he told me about the world. Men were cruel, women were false, there was no justice or truth and people would see my evil and kill me for it.

'"What if Ma comes back?" I asked him one day. "Should I trust Ma?"

'He laughed in my face. "Why would you trust your ma? She was false to me and she abandoned both of us. You are better off to forget her, boy. She was bad, through and through."

'Then he saw my distress because I had waited patiently for Ma so many years, and he stroked my hair and said, "You can trust me and everything I say. I care for you. When you obey, I can ignore the evil in your heart and soul. You are safe with me. Fear not."

'But I did fear, very much, because he was coughing blood every day and night, and he was thin and weak, no matter how much soup I spooned into him.

'One day he said to me, "I am not long for this world. Will you mourn me when I am gone?"

'"I do not know what you mean," I replied.

'"Oh, what a creature I have created," he said. He was mocking me. There was nothing I could do.

'"Will you mourn me, when I am dead, as you have mourned your ma?"

'I was confused. " Ma is not dead," I told him. "She will come back."

'"No. Of course not. She is not dead. Will you miss me, as you miss her?"

'Cold fear seized me at the thought of him leaving me. I was shaking and shivering. I cried out, "Please, please do not leave me. I will be good. I will obey."

'"But surely you want your freedom?" He was teasing me, I knew, but I could not stop my tears at the thought of living without him.

'"I want you to do something for me," he told me. "One last thing, then you are free to go where you will."

'"Where would I go?" I was terrified. "I will stay here with you."

'"Yes. You will. You will stay." He was pleased, I could tell and that pleased me. If Pa was happy then I was happy. I belonged to him. He was everything to me.

'"Yes," I said. "I will stay here forever and ever." I could not imagine feeling safe anywhere else in the world. I hardly knew that anywhere else existed.

"'You will,' he said. "You will stay.

"'But first you will kill me.'"

CHAPTER THIRTY-NINE

1994

MEGAN

Sam runs after me, shouting, 'Megan! Stop! You can't go that way!'

I don't stop. I can't stop. I'm running to escape the feelings of guilt, anger, all the sorrow for Ryo, for me, for our baby.

My lungs are bursting, my nose is running, my eyes are streaming tears, and the undergrowth tears and scratches my legs. I'm slowing down. When Sam grabs my shoulder, I turn on him.

'Leave me alone, Sam,' I plead with him.

'It's okay, Megan, don't run. Talk to me, please?'

I know I seem irrational to him, behaving like this crazy girl – the girl whose mind was turned by Sad Events.

'I . . .'

'I'm sorry if I said something wrong, but I honestly didn't mean to. What did I say?'

I remember that I trust him, Sam with his honest eyes, and I try and pull myself together.

'It's just . . .' I still can't explain. I'm entirely without language. Instead I find that tears are coming, fat uncontrollable tears.

'Can I hug you?' Sam asks, warily, like I'm liable to bite, and I nod, and he wraps his arms around me. We stand there for what feels like an hour, just holding each other and breathing. And then he kisses the top of my head and tightens his arms around me and I hope that he sees what I see in that moment – a glimpse of something more, something wonderful that could be there if we want. No pressure. No pretence.

Eventually we break apart. 'Time to go,' I say.

He grins shyly at me. 'Yeah,' he says. 'Pity I have no idea where we are.'

'Oh.' I look around me. No signs. No path. 'I think we must have come that way,' I say, pointing at random at a path.

'Okay,' he says. 'It's just that this bit is roped off. You charged straight past the signs. There's some old mining works here. We need to watch our step.'

'Oh!'

'It'll be okay,' he says. 'We drove north-east out of town,

and the sun is over there, so if we walk in that direction we're going west. I think that'll get us back towards the car park. And there are maps everywhere.'

I hadn't realised it was getting darker. The sun is orange, turning the dancing leaves brown and black, breeding shadows on the ground.

'We'd better go,' I say. I step in the direction that he pointed out, but stumble over a tree root.

'Ow!' I say, as my ankle twists under me.

And then I'm falling into the earth.

CHAPTER FORTY

1904

EMMY

I froze with horror.

He was silent, his eyes trying to find some kind of understanding in mine.

'Tell me.' I forced out the words.

'He trained me to always obey. I had no friends. Nowhere to go. The weeks before . . . he would sometimes use what little strength he had to throttle me, remind me that my life was in his hands.'

I did not know what to say. I could not comprehend making such a choice. 'How could you? How could you kill him?'

'He was suffering bad. He was spitting blood, he could

not eat, his breath . . . He was like a bear in pain. Angry. Tortured. He wanted death. He wanted it quick and all-at-once. Not lying in a bed, starving to death. That's what he told me.

'I remember the feel of the gun as he placed it in my hand. The smooth, cold weight of it in my hot, sticky hands. The sharp taste of old food in my mouth. The way he pushed his head up to the muzzle. "Do it now," he said. And when I hesitated: "Now, worthless boy. Do not worry for your soul. You have none worth saving."

'Then he laughed and laughed, and I pulled the trigger very slow, watching the blood-flecked spittle gather at the side of his mouth, flinching from the stench of his sour breath, hearing that rasping laugh, for the very last time.

'Then he spat in my face.

'I let go the trigger.'

I could hardly breathe as Tom told me his story. I wanted to clap my hands over my ears, scream at him to stop, to shut up, not to tell me these terrible things. But I could not. He needed to tell someone. The best person was me.

'And then there was blood in my eyes, over my face, on my shirt, in my mouth. The thing that used to be Pa lay slumped over the desk. I stood frozen, hearing his instructions over and over in my head.

'Stay with me.

'Never leave me.

'Alive or dead. You belong here in this place.

'They will kill you, as though you were an animal.

'So I turned the gun on myself. I thought there was nothing for it but to end my miserable life. But as I squeezed the trigger, Wolf leapt up at me. The gun was knocked sideways, and it missed me, all except the wound you saw when I first came to Astor. I was bleeding, but I was alive, and Wolf was . . . he didn't want me to die.

'And then I ran. I ran to the forest. There was a cave where sometimes we would go to hunt. I shivered and wept and rocked myself to sleep, but my skin burned with the feel of his flesh and blood, painted on to me. Wolf ran with me, and that kept me warm at night, but I couldn't stop the bleeding and I was getting weaker.

'In the morning I stripped off my shirt, my pants, every last bit of clothing. I felt my way to the end of the tunnel. I looked for water to wash myself, but only succeeded in making myself wet with mud and bloodier still. I kept the gun with me. I did not want to be mauled to death by an animal.

'Then we ran and ran, through the trees, and the brambles bit into my skin, through the light and the dark, to the place where the forest ended.

'And I waited until you came, you and Sadie. But as soon as you appeared, Wolf ran off into the forest, as though he'd done his job in delivering me to the two of you.'

CHAPTER FORTY-ONE

1994

MEGAN

The earth opens up and swallows us both. We fall, like Alice into Wonderland, down into darkness, banging against hard walls, collapsing with a jolt on to a pile of leaves and soft earth.

All the air in my lungs is knocked out of me, and I gulp and gasp. My neck hurts like hell, and my ankle is throbbing.

It's almost completely dark, and the only light filtering through from where we fell is getting darker by the second. 'Sam?' I hiss. 'Sam?' But he doesn't reply. He's lying across me, a dead weight.

'Sam? Oh, God, are you okay? Sam?'

I find his wrist, and feel for his pulse. Yes, he's alive. Still breathing. But he's not responding at all, and when I brush my hand across his forehead, it comes away wet. He's bleeding, I'm sure of it. I investigate further, and find an egg-shaped lump on the back of Sam's head. He must have bashed it against the wall as we fell.

Gingerly I feel around me to try and get an idea of where we are. What is this hole – a cave? An old well? There are rusting metal struts in the wall, and I don't think we've fallen too far. I can still see the sky, but it's getting darker very quickly. What can I do? How can I get help?

I try and think clearly. There are Forest Wardens, who will see Sam's truck. Will they realise that we are lost? Will they come and look for us? How far off the path did we go? Have they got some sort of equipment to find people?

Or are we going to stay stuck here in this hole for ever?

Sam was carrying his camera bag, I realise, and it fell with him. I find it, right up by the wall, after I shift him off my legs and make a pillow for him with my jacket. He isn't carrying as much stuff as usual, and his one camera seems to be smashed from what I can feel, but there's something that feels like it could be a flashlight, and after fumbling a bit I manage to switch it on.

The first thing I see is an enormous spider. I scream loud enough to wake the dead, and it scuttles away. Sam hardly stirs though, and I can see now that the cut on his head is big and the blood is flowing freely. I retrieve my jacket from under his head and hold it against the wound to try and staunch the blood. But it's not enough. Not nearly enough.

'Dammit, Sam,' I mutter. 'You are not going to bleed to death. Come on! Wake up!' But his eyes stay shut.

I look around the hole that we've fallen into. We fell around three or four metres, I reckon, and there are some metal struts in the wall, the remains of an old ladder, so perhaps I could climb out. If I took the flashlight ... but then Sam would be in the dark on his own. And what if the batteries failed in the forest?

There are several spiders on the wall, and I shudder, looking at them. There's also a small bundle in a corner – cloth and a leather bag and a pair of old boots. I wonder how long they've been there? The bag is empty, but the cloth turns out to be a pair of trousers and a shirt, rough dirty garments, dusty and smelly, but bone dry. I peel off my T-shirt and put on the shirt. It's disgusting, feeling the dirty cloth against my skin, but it's warmer, and it means I can use my T-shirt to press against Sam's head. The flow of blood is beginning to slow. I try and make a bandage, tying the sleeves of the shirt at the back of his head. He groans, which I take as a good sign.

I'm talking to him the whole time. 'Sam, wake up ... You're going to be okay. Sam ... I don't know what to do. Should I go for help, or stay with you? What do you think? Wake up, Sam ... wake up ... '

But he doesn't respond.

It's up to me to get help. I'll have to climb out and try to find my way back to the truck. I dig in Sam's pockets and find the ignition key. I could drop old film canisters to try and mark the path. It's not much of a plan, but it's all I've got.

I kiss him on his cheek, breathing in his apple-shampoo smell.

'I won't be long,' I tell him. 'I'll bring help.'

I put the flashlight and the canister cases in to the old leather bag. I leave his camera bag with him. There's a bar of chocolate in there, and a can of Coke. If ... when ... he wakes up, he'll have something to eat and drink. There's a pen and a notebook too, so I write, *Gone for help, Megan*, and wrap the paper around the chocolate.

I try not to think about how dark it'll be and how alone he'll feel. That won't help anyone.

I sling the bag over my shoulder. Then I start climbing, into the night. Some of the metal struts feel loose, and some are so rusty that I fear they'll turn to dust in my hands. My skin is getting scratched and torn, so every step is torture. But I keep going. It feels like I've been climbing for hours.

I reach the top, gasping and wheezing. I'm so unfit! Then I drop a canister to mark the place – and look around me at the absolute darkness. The trees rustle in the wind and the hair rises on the back of my neck. I find the flashlight and turn it on. The beam of light gives me strength. 'C'mon, Megan, you can do this,' I say out loud.

I try and remember which way Sam said was west,

which way to the car park. There was a phone box there, I remember. I just have to find my way back.

'I can do this!' I say, into the silence, into the dark.

Then I start walking, dropping canisters as I go. I walk and walk. And just as I think it's hopeless, that I'm going to die and Sam's going to die, and it's all my fault, it starts getting light. I'm so relieved that I start laughing. I can see a clearing in the trees. It must be the car park!

And I stumble through the trees and into the car park and pick up the phone in the booth. But it's not working.

So I take the keys to Sam's truck – even though I've never driven anything like it before. I've only had a few driving lessons.

But how hard can it be? And I climb into the cab and turn over the engine and experiment with the clutch, and listen to the engine cough and splutter.

And then I start driving, back to the main road.

I never see the other car, before I slam into it.

CHAPTER FORTY-TWO

1904

EMMY

I could hear Mrs Mitchell moving around in the compositing room. She came every evening to bring food for Tom, but never spoke to him. She told Sadie's mother that it scared her to death, to have anything to do with him, that he should be driven out into the forest and left there.

I listened as her footsteps quietened, and the door closed behind her.

'You should go now,' said Tom.

'I will never tell anyone what you have told me,' I assured him. 'Never. You have told the right person.'

He nodded. 'I know. You are the opposite of him.'

'I will think about what we can do,' I said. Because I was

convinced already that Tom would have to leave Astor. He needed to get far away from this place. But I would go with him. That was my plan.

I kissed him one more time, and then left him. What could I do? My mind was racing.

I was deep in thought when I went to open the print works door, so I didn't see the skinny figure of Mrs Mitchell waiting in the shadows in the corner of the room. I gave out a shriek when she gripped my upper arm.

'You brazen girl!' she said. 'You've been with him, haven't you? Have you no shame?'

I pulled my arm away.

'It is none of your business! What are you doing, skulking in corners?'

'I thought I heard you.'

'So you were spying on me! Well, you can go away!'

'You're exactly like your mother!'

I was dumbfounded. What was she raving about?

Mrs Mitchell stuck her bony face so close to mine that I could smell her sour-milk breath. I hated her at that moment.

'Your mother is a whore!'

'You are mad!' I retorted.

'Oh!' she said. 'How dare you! The whole town knows who your real father is. They collude in my humiliation.'

I lost my temper. I pushed her away from me.

'Shut up,' I told her. 'You're an evil woman!'

There was a noise, a loud growling roar. Wolf was roused from his corner, and was at my side. He leapt at Mrs Mitchell, his jaw open, teeth gleaming. 'No, Wolf, no!' I shouted, as he barked wildly and she shrieked and stumbled backwards, falling on to the stone floor.

Tom was running towards us. 'Wolf!' he shouted. 'No!'

He dragged Wolf away. Mrs Mitchell lay moaning on the ground. Had she hit her head in falling? I did not care, I must confess. My only thought was that as soon as she told people what had happened then Wolf would be destroyed.

'Tom, we must go. We must run. She will make sure that Wolf is shot . . . we must save him . . . '

I tugged at the door, and pulled it open. I looked for Jed, the watchman, but there was no sign of him. This did not surprise me, because he was a lazy beggar who liked his liquor.

'But what about Mrs Mitchell?' said Tom, looking back at her.

'We can't wait! Run!' I grasped his hand and pulled him with me.

We ran in the darkness of the night, and I prayed we would not see a soul.

CHAPTER FORTY-THREE

1904

EMMY

There was whisky on Mr Mitchell's breath and a frown on his face, as I pushed past him on the doorstep, dragging Tom behind me. My words fell over themselves. 'Mr Mitchell! You must help us! We must leave Astor!'

Mr Mitchell looked confused. 'What's happening, child?' he said.

'Please. We have to help Tom.'

Mr Mitchell hustled us into his front room, and poured himself another whisky. He downed it in one.

'Tom will always be in danger here. You told him so yourself. He must go – he must leave – and I will go with him—'

All the time I was listening for Mrs Mitchell at the door.

But she did not come. He swallowed. 'Tom, I will do what I can. I will take you to safety.'

'And me,' I said. 'I will go with him.'

'No,' he said. 'That's not possible, Emmy.'

'I will!' I said.

'Then you will put Tom in danger. He needs to disappear quietly, which he can do with my help. But if he takes you with him, then there will be a search. There will be an outcry. People will accuse him of kidnapping you. Imagine it, Emmy.'

My voice was choked. 'I don't care! I will go with him anyway!' But I knew that he was right. Tom had to go away on his own.

'Wait here,' said Mr Mitchell. 'I have some papers that will help.'

Left alone, Tom and I clung to each other. He was shaking. 'I thought you would tell him . . . ' he said, and I replied firmly, 'No. Not for anything. He does not need to know any more than I have said.'

'Why should he help me?'

'He always has,' I said, and this time I believed it. And I understood why, as well.

'I will be in Toronto in six months,' I told him, 'studying at college. Find me there. Then we can be together.'

'I will,' he said, and then we kissed one last time, springing apart as the door opened.

Mr Mitchell returned, and handed Tom an envelope.

'Here,' he said. 'Take this. You need to be as far away as you can get from here, and never come back.'

'You must write—' I started, but Mr Mitchell silenced me with a gesture. 'Not even writing. Not now. Tom has to disappear.'

There was little I could do, under his gaze, so I gripped Tom's hand and stared into his eyes and prayed that he understood how much I loved him. He rested his brow against mine, and I feared he was too weary with fear and confusion to survive on his own.

'Goodbye, Tom,' I said, my voice as brave as I could make it. 'Goodbye, Wolf. Look after him for me.'

Then I turned my back and walked to the front door. It was the only chance for Tom and I knew it.

As I walked out into the night I knew I should go back and find Mrs Mitchell. I must apologise for what I'd done and try and persuade her to keep silent about what had happened that night. And all the time delay her returning home and finding her husband missing.

So I went back along the West Road, to where the print works stood.

Did I see the men as I walked? Later on – much later, decades later – they reckoned that a whole gang of them had run away, back to town, back along the West Road.

But I did not see them. Ghosts and shadows, masked and hidden, they must have slipped past me as I walked on, oblivious.

I was feeling for the key in my pocket, wondering if I should check inside, see if Mrs Mitchell was still there, when I reached the print works. Something made me stop in my tracks, just a few yards away. Was it the smell of smoke, a crackle in the air, or just a feeling that something was very wrong?

I do not know. All I know is that suddenly the darkness roared into light and noise and bricks and glass flew all around me.

And everything went black.

CHAPTER FORTY-FOUR

1994

MEGAN

For a moment I don't know if I'm in London or Astor. I'm lying in a hospital bed, which could be anywhere in the world. Same lumpy pillow. Same weird out-of-body feeling.

And Mom, sitting in an armchair by my side, leafing through *The Economist*.

'Mom?' My voice is so much shakier than I expected it to be that I scare myself.

She drops the magazine right away. 'Megan! Darling!'

'Mom? What are you doing here? Where even am I? I can't be in London, can I?'

She smiles. 'You're in Astor, sweetheart. I haven't stolen you away. You got lost in the forest and then you had an

accident in a truck. Remember now? They gave you seda-
tion and you've been asleep for hours.'

I smile back. It's actually so good to see her. And then I
remember.

'Oh my God, Sam. He's in a cave, he's hurt, Mom, I've
been sleeping and he might be dead, he's unconscious, he's
bleeding, Mom, and it's all my fault.'

My voice is rising, hysterical. I'm fighting for breath,
panicking. I'm swinging my legs out of the bed, trying to
free my arm which remains stubbornly attached to the
drip – ouch! – it doesn't seem a good idea to rip it out.

She doesn't understand me, she's not doing anything.

'You've got to do something! Sam's hurt!'

She grabs my hand. 'Megan, calm down, it's okay. You'll
remember when the sedative wears off. You managed to
find Sam's truck and you tried to drive to get help, but
you smashed into a parked car. You gave the paramedics
good directions though. Sam's got concussion and they've
stitched up his head, and he might have to have surgery.
The two of you fell down an old mine shaft, quite a way. You
were very brave, sweetheart, it must have been terrifying.'

'Surgery?' My voice sounds so weak and scared.

'There might be internal bleeding. We'll know more
soon. Don't cry, darling, it's not your fault.'

I try and think back, and grab a few scattered snapshots.
The truck, grey in the dawn light. The phone that wouldn't
work. And then feeling sick with fear driving the truck, and

the loudest crash, and then people ... nice people ... and saying Sam, Sam, Sam over and over ...

I close my eyes.

'How are you feeling? They thought a good sleep was the best thing for you. They checked you over last night and they said you were okay. Just some nasty cuts and bruises and dehydration.'

'When did you get here? What are you *doing* here? And where's Dad?'

'Sweetheart, I was worrying about you. You wouldn't talk on the phone, and I knew how upset you were about Grammy. I was coming for the funeral – Rob and I, we thought we'd surprise you – but my plane was delayed. I called you from the airport, but I didn't let on where I was. And by the time I arrived, you'd disappeared.'

She's as neat and smart as ever, even in her casual clothes. Designer dark-navy jeans, a white shirt, a gilet, but she's paler than usual, and she's not wearing lipstick. For my mom, that's like going out in her underclothes.

'Where's Dad?'

'He's here too. Just sleeping. We thought we'd take it in turns. But he was here all night, he only left you when I arrived. And he didn't get much sleep when you were missing.'

I blink again. 'We weren't missing for long.'

'Oh, Megan,' she says. 'It was a whole day and a night. I thought we'd lost you. I thought you were gone for ever.'

Then Mom does something she never does. She never did it when she and Dad separated. She never did it when I told her about the baby. She never did it at the clinic, or afterwards, or when I left for Canada.

My mom bursts into tears.

CHAPTER FORTY-FIVE

1904

EMMY

They blamed Tom. Of course they did. Tom had imprisoned Isabella Mitchell in the print works and burned the place down to revenge himself on the town. Both of them burned so thoroughly that neither body was ever found.

He was evil.

He was a murderer.

He was an arsonist.

And all of it printed in the pages of the *Astor Press*. I refused to cut and paste any of it. I vowed that one day I would destroy all trace, all mention of Elijah Brown and the print works fire. I couldn't do it then. But the day that I took over the newspaper I made a bonfire of cuttings, trying to wipe all trace of this story from the records.

I only left the story about when we had found him. I wanted there to be some record left for you, for when I found the courage to tell you.

I didn't mourn for Tom. I looked forward to seeing him again. We would find each other in Toronto, I was sure. But my tears flowed anyway, whenever I thought about the life he had had, the cruelty he had suffered.

And then I realised that I could never go to Toronto. Sadie would be studying alone.

The reason was you.

I understood within weeks that I needed to get married. I was a doctor's daughter. I knew what it meant to start vomiting for no reason, to feel subtle changes in my body.

I turned to the man who had always loved me, who was reliable and strong and who would do anything for me.

I asked Adam to walk with me after church one day. He was concerned about me. 'You are so pale,' he said. 'I know how sad you are. I know you are missing Tom. I am so very sorry.'

I did not want to talk to Adam about Tom. I did not want to lie to him more than was necessary.

I could not allow myself to think about Tom. Every time I did my heart would twist and the pain was unendurable. I was bereft, but I knew Tom was only safe away from here, away from me. It was his only chance. Now I needed to seize mine.

'Adam,' I said, 'I do not believe the fire at the print works was an accident. I believe that someone set fire to it deliberately. They wanted to kill Tom.'

He nodded. 'I think you are right. I have heard rumours ... whispers ...'

My voice was hoarse, barely more than a whisper itself. 'Adam, swear to me that you were nothing to do with it.'

He seized my hand. 'Emmy, how could you ever think that? Of course not! I would never ever do something, anything like that. Of course I would not.'

I could hardly look at him, but I said it. 'I am glad, Adam, because if you had, I could never marry you.'

It took him a few seconds to understand me. 'Emmy? Are you saying ... ? Oh, Emmy, my darling ...'

And as I sheltered in his arms, I knew that Adam was a good man. A man I should be proud to marry. Is it possible to love two people as I did? It must be.

We were married two months later. I told him that I didn't want to wait.

I did not expect to feel joy at my wedding, just relief. But, to tell the truth I was surprised.

I did not feel the intoxicating thrill that Tom's touch brought me, to be sure. But when I stood alongside Adam, in front of the minister, I sensed a concentration of warmth and love in that church, from all the family and friends gathered there. Everyone wanted our happiness, and Adam himself was so full of joy that when he repeated his vows to the minister, he was almost laughing.

I looked down at the bouquet that Sadie had made for me, the delicate white flowers of the bloodroot, and the dark green bearberry leaves. It was so beautiful that I felt new hope. Surely I could take all this love and make a life worth living with Adam?

And, to be honest, I was glad to be leaving home. Things were awkward between Mother and me. We both had secrets, and we did not want to confront them.

The day of my wedding I decided I would try and forget Tom. I would not ask Mr Mitchell what had become of him. I would not think of Tom, or speak of him. Slowly the memories would fade.

Sadie had helped me to dress that morning, with tears in her eyes as she combed my hair into careful curls. 'I wish you were coming with me to college,' she told me. 'I wish we could have had that year. But to have you as my sister has always been my dream.'

I squeezed her hand. 'Sadie, I am sorry. I have neglected you, these last few months.'

She shook her head. 'I understood,' she said. 'Tom changed everything. I am sad that he died, but I must confess I am not sorry that he is gone. He bewitched you, Emmy. Now you are returned to us.'

I could say nothing. I just prayed in my heart that Tom was safe and far, far away.

Adam was my future. Adam was my world. And Adam would be the father, the one and only father, to the baby that I knew was already growing within me.

He knew, I think. But he never said a word. All our years together, he never once questioned me. And once we were married, he loved my baby as his own.

And that baby was you, my darling Jesse.

CHAPTER FORTY-SIX

1904

EMMY

'Who do you think the baby looks like?'

That's what my mother asked me, when she laid you in my arms for the first time. You, Jesse, with your little button nose, and your blue eyes, your pink cheeks and all that dark hair.

'He looks like a baby,' I said, exhausted from the pain and the effort of pushing a whole new person into the world. I felt so strange, as though my old, strong body had been taken away from me, and replaced by something soft and weak and empty. 'A tiny, little baby.'

'You'd expect him to be small,' said Mother, 'as he's

arrived a little bit early into the world. But he's a good size for all that. A five-pound baby.'

'Is that what he weighs?' I asked. I must have been more tired than I realised because I hadn't seen her weigh you. But you were clean and washed, and swaddled in a white blanket knitted by Adam's mother, so she must have weighed you when you were just born, shouting to the world, all covered in blood and muck. You reminded me of Tom. Of course you did. All naked and bloody and wordless and needing my help so badly.

'I reckon he's a look of Adam around the mouth and nose,' said Mother. 'And hair like Sadie and Susannah.'

'And his forehead is like my father's photograph,' I said. 'William Murray's forehead.' I stared her straight in the eye, with my brown eyes, so like Mr Mitchell's, and she looked away.

'Emmy ...' Mother's voice was uncharacteristically uncertain. 'Perhaps we should talk. Now that Mr Mitchell is free – I am sure you will understand—'

'We should not,' I said.

'Are you sure? There is so much that I should explain—'

'You should not,' I said. 'The baby's name is Jesse,' I told her. 'Jesse, for Adam's grandfather. Jesse William, for my father too.'

I closed my eyes, and thought of Tom, and felt as though a knife were cutting me from inside my heart. But there was no point allowing myself to think like that, so I concentrated on Adam, waiting patiently to be allowed to see his new baby son.

'Are you ready to see him?' asked Mother.

I nodded, and then shook my head. It was not that I did not want to see Adam, of course I did. He had done nothing but love me since the day I had agreed to marry him. I knew he would love you too, Jesse, and be the best father in the world to you.

But I also know that the minute Adam saw you would be the minute I started to lie to him. And to everyone. And to you, my darling boy, to you as well. So I wanted a few minutes alone.

Mother stroked my hair and said, 'I'll leave you two together, and go and break the news. I'll tell Adam to come to you in about fifteen minutes.'

I nodded again, scared to speak in case the tears came. When she'd gone, and we were safely alone, I rocked you and kissed you and remembered that sweet night with your father.

And I thought of one more thing that he had told me. That Elijah Brown always called him 'boy' or 'you', until he near forgot the name his mother had given him. And how he'd tried to forget it, because Tom was the new name he wanted for himself.

But his real true name was Jesse, and that was why I gave you that name. It was just my good fortune that it sat there in the Harkness family bible.

I never told a soul of Tom's true story until now.

I am only telling you, Jesse, because I want you to know whose son you are.

CHAPTER FORTY-SEVEN

1994

MEGAN

Mom wants me to come back to London with her, but she accepts it when I say, no, I'm staying on.

'I do miss you, Mom, honest, but it's good to be here right now. I'm getting myself together for starting uni next year.'

'Well, as long as you're not going to drop out on me,' she says, buttoning up her Burberry mac and painting on a Chanel mouth. 'I couldn't bear it if you wasted all that promise, Meg darling. You're not going to waste your life in a small town like this, promise me.'

I laugh at her. She's such a fighter, my mom. I don't

really appreciate what it took for her to get from here, Astor, to become what she is, who she is. She's worked so hard.

'It's okay, I'm still going to uni. But I might apply to some places in Canada. I love Astor. It's actually beautiful. And there's a lot more going on here than there was in your day.'

'I always did exactly what I wanted to do, so I suppose I should understand when you do the same,' Mom says. 'Anyway, I've been talking to Bee. She's dying to come to the UK. I've offered to fly the two of you over in the spring, so she can see the sights.'

'Cool!' I say. 'She'll love that!'

I wish Sam could come too, but I know he'll never leave Lexi. I've been to see him a couple of times at the hospital, but he was barely conscious. I felt so guilty that I'd mostly stayed away. Bee's told me he's coming out today, but I'm not sure when I should call him.

There's a ring at the door, and Grandma Vera calls up, 'Sandra! Your taxi!'

'Well,' says Mom. 'This is it.' She hugs me, a bone-cracking, fierce hug, a tiger grabbing her cub. 'Now, call me, okay? Or I'll have to come back over, and this time I'll be taking you home with me.'

'Sure,' I say. 'No sweat. Don't work too hard.'

She fishes around in her bag. 'Megan, this came for you. I wasn't sure . . . but I have to pass it on.'

I look at the airmail envelope: our London address in Ryo's writing. 'I don't want it,' I say.

'Just hold on to it for a bit,' she says. 'It might help to read it, you never know.'

When Mom's gone off to the airport, I pace around the house, bored, almost wishing I had gone with her. She's got so much energy packed into her tiny frame that the house seems sort of dim and cold without her.

'You're going to miss your mom,' says Grandma Vera. 'She's not changed at all. I remember her as a scrawny little teenager, sitting at my kitchen table, telling me how she was going to escape from Astor by going to the top university in Canada.'

'And she did it!'

'She certainly did. Best grades in her year. Then she was top student for Economics. Little Sandra. What she lacked in height, she made up for in pure determination.'

'It's sad she's got no family left here now. I mean her mom. I think she feels a bit overwhelmed by Harknesses when she's here.'

'It was only ever Sandra and her mother, and they didn't have the easiest time,' said Grandma. 'Her ma worked every hour she could, cleaning folks' houses. Sandra and she never had much in common. Mind you, neither did Sandra and your pa. I was pleased when they married, but I wasn't surprised it didn't last. Sandra will do better with the new one she's got now.'

'Oh, him,' I say scornfully. Fernando with his long hair and his guitar and his shy smile and Colombian accent. 'He's about ten years younger than she is.'

'Sometimes it's better that way,' says Grandma. 'Now, I'm going out to my charity committee meeting tonight. How about I take you round to see how young Sam's doing, on the way?'

'Oh! But I thought he wasn't well enough for visitors.'

'I called earlier. They reckon he's strong enough now. He's been home a few days. He's weak, but getting better all the time.'

Grandma remembers the way to Sam's house. On the way she tells me about when his mother died.

'Oh, it was a tragedy. Kevin was such a nice boy, and he adored Caitlin. She was a beauty, a singer, she could have done anything. But she had Sam very young, and then Lexi, and she loved those kids. I can't bear to think of it.

'Lexi was little, and Sam was a quiet boy. No trouble, but didn't give much away, you know? It was hard to comfort him. All he wanted to do was look after his little sister.'

The house is a small one at the end of a long track. It's been neglected, you can see the paintwork is chipped and dirty, the yard is a mess and there's a truck parked at the front with four flat tyres.

'Thanks, Grandma,' I say, getting out of the car. 'I'll find my own way back. Maybe I'll call a taxi.' But she shakes her head and says, 'I'll come back for you in an hour. You don't want to tire Sam out, and you're still not one hundred per cent yet.' I'm quite relieved as I knock on the door.

Lexi opens the door, a whirl of ribbons and tulle. She's dressed as a ballerina, with her hair cascading from a central top knot.

'Hi Lexi,' I say, nervously. 'I came to see Sam.'

'Megan!' she says, and she jumps forward and hugs me around the middle. 'You saved my Sam!'

'Well, not really,' I tell her. 'We saved each other.'

There are more ways than one of saving someone after all.

She gazes up at me, and I can see Sam's dark brown eyes. 'Thank you.'

'That's okay,' I tell her. 'Any time. Can I see him? Is he well enough?'

'He might be asleep,' she tells me. 'He sleeps all the time now.'

She leads me through the house, which is shabby, but homely. The carpets are threadbare and the furniture looks old, but it smells of fresh air and furniture polish, and there's a gallery of Lexi's paintings and Sam's photographs on one wall.

Lexi shows me her fingernails, painted silver and cyclamen pink. 'Aunt Alice did them,' she tells me, proudly. 'She's staying with us right now. She's the best.' Aunt Alice is coming out of Sam's room as we're about to go in, shutting the door behind her. She's whippet-thin with spiky hair, but her smile is welcoming.

'Megan? We've got so much to thank you for.'

Lexi prances around us. 'I already thanked her! She saved Sam for us!'

'She did, and now maybe she can cheer him up a bit.' She lowers her voice. 'He's taking it hard, the whole accident and all. Blames himself for taking you out there. He's worrying all the time about Kevin and Lexi . . . who's going to look after them . . . it's wrong, really for such a young boy to have these worries.'

I have no idea what to say, so I stay quiet.

'I've offered to have them come to me in Saskatoon. He is my brother, after all, and there's room for them. Sam could come too, except I'm not sure he wants to. He's fought so hard to keep this family together, and I don't want to interfere with that. But, you know, I'm not sure that the doctors here are treating Kevin too well. I'd like to go with him to see the specialist. See if there's anything that might help the poor man.'

I open my mouth, but she's clearly more of a talker than a listener.

'Now I'm retired I've got time to look after them all. And Lexi needs a woman to look after her. It's just not the same in a household of men, eh darling?'

'Is Sam really well enough to see me?' I ask. Maybe all this talk is a way of putting me off.

'He'll be made up to see you! He's been worrying about you, poor kid. Come on, Lexi now, let's make those cookies we've been talking about.'

Left alone and suddenly shy, I knock at Sam's door. 'Yeah, come in,' I hear, so I push the door open and walk right in.

He's dressed in sweatpants and a baggy T-shirt, which covers his arm which is all strapped up. He's got a dressing on his head. His hair's been shaved around the head wound, and his eyes are huge in his pale face.

I'm speechless for a moment.

'I'm a mess, right?' He grimaces. 'I'm going to have to get a buzz cut when they take all the bandages off.'

'It'll suit you.' I sit down on the edge of the bed. 'Is this okay?'

Sam's room is almost bare of personal stuff. No books or pictures, just a bed covered in a tartan rug, an ancient brown chair, a small television perched on a green-topped card table. There's a shelf with a few framed photographs. A woman who must be his mother. Lexi's latest school photo. An old picture of Sam and Lexi with Kevin, but not the shambling angry drunk that I saw that one time. A smiling, laughing Kevin, with Lexi on his shoulders and his arm around Sam, just as though he was his own son. Looking at it, I understand why Sam stays. Why he tries to keep his ruined family together.

Sam follows my gaze. 'They put the pictures here when I came out of hospital. I was waking up a lot at night, having bad dreams, you know. The nurse said it'd be useful to see something right away so I knew I wasn't in that place anymore. And I have to have a night light. I'm like a scared little kid. Have you had nightmares?'

'Not really,' I say, skirting around the fact that I've been taking pills to help me sleep for the last few months anyway.

'Just me then. The stuff they give me seems to make it worse.'

'You were there a lot longer than me. You were really brave; I didn't even realise how bad you were hurt. Sam, I'm so sorry. I shouldn't have left you.'

'It's okay. You went for help. You got help. I wouldn't want to be the one wandering around trying to find my way with a flashlight that could've run out of battery at any time. Much better to be safe and sound and waiting.'

'Did you wake up and find me gone?'

He pauses, and I know that he did. 'It was okay. Kind of tickly though, with the spiders.'

I shudder.

'They kept me company. Hey, did you see we made the paper?'

He hands me a copy of the *Astor Press*. Ed's by-line is on the front-page story – *Couple Lost in the Forest* – which makes me cringe.

I roll my eyes. 'So, how're you doing? Apart from the nightmares.'

'Getting better. I'm looking forward to getting back to normal.'

'What is normal though?' I ask and then feel stupid.

'Well, not stuck in this room, for a start. I can go back to my own place.'

'What place?'

'I've got a trailer, out back. All my own. This is just a spare room. Usually that's where Lexi's aunt would stay, but this time she's had to sleep in Lexi's bottom bunk.'

Lexi's aunt, I notice. Not Aunt Alice.

'She says she wants to take Lexi and Kevin back to Saskatoon,' I say, slightly nervously.

'Yeah. I've heard her. Thinks she can do a better job than I can.' He shakes his head. 'Well, maybe she's right. I don't seem to be doing much that's right.'

I seize the moment.

'Look, Sam, I need to explain.'

'Explain?'

'Why I ran away. Why I got upset.' I can feel myself shaking as I say this, and Sam notices too, because he puts his hand on mine.

'Megan,' he says. 'You don't have to tell me anything. You really don't. But the first time I ever saw you, you were crying, and now you're nearly crying, and I'm not afraid of tears. I've had a lot of experience.'

'It's just. What you said about how your mum could've got rid of you.' I stop, take another breath. 'Before I came

323

back to Astor, I was pregnant. An accident. I was only a few weeks gone when I had an abortion. I thought I was okay with it. My boyfriend, the baby's father . . . he couldn't deal with any of it. He left.'

Sam takes a sharp intake of breath. 'Oh, Megan. I'm so sorry. I'm an idiot. I didn't mean to be so judgemental.'

'I don't have doubts – well, not many, but hormones, you know. And my parents separated this year as well, and somehow nothing seems permanent anymore. Like I'm losing everything. I'm sorry, I shouldn't have shouted at you.'

'Nothing to apologise for,' says Sam. 'And you're not losing everything,' he says. 'You did what was right for you. That was your choice. You don't have to apologise to anyone. Least of all me.'

I feel a little less shaky.

'I know, I mean I'm not doubting my own decision, you know? I did the right thing. It's just that I'm sad about the way it all worked out, and I feel stupid and careless for letting it happen in the first place. And I really loved Ryo, and now I don't know how I feel. I mean, if it hadn't happened we'd still be together. I feel it was my fault that everything went wrong.'

'Don't be so hard on yourself. It happens. We all make mistakes. Your boyfriend was at least half responsible,' he says.

'Yeah.' I nod. 'But I'd have stuck with him, if he'd been the one to get pregnant.'

'Yeah, well, maybe he's really regretting taking off,' says Sam. 'I mean, he must've been through a lot of thinking now. He probably wishes you would talk to him, or give him another chance or whatever.'

'I doubt it,' I say, but I can't help thinking of Ryo's letter, still unopened, shoved into my T-shirt drawer. Could he be asking for another chance? What would I say? Despite myself, I know I'm half smiling.

'You really like him, hey?' says Sam, softly.

'I did,' I answer. Now I feel really confused.

'I can't believe he'd turn his back on someone like you,' says Sam – sweet, kind Sam. But what if Ryo does want another chance? He is my soulmate, after all. Maybe we've been through all this agony for a reason. Maybe everything that has happened was a test?

I gather together my stuff. 'You look exhausted,' I say, which is true. Sam's very pale and he's sunk back on his pillows. 'I'll let you rest. But I'll see you soon.'

'Sure, Megan,' he says. 'Goodbye.'

And while I'm dithering about whether to kiss him goodbye or not, he closes his eyes, so I just have to tiptoe out of the room.

CHAPTER FORTY-EIGHT

1994

MEGAN

Bee's helping me pack my bags. Dad's house – our house – is finally ready to move into.

It's turned from a neglected wreck to somewhere that feels like it could be home. Dad's knocked down walls, scraped off wallpaper, pulled up carpets. It smells of new paint and onions (Grandma has placed raw, peeled onions around the rooms to absorb the smell of the paint).

All those years, living in rented apartments, and now we have built-in bookshelves to fill, and a kitchen where Dad let me choose the colour scheme (pale yellow walls, the colour of vanilla ice-cream, and light wood units).

My room has grey blue walls and white-painted

floorboards, a comfy bed covered with an indigo bed-spread, and a view out over the forest. I thought the colours would reflect my sadness, but actually the room makes me feel calm and peaceful, and the blue reminds me of a spring day when the clouds clear after a shower.

Dad and I have talked a lot since I came out of hospital. About Astor, and what it means to him. And Mom and how he doesn't bear her any grudges. 'We just grew out of being in love with each other,' he tells me, 'but that doesn't mean we were a mistake. It just means that now is the time to go in different directions.'

That's helped a lot. I've also realised that I can save myself a lot of misery by treating my parents like human beings, and not trying to make them into something that I want them to be.

I'm explaining all this to Bee as we're packing my stuff, and she's telling me about this guy Dexter from the *Astor Press* art desk that Ed introduced her to, and he really loves her cartoons, and thinks they might run them, which is completely brilliant.

And then she finds my folder full of our research about Tom, the wild boy.

'What's this?'

'Oh, just some stuff that Sam and I were researching.'

'Tom?' she said. 'I wish you'd asked me.'

'What do you mean?'

'Grammy used to tell me about Tom.'

'But Aunt Betsy said she never used to talk about him.'

'I think she got a bit lost in time,' says Bee. 'She used to call me Sadie a lot. And she'd talk about Tom. Teaching Tom to read and Tom and his spiders. And asking me if I ever saw Tom in Toronto.'

'Spiders?' I ask.

'He loved them, apparently.'

'And what else?'

'How he went away, and how much she missed him, but it could never be.'

'He went away?' I asked. 'Do you mean died? It says in the cemetery that he died.'

She shrugged. 'Grammy said "went away". And she also said that Mr someone, Mr Michael? Mitchell? He knew, but never told her he knew.'

'Oh,' I say. I feel a bit jealous of Bee. I wish I'd had more of a chance to be around Grammy and ask her questions.

'And she told me all about Sadie, her sister-in-law, and how Sadie went to college and she couldn't, and how close they were when they were kids, but then Sadie went away too, and she became a teacher and Grammy was stuck at home having kids, and it made me think of me and you, Megan.'

'How d'you mean?' I'm trying to think how to bring the conversation back to Tom.

'Well, you're going away to uni, and I don't want to be stuck at home, here in Astor. So I've been getting together a portfolio, and I'm applying to art school. Probably in Toronto, but maybe somewhere else. There's a great graphic design course in Montreal, Dexter was telling me about it.'

'Oh, wow, Bee, that's amazing!'

We hug. And then I confess. 'But actually, I'm not even sure I will be going to uni. I'm sort of screwed up at the moment. I don't feel sure about anything.'

Bee looks me in the eye. Really looks at me. 'You know, Megan, I think you're not telling me something. And it's awfully hard to be a good friend when you're working with half the available information.'

'I know! I'm sorry. Okay, here it is.'

I tell her everything. The whole story. And she's so understanding and loving and sad for me, but also completely supportive, that I can't believe I didn't tell her before.

I tell her about what happened in the forest with Sam. And about Ryo's unopened letter. And about Sam.

The feelings I'd been having about Sam. Around Sam. With Sam. And how now I don't know what I want, or need.

'Time on your own?' she suggests. 'Just Megan? Working out what makes you happy?'

'I know you're right,' I told her. 'In my head. But there's all this unfinished business with Ryo. And Sam, it sort of feels like there could be something really—'

'Open the letter,' she commands. 'I can't bear it. Open it and you'll know.'

And I feel like I can actually do this, with Bee there. So I get it out from my drawer, and slit open the thin envelope.

She sits patiently while I stare at Ryo's neat handwriting. He hasn't written much.

There's a bit about Tokyo, and what it's like at uni. He asks about London and all our friends – I guess no one's told him I'm in Canada. And then, just this:

I feel like I really let you down, and I don't know how to say sorry.

I couldn't be everything you needed me to be, because I couldn't even figure out the beginning of what that might be.

I thought we could just ignore what had happened, and go back to before it happened.

But I guess you can't reset your life. You have to keep going forward.

Our love was a flower, and it will always bloom in my heart. It was a rainbow, that only shone while the rain and sun collided. It was a leaf that fell to the ground when autumn came.

One day I will write a song that will make you proud. One day I will find the words and music to make sense of all of this.

Until then

Remember me.

I try and imagine Sam saying anything like this, and fail. I think about how deep I always thought Ryo was, how poetic, how intense. And then I start to laugh, not at him, but because I *know* I'm over him. I'm not going to be pining for Ryo all my life. The sadness I've felt – it was real, but it's over.

'What does it *say*? Can I read it? I guess it's good news?'

I can't even bear to show her what an idiot I've been.

'Nope,' I say, crumpling the letter into a ball. 'It's okay. It's over. Really over.'

'That's good!' she says, and she's such a good friend that when I lob the ball of paper into the garbage bin, she doesn't even grab it to take a peek.

'So, Megan, what about Sam?'

I remember the look on Sam's face when I told him about Ryo. I think about the way he just closed his eyes at the end of the conversation.

'I don't know,' I tell her. 'At least – I don't think he's an option. I've really messed up.'

CHAPTER FORTY-NINE

1904

EMMY

There was an inquiry, of course. Some people pointed fingers at Mother for nurturing a dangerous arsonist, others swore blind they'd seen Tom and Wolf skulking in the shadows of the forest. But Mother paid for a stone to be placed in the graveyard, stating unequivocally that Tom was dead, and so he was.

Mr Mitchell must have told her the truth, but she and I never acknowledged it. We never acknowledged anything. Bit by bit I'd pieced together the truth all by myself, but the lies – from the husband and father who never was, to the very many nights spent at the hospital – were too many to unravel. Better to let it be, and smile and cheer when she and Mr Mitchell wed, a decent eighteen months after the death of his wife.

It took years for the truth about the fire to emerge. People talked. People felt guilty. There was a deathbed confession from Jed, the bribed lookout. Mr Mitchell – Wyngate, I called him by then – sought justice and recompense from the masked men who torched the print works, and killed his wife inside.

I never told a soul how we had left her lying on the ground. I was haunted by the memory, and I tried to remember if she was moving ... crying out ... conscious ... when we made our escape. I am almost sure that she was. It was not my fault, I told myself.

I do not know why she did not come after us. But if she had, would Tom have escaped? What would have happened to me?

And besides, I was not the one, the two, the many, with the scarf around my face, bribing Jed to turn a blind eye, setting fire to a building packed with the explosive petroleum that powered the presses, sending glass and bricks and poisonous smoke spewing into the air.

All for the hate of a boy from nowhere. And for a newspaper that told the truth.

So I am confessing this only to you. It may be that Isabella Mitchell died because I pushed her. And I have felt guilty all my life.

When Wyngate Mitchell was taken ill that last time, he

explained to me that he was leaving the newspaper business to me. 'Because you are the nearest thing I have to a daughter,' he said, and I still said nothing. But I thanked him, and kissed his brow, because I had seen that he and Mother truly loved each other. Theirs was a meeting of minds, as much as anything else, and she so enjoyed debating with him.

'I had a son once,' he told me. 'Matthew. He only lived a few days. I think his loss was what turned Isabella's heart to stone. She could not bear to love again.'

'Maybe,' I said, although I thought it was more likely that Isabella Mitchell's nature turned sour and angry when she realised that her husband loved another woman, had a daughter by her and had engineered her coming to Astor.

'My son Matthew died,' he said, 'but his name lived on.'

'It did?'

'I gave Tom his birth certificate,' he said. 'And letters of recommendations to printers . . . so he should have a name and a job. And I gave him money, and I put him on the train to Toronto. I did all I could . . . and I know that he got there . . .'

So Tom had communicated with him, and not a word to me? I could not believe it.

'Is he well?' I asked. 'Is he . . . has he married?'

'Oh, it was not Tom that wrote to me,' he said. 'Emmy . . . I am so sorry . . .'

And he handed me two envelopes.

I saw that the letters that he handed me came from the Canadian army, and I did not ask any more. We had seen the same when the news came about Eben.

'I don't want them,' I said.

'You must take them,' he said. 'For Jesse.'

So I took the envelopes, and I put them away for you, Jesse. I know what they must say. I never wanted to know the details.

CHAPTER FIFTY

1994

Megan

Sam has recovered enough to be taking pictures again. He's covered a few jobs for the *Astor Press*, and he's still covering gigs at the Old Hospital.

I know this from Bee, who's really hit it off with Dexter-from-the-art-desk. And I glimpsed Sam in the distance last week when we went to hear a local band.

He hasn't rung me. He hasn't come to see me. And I'm pretty sure he never wants to see me again.

Which is fine. I'd be crazy to get involved with someone here in Astor, and I'm on the rebound anyway. I need time to be on my own. I'm actually enjoying feeling free of love. My heart isn't aching for Ryo anymore.

I just miss Sam's company, that's all. I feel like I screwed up, and I'd go over and try and make up with him, except he probably wouldn't be there, he'll be working or busy with Lexi, or something and, knowing me, I'll say the wrong thing.

What even is the right thing to say?

So, I've been thinking about what comes next and looking at prospectuses for Canadian universities. Maybe Bee and I will end up in the same city. Maybe we can achieve what Grammy couldn't. I like that idea.

And I've been helping Dad sort the house out, and sift through the documents and books that have come to him now that Grammy has died. Aunt Betsy brought a load over yesterday. 'You're the family archivist,' she said. 'I'm never going to have the time to go through all these, but Mother was adamant I shouldn't get rid of them.'

'You take that stack, and I'll look at these,' says Dad, gesturing at some dusty box files. Lucky I'm wearing old clothes for decorating; it doesn't take long for the grime to transfer from the boxes to my hands and face.

Box file one is full of letters, from Grammy to her husband, from when he was a soldier in the First World War. I read a few with tears in my eyes. Their love is so clear, in the gentle, respectful way they communicate. He asks after her and the children, he is sketchy about the detail of his life. It's only by looking at the dates and places – France, Belgium, 1915, 1916 – that I know about the horrors he is protecting her from.

The second box is full of school reports and written work, and children's pictures and photographs. 'Look, Dad,' I say, showing him a picture of a tractor and a chicken. 'Your dad drew that.'

Dad takes it from me. 'That's just brilliant to have,' he says. 'We'll have to frame some of these.'

I could ask Sam to photograph them, I think. But I'm not even sure if we're friends anymore.

'Or should we just get rid of all of this stuff?' says Dad. 'Am I ridiculous, hanging on to the past? Looking for something – I don't even know what I'm looking for.'

'What do you mean?'

'It's just that I never felt I knew my father very well. He was away so much, and even though he wrote often, he was a very reserved person. And then, when I grew up, I went away. We never talked, not properly ... we were like strangers to each other. Now I'm searching for the father that I never really had.'

'Oh, Dad. I never realised.'

'Why should you? But you know, one thing that's come out of all the bad stuff that's happened this year, is that I get another chance to be around for you, Megan. I love you so much, and so does your mom. I hope you know that.'

'I do,' I say. 'I really do.'

We carry on looking through the boxes of stuff for half an hour, and then Dad goes off to make us some lunch. I need to go and clean myself up a bit, so I just peek into box number four.

It's packed full of cassette tapes. There's a piece of paper folded on the top. 'For Jesse' is written on the outer fold. The handwriting is Grammy's. I unfold it.

I thought it was kinder to keep the truth from you, but now I'm doubtful. I was only trying to protect you. I was only trying to do the best I could. Forgive me, my darling. Forgive me.

Intrigued, I take the box with me to my room where there is a cassette player. Luckily the tapes are clearly labelled, again by Grammy. I find number one, and put it into the slot.

The tape crackles and hisses, her voice is younger and stronger. It's as though she's at my shoulder.

He was naked and bloody as a new-born baby, and just about as ugly too. He was so skinny that his head seemed oddly big for his body, his features too large for his face. His hair was shoulder-length and tangled, matted with dust and twigs. His face and limbs were scratched and scarred and rotten with dirt. The mud and blood had dried and mottled like rust on an iron gate, all apart from a fresh wound to his side which bled rapid and red. He gripped it with one hand, trying to stem the flow, but the blood oozed through his fingers.

My fumbling fingers stop the tape. I'm shaking. I gather up the box. Never mind my dirty face and hands, or the grime on my clothes. I rush down the stairs.

'Dad! Dad!'

He looks up from the salad he's chopping. 'What's the matter, pumpkin?'

I can hardly get the words out.

'I've found something . . . something important. Grammy made some tapes – they could tell us so much – but I have to listen to them with Sam. Then I can tell you properly, but now – will you take me to Sam's house, now? Please?'

CHAPTER FIFTY-ONE

1994

MEGAN

Dad drops me outside Sam's home. He wants to stay, to check Sam's in, but I insist he leaves.

'It's okay,' I say. 'Sam might not be in, but I can leave a note for him. I'll find my own way home.'

I have the cassette player and headphones. If Sam's not in, I'll find somewhere to wait for him and start listening myself.

I knock at the door. I'm all churned up with excitement and nervousness. 'We're going to find out about Tom!' I imagine myself saying. 'We're going to know the whole story!'

But the longer I wait for someone to answer the door,

the longer I worry that Sam's going to say, 'So what? I'm not really interested in the Wild Boy at all. It was just an excuse to get close to you, and you didn't even really notice, because you were still in love with your ex.'

At last! The door is opening. But it's not Sam, and it's not Lexi or her aunt Alice either. It's Sam's stepdad, frowning at me.

I take an involuntary step backwards. 'Is Sam home?'

'How would I know?'

'Oh – I just thought—'

Kevin must be six foot four at least, a stocky bald man with a scar which runs from the top of his skull, all the way down to his nose. It gives his head a strange, patchwork appearance, like a child's Play-Doh model that they've made and remade and got bored trying to perfect.

'Don't worry,' I say. 'Maybe I can just leave him a note?'

'His truck's not here,' says Kevin. 'So most probably he's not.' He pauses to think. 'You must excuse me, miss. My memory's not what it used to be.'

'I'm Megan,' I say. 'Sam wasn't expecting me. Maybe I can just leave him a note?'

I've confused him, I can see. He takes his time, picking over my words.

'You want to come in?' he asks, eventually.

I don't – I'm a little bit scared. What if his mood turns? Is he actually safe to be with?

We walk through the house to the kitchen. He opens the

fridge and asks if I want a beer. 'I'd like a Coke,' I say, worried that I'm about to say the wrong thing, but he finds a can for me and opens a beer for himself. We drink standing up, awkwardly silent, until he shuffles to the door and says, 'Come and sit down. I was just watching the TV.'

There's some quiz show on the television, and we watch it together until it finishes. Then he switches off. 'I love that show,' he says. 'You learn a lot watching it. Lexi likes it too.'

'Is Lexi at school?' I ask. His face lights up with a smile. 'That's it!' he says. 'Lexi finishes early today, and Sam's gone to take her to a dancing class. That's what he told me. "Lexi's going to dance. We'll be back later."'

'Oh, cool,' I say. 'Maybe I should just leave that note?'

'No, they will be back later! After dancing! Lexi loves her dancing.'

'She's very good,' I say. 'She showed me.'

Now Kevin's worked out where Lexi and Sam are, he can't talk fast enough. Or could that be the beer loosening his tongue? He tells me how proud he is of Lexi. Poor Sam, I think. He must always feel second best.

'And Sam, he's such a great kid too. He takes photos, you know. Amazing! He gets money for them! Such a talent! They always said bad things about him at school, but I knew he could do it. I knew he would show them!'

Kevin's face doesn't look so bulbous and strange now he is smiling.

'It's great he's working for the newspaper,' I say.

343

Kevin shakes his head. 'It's not right. He should work for big papers and magazines. I've told him so. He needs to go to the city, to Toronto. Prove himself. I can look after Lexi.'

'Can you?' It comes out before I can help myself.

'With the help of my sister. She lives up in Saskatoon, you know. Did you meet her? She's kind of bossy, but she makes good pancakes.'

'I . . . yes . . .'

'Sam was lost. Lost in the forest. Me and Lexi, we were so scared, but Alice looked after us until Sam got found.'

'That was my fault.' I choke out the words, but he just looks puzzled and says, 'He's all safe and sound, miss. He's good and healthy now. Don't you worry about Sam. He's just sad because he liked a girl and she don't like him back.'

'Dad!' Neither of us heard Lexi and Sam come back. She bursts into the room to hug Kevin tight, and I spill my Coke in surprise.

'How was your class?' says Kevin. 'Show me what you learned.'

And then Sam's in the room and I'm too embarrassed to look at him properly, because now I see his big brown eyes, and his sweet smile, all I can think is what an idiot I have been.

'Megan?' he says.

'I found some stuff I thought you'd be interested in.' I remember my dirty face and clothes. 'I just came round right away. If it's not a good time, I can come back some other day.'

'It is a good time,' he says. 'You guys are okay, aren't you, if Megan and I go out to the trailer?'

'We're good!' says Lexi.

Sam's trailer is like a little wooden cabin inside, with green-covered seats and a bunk to sleep on. He keeps it very neat, and he's stuck pictures all over the walls, so it's a capsule gallery. I feel it's rude not to admire them – they're his shots, clearly; a lot of them are of bands.

'Great pictures,' I say.

He ignores the compliment. 'So you met Kevin. Did he live down to your expectations?'

'He seemed very nice,' I say, shocked at his bitter tone.

'So you weren't scared? He didn't attack you?'

'Look, I was scared, I've seen what he does to you when he lashes out. But now I've met him – he seemed so nice. And he seems to really love you.'

'He does,' Sam agrees. 'Everyone thinks he's a monster, but that's because they don't understand him at all. He's like a big kid really. It's not his fault.'

'But it's a lot of responsibility for you.'

He sighs. 'Not if I let them go to Saskatoon.'

'Let them go?'

'That's how it feels. I mean, I could go with them, but then ... I don't know. When do I get a life, Megan?'

'You can always go and see them.'

'It's not the same. But yes, I can. Anyway, you had something to tell me?'

'I found something that you might be interested in . . . ' I start. And then I stop. 'I mean, how are you?'

'All mended,' he says.

'I thought you'd call me,' I say, and then feel myself get hot in the face.

'I thought you were telling me not to.'

'No,' I say. And then, 'Doesn't it get very cold in this trailer in the winter?'

'Oh, I don't sleep here in the winter. So what did you want to tell me? What's in that bag?'

I pull out my cassette player.

'It's the Wild Boy. I mean, it's Grammy. She made these tapes and I just found them, and I had to bring them right over to you. I thought you'd want to – I mean, I didn't want to listen to them without you.'

'You didn't?'

'No, I thought . . . ' I gulp. 'Sam, I really have missed you these last few weeks.'

'I missed you too.' His voice is still wary. But he's moved a step closer.

'I realised that I don't love Ryo at all,' I say.

'You don't?'

'He's so pretentious. And shallow. And just wrong for me.'

'Oh.'

'And that feels good! I'm so happy that I've realised.'

He's even nearer now. Near enough for me to put out my hand and touch his face.

'Can we just spend some time together? Like lots of time?'

'That would be good,' he says, but his voice is all muffled because he's talking into my hair, and there's no distance at all between us now, his arms are round me, and I feel like I've come home.

Some time later, we start listening to the tapes. We listen to one after another, after another, curled up together on the green seat. We take a break to make supper for Kevin and Lexi, and for me to call Dad and tell him not to worry about picking me up. 'Sam will drop me back,' I tell him.

It's 2 a.m. by the time we're all finished.

'So Tom – he was your great-grandfather? You're not really a Harkness at all!'

'Sounds like it,' I say. I *knew* there was a reason why the Wild Boy felt somehow connected to me.

'And the woman they found, the body – could that be Tom's mother?'

'I think it must be. That man – Elijah Brown – he shot her, and hid the body and lied to poor Tom, all those years.'

'Why would Tom have stayed?' says Sam. 'That's what I don't understand.'

'I read a magazine article once about something called Stockholm Syndrome. Where people who are held prisoner . . . hostages . . . they love their captors. They sort of can't help themselves. I don't think Tom loved him, exactly, but he couldn't imagine life away from him. He was a prisoner of his own mind.'

'Poor guy.'

'What did she mean?' I say. 'What happened to Tom? She says there are letters, but I don't see them.'

'*We had seen the same when the news came about Eben,*' says Sam. Then he reaches up and pulls down a folder. 'Look . . . here . . .'

It's a picture of the Astor War Memorial. Ebenezer Harkness. Died 1917. Vimy Ridge.

'Oh! No!'

'Thousands of soldiers did die. I mean if you were a young man you were pretty lucky to survive.'

'Poor Tom. And poor Emmy. I wonder if she ever did open those envelopes.'

'They're not here.'

'There are lots of boxes.' I stand up. 'Come back with me, and we can look.'

Sam stretches. 'I'll drop you home but I'd better not stay. I need to be around here for Lexi and Kevin.'

Is he just making an excuse? But then he drops his head down to mine, and I feel his lips softly brush my own, and I know that I can trust him. And somehow we'll find a time and a place to work out what we mean to each other.

CHAPTER FIFTY-TWO

1994

MEGAN

Dad has the letters, it turns out. He'd filed them away with the other papers relating to Wyngate Mitchell, with no idea of their significance. Once I'd explained and he'd listened to the tapes himself, he found the right pile.

'I had no idea,' he said. 'They talk about a Matthew Mitchell. I thought that was just a relative of his.'

'Don't tell me what they say!' I begged. 'I want to read them with Sam.'

So we open them together. We've driven out to the house where Tom's mother's body was found, and we sit outside in Sam's truck, reading words that were written seventy-six years ago.

Belgium 1918

Dear Mr Mitchell

It is with the deepest regret that I write to tell you of the death of your dear son, Matthew Mitchell, known to us all as Tom.

Tom fought with conspicuous bravery for King and Country and you can be very proud of his memory. He never flinched in his obedience to orders. His death came about as he tried to help a comrade who had been wounded in No Man's Land. Tom was hit by a shell, and later died of his wounds.

Take comfort from the knowledge that he died for a worthy cause.

I enclose a letter, found among his possessions.

With deepest sympathy
F C Adkins, chaplain

Dear Emmy

All the fellows in my company are writing post mortem letters, to be sent home if we should die. Life is short in these parts, and so I have followed their lead. I hope that at least one person will remember that once I was alive. I hope that person is you.

I have seen so much suffering, that in a way our lives here make more sense to me than normality. We live, we obey, we die. We kill on command. I hope it is in a good cause, better than anything I have known in the past. I tell myself I am defending you and your family, and that gives me courage.

Sadie told me that you had married her brother and were carrying his baby. I understand that I was never good enough for you. I hope you are very happy. You only deserve the best, and I could never hope to give you that.

I will never forget your kindness and all that I love about you. You are brave and kind, you are beautiful like a hawk, you are everything good that I knew in my life.

Do not forget me, Emmy, because I will never forget you.

Your obedient servant

Tom

CHAPTER FIFTY-THREE

1995

MEGAN

Today is the day my baby was due.

It's something and nothing. Of course, we might never have got to this point. The baby could have been born before, or after or never. But this date is the only one that I have. The due date.

I'm still in Astor. Mom thought the cold winter would put me off, and it is fierce, but it still feels like the place I need to be. A year in Astor will be enough for now, though. I'm already planning ahead, looking outwards again, thinking about my future.

Sam's found bloodroot flowers for me, even though it's early for them. They look like little white stars. I've arranged them with holly leaves, in a tiny bouquet. I'm going to put it on Grammy's gravestone. I've kept some for Tom's stone too.

There's a new grave that's been dug, and there's going to be a burial soon. Mattie, the girl with no surname. Only a few people outside the family – Dr Sweet, Sam – know that her DNA is linked to me, which pretty much confirms that she was Tom's mother. Everything linked together, Grammy's tapes and Tom's letters and the DNA tests. Dad's trying to find out more, he's been writing to a historian in Chicago who specialises in social history. Apparently, the resorts were famous around a hundred years ago. And there was one with a parrot called Freddie, run by a Mrs Peggy O'Malley. Dad's quite confident he might find out more about Mattie. He's planning a trip to Chicago in the spring.

We told Rob at Christmas. He came to Astor and Mom flew out for New Year's Eve, and it was weird and strange, but somehow okay, even though Fernando came with her. Seeing that he was incredibly nervous about meeting us, and watching Mom with him, seeing how relaxed she was, somehow softer and, well, happier, I couldn't resent him anymore. I thought of Emmy, and how she'd had to accept that her real parents had lied to her all her life. Families are complicated. She found a way of coping, and so will I.

I'm going to university, and I'm going to be a doctor and I'm pretty sure now that one day I will specialise in women's health. I want to help women feel listened to and cared for, whether they are old or young, rich or poor. I'm not sure what shape that will take, but I know I'm going to meet patients and think of all those women in my past. Emmy and Elizabeth and Mattie. Even sad, sour Mrs Mitchell. And Sadie, who lied to Tom and to Emmy, and must have thought she was doing the right thing.

Each with their story to tell and their secrets to hide.

I'm going to study here in Canada. In Toronto, where Emmy and Tom fought a fire that could have consumed the whole city. Bee's coming too, to study graphic design. And Sam's having interviews right now for a job on the picture desk at the *Toronto Star*. Lexi and Kevin are going to Saskatoon, and Sam's going to visit them there a lot. As much as he can. Every weekend if necessary.

But right now, he's here, at my side. And as I put the flowers on Tom's grave, I turn and hug him. 'You all right?' he asks and I bury my head in his coat, and nod. 'Yes,' I tell him. 'I'm all right.'

'Want to head back?'

'Give me a moment,' I say, and I pick my way back over to Grammy's grave, and put my hand on the new gravestone.

'Thank you,' I say. 'Thank you, Emmy. You've taught me how to live.'

ACKNOWLEDGEMENTS

I started telling myself the story that became this book when I was about 12 years old. It was the story I told myself to help get to sleep. I started writing it six years ago (cue sleepless nights, as it lost that particular power). Seeing it published feels like the end of a very long journey, mostly spent stumbling around in a dark forest with very little light.

Many people have read, commented and encouraged me along the way. Thank you all so much. Every single one of you helped lighten the way. (Lee, Emma, Lisa, Susie and Sheena, you helped at especially dark hours)

My agent Jenny Savill believed in this project for a very long time, thanks as ever for your support, your advice and your honesty. And thank you to everyone at Atom who worked so hard to make it the best book possible, particularly Sarah Castleton, Olivia Hutchings, Emma Clements,

James Gurbutt and Ellen Rockell who designed a cover so beautiful that I may have to frame it. Thanks also to Imogen Russell Williams for great advice at a crucial stage.

Sean Cummings helped with all things Canadian, sending me fascinating books and answering many questions. Sean, I can't thank you enough. And thank you to my many Canadian Facebook friends who helped with everything from flashlights to university application dates. This Canada though is *my* imagined Canada, so all errors are very much my own.

I read many books while researching this book, and was indebted to the library at the St Bride Foundation which specialises in books about the print industry. One of the books that I found there was Wilfred H Kesterton's *A History of Journalism in Canada* (McClelland and Stewart, 1967), which gave me ideas for about 20 different books.

Another book that helped me in picturing Tom's early life was *Sin in the Second City: Madams, Ministers, Playboys, and the Battle for America's Soul* by Karen Abbott (Random House, 2007) which was a completely fascinating read, highly recommended.

Juliet Walsh bid on the Authors for Refugees auction to name a character in this book. She gave me her daughter's name – Bee Patience – a wonderful gift of a name. As Bee says in the book, 'it's virtually an instruction'. Thank you, Juliet and Bee, and my friend Fiona Dunbar who organised the auction for a cause that is all too urgent.

Like Emmy, I started my career in newspapers as a teenager, and while I was writing this book I went back to work at my very first newspaper. Thank you to all my colleagues at the *Jewish Chronicle*, then and now, for reminding me why I love journalism. Special thanks to Jenni Frazer. No one could ask for a better mentor.

For encouragement, wisdom and laughs many thanks to all my wonderful friends. I'm not going to name you because I'd be mortified to miss anyone, but I am very lucky to have you in my life.

Thank you to my readers, to the wonderful bloggers who review my books and to all the librarians and booksellers who do so much to promote reading. Many thanks to Kate and Noa in the LRC at Highgate Wood School, where I am proud to be Patron of Reading. And hello to the school's fabulous Reading Groups which are packed full of brilliant people with a lot to say about books.

So much love and thanks as always to Mum and Dad, Alun, Deborah and Jeremy, Josh, Avital and Eliana.

Laurence, Phoebe and Judah, I couldn't do any of this without you (but I'd probably do something else a little more quickly). You are the stars in my sky.

Our son Daniel was stillborn 19 years ago. He will always be my inspiration, but I thought of him more than ever for this book which is so very much about mothers, babies and loss.